LAMENT

for a

Lounge Lizard

A Fiona Silk
Mystery

LAMENT
for a
Lounge Lizard

A Fiona Silk
Mystery

Mary Jane Maffini

RENDEZVOUS
PRESS

Cover art: June Lawrason

Le Conseil des Arts | The Canada Council
du Canada | for the arts
depuis 1957 | since 1957

Napoleon and Company acknowledges the support of the Canada Council for the Arts for our publishing program

RendezVous Crime
an imprint of
Napoleon & Company
Toronto, Ontario, Canada
www.napoleonandcompany.com

2nd printing
Printed in Canada

11 10 09 08 07   5 4 3 2

Library and Archives Canada Cataloguing in Publication

Maffini, Mary Jane
Lament for a lounge lizard / Mary Jane Maffini.

(A Fiona Silk Mystery)
ISBN 1-894917-02-2

I. Title. II. Series: Maffini, Mary Jane Fiona Silk mystery.

PS8576.A3385L35 2003   C813'.54   C2003-902839-9
PR9199.3.M235L35 2003

ACKNOWLEDGMENTS

I would be lost without insights and inspiration from the usual suspects: Mary Mackay-Smith, Linda Wiken, Sue Pike, Vicki Cameron, Joan Boswell and the late Audrey Jessup. Jane Plastino, Lois O'Neill and Giulio Maffini generously offered their encouragement and eagle eyes. Virginia and Barry Findlay and Victoria Maffini Dirnberger and Stephan Dirnberger have the most unusual information at their disposal and are always happy to share. I thank Leona Trainer for her faith in me and my projects. My publisher, Sylvia McConnell, and brave editor Allister Thompson continue to be surprisingly calm and good-humoured. Bob McConnell merits a special *merci beaucoup*.

It should be no great surprise to anyone that any errors are my own.

A word to the wise: St. Aubaine, Quebec, is a fictional community. It is not like any place that you've been. Don't bother calling your lawyer.

Liberty, equality, privacy. You can keep fraternity.
-Fiona Silk

Dogging Your Footsteps

When walking your pooch
Make sure you take care
To scoop up the poop that is sure to be there
Wherever you choose to be strolling beware
For the ooze on their shoes could drive others to tear
Out your hair

-Benedict Kelly

Marci Glickman's 2003 Gourmet Guide to Best Getaways in Small-town Canada

St. Aubaine, Quebec

Scalloped along the banks of the **Gatineau River**, *mountains looming in the distance, this picturesque community of two thousand has grown from a simple village settled late in the last century by brawling French-Canadian and Irish loggers. The main streetscape features authentic examples of the traditional Québécois-style house with its steep roof, prominent dormer windows, and full-length front veranda. The origin of the name seems shrouded in mystery: Is it a historical mispronunciation of the martyred St. Aubin? Since Aubaine means, among other things, 'godsend' and 'windfall', perhaps it reflects its early inhabitants' delight in the setting. Today's bilingual village continues the best of its English and French traditions and certainly delivers on its name.*

In early parts of this century, **St. Aubaine** *was a favourite summering spot for the well-to-do from Ottawa. Summer homes ranged from magnificent Victorian structures, complete with gingerbread, to simple riverside cottages. Many of today's coveted riverside residences began as converted cottages.*

Services of the **Upper Gatineau Railway Line** *have been restored and day trippers can make getting to St. Aubaine half the fun by connecting with the train in Gatineau from May 1 to October 15th. After disembarking, history buffs will head for the lovely stone structures of* **Christ Church** *(1789) and* **Église St.**

Mathieu *(1704)* *and their historic graveyards. Visitors can savour home-made scones, fresh-fruit jams and fragrant Earl Grey in **Thé Pour Deux** while enjoying the breathtaking expanse of the Champlain rapids. **Le Bistro Bijou** shares the river views and adds a very fine espresso (in all the popular variations) and a rich, dense, chocolate mousse cake that must have resulted from a pact with the devil. No, they don't give out the recipe. We tried.*

*You can take home a taste of St. Aubaine from **L'Épicerie 1759**, a unique foodshop featuring local maple syrup in the form of liquid, candy or fudge, unusual homemade baking and a variety of surprising health food products. Shopaholics cruise the craft and antique shops across the boardwalk from the marina with its cluster of sail boats. Browse through exclusive designer ladies' wear at **Boutique Réjeanne** and delightful Irish imports at **Forty Shades of Green**. **La Tricoterie** features one-of-a-kind designer sweaters from "Evening's End". Look for original water-colours, oils and acrylics, pottery and glass at **Le Mouton Noir**. Or join the flocks of bargain hunters at the "factory outlets" on the perimeter. St. Aubaine is more than shopping and snacking and sailing: If you decide to make a getaway weekend of it, check out the romantic ambience of the local Bed and Breakfasts in our listing. For sensuous comfort and fabulous hospitality, you can't do better than **L'Auberge des Rêves**. Top off your visit with a memorable dining experience at **Restaurant Les Nuances**, an elegant dinery in a Victorian mansion. It's a tribute to Chef Pierre Valentin that the lights on the dramatic riverscape scarcely distract from the wonderful food.*

*Many poets, musicians, and artists make their homes in this community. Check local listings for literary happenings and readings. Don't miss the live music at the **Pub Britannia**. Up and coming bands play to a packed house on most weekend nights. Entertainment ranging from traditional fiddle, country blues,* rock, stand-up comedy and the occasional string quartet pulls in fans from near and far. There's never a dull moment at the Britannia.

Skiers and snowboarders have unparalleled access to the slopes of Mont St. Martin. Lovers of the outdoors will also enjoy the trails for nature walks and hiking in summer, cross-country skiing and snowshoeing in winter. For the other three seasons, avail yourself of the well-groomed bike path that hugs the river for more than five miles. If you're energetic, climb the rugged woodland trail to the **Findlay Falls,** but allow yourself a full day for the experience: those who make it claim the spectacular 360° view of falls, river, mountain, forest and farmland is worth every ache and pain, especially in autumn! Bring your binoculars.

Whenever you go, remember: like all our getaways, **St. Aubaine** is warm, welcoming and very, very safe.

One

I wasn't expecting a man in my bed. Especially not one who brought his own bottle of Pol Roger and two champagne flutes and had the good taste to have a Chopin nocturne playing on the stereo. But there he was. Light from my bedside lamp washed over Benedict Kelly's bare torso as he lounged against the headboard of my antique four-poster, his famous lips curved in a smile.

I sagged against the foot of the bed and squinted at him. No question, it was Benedict, all right. Naked as a jay.

Being more or less three sheets to the wind myself, I leaned closer to get a better look and hiccuped softly in surprise. The light warmed the pale blue sheets, glinted off the glass in Benedict's hand and illuminated Tolstoy, my so-called watchdog, zonked out at the foot of the bed, snoring.

On my bedside table, a yellow rose lay next to a box of chocolate truffles. Looked like Benedict believed candy was dandy, even though liquor was quicker. That night, he wasn't taking any chances. The rose must have been for insurance.

It somehow crossed my soggy mind that good champagne, roses, music and soft lighting were not really Benedict's style. He'd prefer to seduce you with a shot glass of Jameson whiskey, take-out fries and a promise to get your poems published.

But I had to admit, Benedict had never looked better. Rumpled and Irish and wild, with his grin a little more crooked than usual.

Too bad he was dead.

No. That couldn't be. I reached over and touched his face. He was too cold to be alive. I fumbled for a pulse. No pulse.

I crumpled on the floor and passed out, maybe from the shock of that cold cheek, maybe from my night on the town, it's hard to say. When I opened my eyes again, a rosy dawn streaked the sky. A hangover drilled in my head. Tolstoy continued to snore, a smile on his sleeping Samoyed face, dreaming of Frisbees, most likely. And Benedict still grinned from the bed. As dead as ever.

I hoisted myself up by the footboard and gave Tolstoy a little shake. He whimpered but didn't wake up.

I slid back to the floor and asked myself the key questions. Who had drugged my dog, killed my old flame and left me to inform the St. Aubaine police about the dead poet in my bed?

Two

The detective from the St. Aubaine Sûreté followed a pair of jumpy patrolmen, who were used to shoplifters and speeding tourists but who had never seen a corpse before. I'd expected the police to bring reassurance and restore equilibrium.

Not this guy.

He was slightly smaller than a grizzly, with the same type of personality. First thing in the morning, and he already had a good start on his five o'clock shadow.

His name was F.X. Sarrazin. He addressed me as *madame*, but he must have learned English from his mother to speak it that well. He stalked around the four-poster. His dark looks grew darker, and his seventeen-inch neck swelled. My so-called watchdog followed him, wagging his tail. Tolstoy was fully recovered, and he does love strangers.

Sarrazin glowered at the sheets and at Benedict and at me. I'd seen him around St. Aubaine, which, when the tourists aren't in season, is small enough to see everyone, whether you want to or not. He seemed to hold me personally responsible for disrupting the routine of the St. Aubaine constabulary.

Every two minutes he wrote in a little white notebook. Something told me I wouldn't like the contents. Perhaps he had trouble believing I didn't have the slightest idea how Benedict had gotten into the house. Perhaps he found it hard to accept I hadn't seen Benedict for seven, maybe even eight, years. Perhaps he thought this was exactly the kind of social clumsiness you could expect from the English.

He didn't seem keen on my unknown murderer theory. Probably because not a single person had been murdered in the eighteen months since I'd moved back to St. Aubaine. When I'd dialed 911, I must have ruined some perfect local record.

Let's just say I found it difficult to communicate with Sergeant Sarrazin. Everything about him aggravated my hangover, but in particular the way he had of humming "I can't get no satisfaction."

I was glad when the coroner arrived and distracted him. I escaped to the kitchen and made coffee. While it perked, I stared out the window through a curtain of rain. My two dozen maples were still green, but the stand of oak had changed to gold. An early start to the famous Gatineau autumn.

Then it hit me. Benedict would never see the Gatineau colours again. I leaned against the counter and closed my eyes. Until Sergeant Sarrazin thundered into the kitchen and sniffed the air.

"That coffee?"

I carried two mugs of very strong, very French roast to the pine table without making eye contact with him. I was concentrating on keeping my hands steady. I was no fan of the late Benedict Kelly, but his death had left me seriously shaken. It was bad enough to have Benedict's body still lying in my tiny, perfect converted cottage on the Gatineau river. It made matters worse having some cranky detective making himself at home in my kitchen. Especially since he kept picking the dead leaves off the philodendron in the corner.

He turned away from the plant, flipped to the next page of the little white notebook and clicked the top of his ballpoint.

That would make a nice note: "Suspect fails to water plants." Just the kind of crime you'd expect in St. Aubaine.

"What did he do?" Meaning Benedict.

"He was a poet and a philosopher," I said.

"Is that a fact? But I meant what did he do for a living." He picked up the mug and glowered at it.

I glowered a bit myself. My hangover clanged. I was distressed by Benedict's death. I really wanted to go to sleep, not to cope with someone who looked like he'd been interrupted mid-hibernation.

"I don't know, Sergeant. I've told you already I haven't seen him for years. Seven, no, eight, to be exact."

"So you don't know what he did for a living?"

"I'm fairly certain he was still a poet and a philosopher."

And a lounge lizard, some people would have added.

"Where'd he live?"

"He used to have a cottage up past LaPêche. I haven't seen him for seven or eight..."

"Yeah, yeah, you've made that point." He turned his head so he could glare out the window at the maples.

I'd stopped thinking of him as Sergeant Sarrazin and switched to plain Sarrazin. It let me feel a bit more in control.

"How'd he get here? You drive him?"

"I didn't drive him. And I have no idea how he got here."

My house was a long way from anywhere Benedict was rumoured to hang out. Of course, he might have walked from the Britannia Pub. But Benedict never walked anywhere.

There was no sign of his car.

"Did he use his own key?"

"He didn't have a key. I haven't seen him even once since I moved back to St. Aubaine."

I knew Sarrazin didn't believe me. I could sense that cranky

8

glare, even though I still couldn't make eye contact with him. I didn't feel much like looking at anyone. And I certainly didn't want anyone looking at me. My eyes were red, my hair was even wilder than usual, my tongue felt breaded and fried. Anyway, the long eye of the law had glared at me enough for one day.

Still, it was in my interest to help the police. "He used to spend a lot of time at the Britannia Pub."

"The Britannia." His expression probably captured the typical cop's view of the Britannia: a hotbed of college kids, small-time crooks, cheap drugs, beer by the quart, smuggled cigarettes, dollar-a-game pool and roof-rattling good music of any kind you could mention. Plus poets, writers, sculptors, artists and other low life.

"Right."

"Any names?"

I shook my head. "I haven't been in the Britannia for years, since I stopped seeing Benedict."

"Anyone else who might know what was going on?"

I hesitated. I could feel those bear eyes on me. "His girlfriend, Bridget Gallagher. She owns the Irish shop by the Marina. She's a very nice person. Oh, God, someone will have to tell her." I really hoped the someone wouldn't be me.

*　　*　　*

It was eight o'clock when the coroner finished with Benedict. She came to the kitchen door, holding her spiral notebook in a long, elegant hand. She was about thirty-five, trim, with an elaborate hairdo, dark brown with several shades of highlights, the type that set you back a bundle. Her name was Lise Duhamel. And a little thing like a dead man at dawn wouldn't rock her socks.

"I'm finished now, Ms...um."

"Silk. Fiona Silk." We'd been through that when she'd arrived. I got the unspoken message she'd seen my type before, in formaldehyde.

"Hello, Frank. Off the top of my head, I'd estimate *monsieur* has been dead between eight and ten hours. No guarantees," she said, flashing a bit of dark stocking as she sat down.

Eight to ten hours. That put Benedict's death between ten o'clock and midnight.

That earned me another bear look. "Why didn't you call us as soon as he died?" Sarrazin said.

"I told you. I was with Dr. Liz Prentiss at Les Nuances all evening. I found him after I got home." I glossed over the passing out on the floor part.

"Heart attack, I imagine," Sarrazin said firmly to Dr. Duhamel. Still rooting for natural causes. Keep the village's record clean. Minimize paperwork.

Dr. Duhamel wrinkled her nice nose and chuckled. "Heart attack, Frank? Oh, I don't think so."

I tried my luck with her. "Definitely not a heart attack?"

She answered as if Sarrazin had asked the question. "It will take an autopsy to be sure, but I think he had some serious internal injuries."

"Really?" he said.

This time I made eye contact with him. "I told you. Someone murdered him."

Sarrazin rubbed his chin. He looked at me as if he suddenly realized I wasn't playing on the same team.

"Well, not *me*," I said. "Somebody else. I called you, remember?"

I found myself dropped from the discussion. Sarrazin and Dr. Duhamel moved to the front hall and lowered their voices.

I had to creep into the living room, press myself against the wall and strain to hear.

"Are you telling me he ended up in that bed *after* he died of a beating? That what you're saying?"

"Don't laugh," Dr. Duhamel said flirtatiously. "It looks like that's what happened. The body was definitely shifted after death."

"You sure?"

"Oh, yes. Might not have even died here. No sign of violence in the room, no blood."

I found myself gasping for breath when I finally exhaled. I did my best to gasp quietly and keep listening.

"These kinds of things don't happen in St. Aubaine," he said.

"They do now," she said. "We have pretty good indications he died of a broken neck. Plus some other serious injuries which he didn't get falling into that four-poster. I'd say he'd been roughed up very, very badly by someone who knew how to hurt people and not leave marks. Naturally, we'll have to wait for the full autopsy."

Sarrazin said, "*Merde.*"

She chuckled again. "But it won't take an autopsy to tell us someone stuck that cute little smile on his pretty face. Krazy Glue, if you ask me."

Three

At some point, St. Aubaine village council must have had a financial surplus, and they'd blown it on the cop shop. Automatic key cards, bullet-proof glass, an intercom system to talk to the desk staff, this police station had the whole shebang.

"Expecting a siege?" Since I'd started to believe this was all a bad dream anyway, why not be flip with the detective?

"Everybody's a comedian," Sarrazin said. He slipped his magnetic card into the door.

I was on my way to be fingerprinted, photographed and interviewed. Oh well. At least I had that hangover to keep me warm.

The interview room was the sort of place you might expect from the mind of Kafka. The interview too. It varied on the theme of: "Yes, I do think someone else killed him and planted him in my house afterwards. No, I don't know who or how or what the motive was."

"Why would that be?" Sarrazin asked me for the fifth time.

"I have no idea. I told you I haven't seen the man for..." I hoped the tape recorder picked up the outrage in my voice.

"Yeah, yeah, we've been there. But, it was your bed, so you can see why I'm interested." He had a tough time getting away from that bed business.

I stared at the blue ink on my fingertips. I would have a

tough time getting away from that too. "Somebody killed Benedict, and you're hassling me. That somebody is on the loose now. The way he died, it would have to be a psycho. You should be more interested in that."

"What about his girlfriend? Is she a psycho?"

"Hardly. Bridget's a lovely person. Plus, she's just a little bit of a thing. She couldn't lift him, let alone beat him to death. You'll figure that out yourself when you talk to her."

"You know, I kind of like the idea that you killed him."

"Let me remind you that I was..."

"We'll soon check that, won't we?" He switched off the tape recorder and stood up. "Don't stray far," he said.

*   *   *

Back home, between my desperate hope that I was dreaming and my fascination with the police photographer and the crowd of forensic technicians picking over the house, it was hours before I strayed anywhere.

At ten o'clock, the ambulance attendants wheeled the late poet and philosopher, encased in a black vinyl body bag, out through the front door.

Except for Tolstoy, I was finally alone. But I desperately needed a break from thinking about Benedict. I switched on the radio and caught the tail end of the CBC National news. "The controversial poet, Benedict Kelly, was found dead at the home of romance writer Fiona Silk in St. Aubaine, Quebec today. He was forty-seven. Last week's announcement by the Flambeau Foundation that Kelly had been the first winner of the Flambeau Memorial Prize for Poetic Literature created an uproar in the literary community. Police are investigating."

"Be serious," I said to the radio. Benedict? *The Flambeau?*

Canada's rarest and richest literary prize? Hardly. A sick joke maybe?

How could I have missed that news? Well. Easy. When you're a writer with a non-performing manuscript close to deadline, and you're thinking about using your drop-dead emergency cash roll to buy food, you let your newspapers pile up, you don't turn on your radio, and you don't own a TV set anyway. Your former-almost-lover wins the Flambeau, and you don't even hear about it.

The Flambeau! It never occurred to me that Benedict was churning out serious poetry. I'd figured his efforts were props for enticing girls out of their skivvies and for encouraging Irish expatriates to pay for his drinks. And here all along they were serious works of literature. It just goes to show you.

The Flambeau was an erotic dream for poets. A serious pile of cash donated by the philanthropic widow of an industrialist. Of course, a lot of good it had done Benedict.

*   *   *

That's the trouble with national public radio. It gets around. I wasn't the only one who heard it. My ex-husband-to-be didn't start with any of the more conventional conversational openings. "This is a singularly inconsiderate and flagrant thing to do, even for you, Fiona. This kind of behaviour is bound to impact your divorce settlement negatively."

"Leave a message after the beep," I said.

"And don't pretend you're not there. I know better."

My divorce settlement. Just what I didn't want to discuss. I needed a clear head to talk to Philip. And if I'd had a clear head, I never would have picked up the phone in the first place.

"Rats," I said. "I thought you were in Vancouver."

"Even three thousand miles away, Fiona, you manage to embarrass me."

Embarrass *him*? I loved that.

*   *   *

I was still distracted by the idea of Benedict's body, the Flambeau thing, my blue fingertips, and Philip's call when I realized Tolstoy was three hours late for his morning outing.

"Good dog. Keep those legs crossed," I said, fishing out my rain gear. And his Frisbee to make up for the long wait.

Flashbulbs went off in my face as soon as I opened the door. I did my damnedest to slam it before the trio of reporters reached my front steps. "Ms. Silk, how does it feel...? Ms. Silk, have you any comment...? Fiona, can we get a shot of the four-poster?"

Someone jammed his foot in the door.

Tolstoy recovered from the shock before I did and managed a convincing bark. The foot withdrew. Twelve minutes remained of my fifteen minutes of fame, and I didn't think I could live through them. For once I was glad I had no living relatives, if I didn't count Phillip, and why would I. Still I needed a solution to the reporters on the doorstep problem, or Tolstoy was going to have a long wait for relief.

*   *   *

It wouldn't be the first time I'd asked Hélène Lamontagne, my good friend and closest neighbour down the road, to bail me out. Hélène is *pure-laine* Québécoise, charming and elegant. Plus she's beautiful, a size four, with surprisingly becoming burgundy hair and a flair for the dramatic. She's also one hell of a community organizer. Never mind. I like her anyway. In spite of the fact that her wretched husband had been trying to oust me from my little converted cottage on its two-acre riverside lot ever since I'd moved in two years earlier. He might have been sleaze personified, and I might have hated the sight of him, but Hélène's a different matter.

"Fiona! I have been so worried. I phoned and phoned and you didn't answer," Hélène said.

"I'm not answering the phone," I said.

"But what is this terrible news?"

I summed up my shock, paranoia, acute embarrassment and desire to evade the media.

"*Oh là là*," she said. Before I met Hélène, I would have sworn nobody outside of the movies ever says *oh là là*. But Hélène sometimes even adds an extra *là*.

"It is a shame. Right after he won such a big prize too. But Benedict was always trouble," she said.

"No kidding. Which reminds me, do you still have any newspaper write-ups about Benedict winning the Flambeau?"

"In the *recyclage*."

"Good. Recycle them to me. I need them."

"And now you will need new sheets too."

"Not only that, but Tolstoy needs to pee, and I need a diversion."

"*Pas de problème.* Leave it to me. By the way, did I mention I still need volunteers for the Charity Auction next month?"

"Anything," I said. "Just get those turkeys off my lawn."

*   *   *

The media vans peeled out of my driveway, three seconds after

Mme Jean-Claude Lamontagne, glamorous wife of St. Aubaine's most successful developer, let it slip to a reporter that she'd just sighted Fiona Silk, prime suspect, pawing through the black push-up bras over at the Boutique Minou. As soon as the vans disappeared, Tolstoy and I dashed out. My mind was on Hélène's discarded newspapers. Tolstoy's mind was on lower things.

* * *

Too bad there's no answering system for doors. People could leave little messages, and you could let them know whether you were in...or not. Hi, this is Fiona and I never, never, never answer my door, but go ahead and leave a message if it makes you happy. Knock, knock...Hi, Jack here, I want to read your meter...give me a call...Hi, this is your newspaper carrier, you owe me for July and August and...Hi, how well do you know your Bible? I'd like to tell you how you can find peace and contentment. I'll be back next Saturday morning at about seven-thirty. Hi, this is the media. We'd like to smear this story all over every front page and television set in the country. How about opening the door and spilling your guts?

But Dr. Liz Prentiss doesn't stop just because you don't answer. When I finally capitulated, she breezed through and slammed the door on a ferret-faced reporter just back from a wild goose chase to Boutique Minou.

She said, "Get me a drink on the double. The police have been trying to poke holes in your so-called alibi."

What are best friends for?

Four

"What do you mean *'so-called* alibi'?"

"I'm your alibi. Remember? And the local hotshots just blew a lot of the taxpayers' dollars trying to catch me in a lie."

"Okay, but why *'so-called'*?"

"Get a grip. Your hands are shaking. Make sure you don't spill my drink."

She was right. My hands were shaking. After all, she is a doctor (even if no one can figure out when she keeps office hours), and doctors are trained to recognize things like shaky hands.

"I've been *fingerprinted*. I've outrun the media. I'll never be able to sleep in my bed again. I can shake if I want to. What do you mean 'poking holes in'?"

"Relax. They're just doing their job." Easy for her. She was already fully relaxed in the bean-bag chair in my living room, swilling the final two inches of my last bottle of Courvoisier.

"Yeah, but 'poking holes' in. I don't like the sound of that."

Liz rubbed Tolstoy's belly with her foot.

The phone rang for the thirty-seventh time. Tolstoy perked up. He loves to hear the voices recording their cranky little messages.

"I hate it when you don't answer the phone."

"I've had a rough day, Liz."

"Who hasn't? You know, this is the sort of thing we can

anticipate from now on. Now that we're forty-five, we have to accept the fact we'll be surrounded by death and decay."

"Speak for yourself. I won't be forty-five for six months. I don't expect it to lead to a flurry of corpses in my bedroom."

"I think you know what I mean. We have to come to grips with our own mortality." She tossed back a slug of Courvoisier.

"You come to grips with your mortality, if you want to. And don't rule out cirrhosis of the liver as a contributing factor while you're at it. I'm trying to figure out what happened here last night."

"See this?" She grabbed hold of the skin at her jaw and pulled at it. "My chin line. Look at it. It's disintegrating. You know what they call these things?"

"No. I'm more interested in who might have murdered Benedict. You know, since *I* didn't and my so-called alibi is having holes picked in it."

"Poked in it. They call them dewlaps," she said, still tugging at her chin. "They start to develop around our age."

"Your age," I said. "I'm six months younger, remember? Anyway, let's deal with the Benedict thing first. I can't figure out who could have killed him."

Curled up in the beanbag chair, with her rumpled short black hair, tight black jeans, bare feet, and red toenails, Liz reminded me of a sexy, self-centred cat.

"Just about anybody probably wanted to. Are you telling me you never felt like killing him?" Liz said, barely holding back a yawn.

I ignored a new banging on the front door. "Not in the last seven years. But I take your point. So the cast of possible villains is roughly the population of St. Aubaine."

"Yeah, that's a problem. Anyway, my chin line is…"

The banging on the front door escalated. I said, "In the

greater scheme of things, I really don't give a flying fig about your chin line."

"No need to be nasty."

"There is a need to be nasty. My home's been violated. Large strangers have snooped in my medicine cabinet and wastepaper baskets. The coroner was rude, and the police are poking..."

The front door opened by itself. Flashes went off. A ragged fringe of ginger hair shot in. The door slammed behind Josey Thring. Voices clamoured.

"Oh, no, you should have locked it," Liz said to me.

"I thought I did lock it."

"Hi, Miz Silk. I figured you couldn't hear me knocking with all the racket outside." Josey said. "Jeez. You got every TV station in the region out there. Even some from Ontario. Gonna be a big job to get that lawn repaired."

Josey may be only fourteen, but she runs her booming business, THE THRING TO DO, out of the ramshackle cabin she shares with her Uncle Mike in the backwoods of St. Aubaine.

Josey provides services in gardening, repairs, errands and anything else anyone wants done, legal and notso. For a fee. For the record, Uncle Mike is St. Aubaine's leading drunk.

"How did you get in?"

"Jeez, Miz Silk. A dead guy. In your *bed*." Her freckles stood out in sharp relief. Visions of business opportunities must have been dancing in her head, like sugarplums.

"It's two o'clock. Aren't you supposed to be in school?"

"No school today. It's a Professional Development Day for the teachers." With those round blue, unblinking eyes, you'd almost swear she was telling the truth.

"In September?" On one hand, it wasn't my business if Josey attended school, but on the other, I didn't want her hanging around for a cozy chat about the corpse. On the third hand, I didn't want her spilling any of my personal details to the gang on the lawn.

"I'm pretty sure it *is* a school day," I said.

"What's this thing you have about school days? You know, there's other things besides formal education. What about educational experiences?"

Liz snorted into her Courvoisier.

"Jeez, Miz Silk. I thought you might need some chores done. I'm raising funds for the field trip. Remember? To France. That'll be a major educational experience."

"France?" Liz will argue with anybody. "France? You don't need to go to France to have an educational experience. You live in the best country in the world." Liz has never gotten over the last referendum. She still feels the threat that Quebec could separate from the rest of Canada.

Josey didn't even blink. "Sure, Dr. Prentiss, but France…"

"But France nothing. What about Canada? You want educational or cultural experiences, you can find them right here."

"Yeah, sure. Anyways, France is like the seat of civilization." It took more than Liz to get Josey down.

"I believe you mean Greece. Possibly Egypt. You could even make the case for China. France is a non-starter."

"France is supposed to be very beautiful."

"France is beautiful? You don't think we've got beautiful? What about our Gatineau Hills? What about our river? What about the Findlay Falls? You've been there?"

"Liz, I don't think…" I didn't want Josey planning trips up the Gatineau Hills to the Findlay Falls with me panting along behind her.

"That's not educational," Josey said.

"Sure it is. Historic caves. Arrowheads and rare birds and crap. Unique to this area. Look through your binoculars. You have more educational experiences than you can use."

"I don't have binoculars. Anyways, I can do that stuff any time. France is something special. I even got my passport."

"I give up." Liz turned back to her Courvoisier.

I was stunned. How did Josey get a passport? Her only local relatives were her grandmother, currently doing a stretch for senile dementia in the Hôpital St. Mathieu, and her Uncle Mike, renowned for his inability to remain upright in public places.

"So anyways, I got enough for my ticket, but I need a bit for expenses. That garden of yours needs a good fall clean-up before the ground gets any soggier. And today I figured you'd need help keeping people away." She flicked a glance at Liz.

Liz snorted again.

"I have to think about the garden." Meaning I wasn't sure whether my bank account could handle a good fall clean-up.

"And firewood. I can get you a deal. Money under the table."

"Absolutely. But you know, now that I think about it, I'm positive it is a school day." I hustled Josey toward the front door. "You can get in a lot of trouble playing hooky."

"Speaking of trouble," Josey said. "That Dr. Prentiss is some grouchy. I thought she was supposed to be your best friend."

"She was just making a point about other educational experiences. She means well."

"No, she doesn't. She's bossy and sarcastic and mean."

And self-obsessed, I thought.

Josey added, "Not just to me, to you too, Miz Silk. I've heard the way she talks to you, for months now. I don't know why you put up with that."

Not that I really had to explain the behaviour of a middle-aged physician to a kid who had decided on her own initiative to elbow her way into my life, but I tried. "Dr. Prentiss has been my best friend since Grade Six. She's bailed me out of I don't know how many situations. She's always been there for me."

I didn't tell Josey what a rock Liz had been when my so-called marriage was disintegrating. Or how I'd cried on her shoulder during every disaster of my adolescent and adult life. I wasn't about to betray her by announcing that she was not handling her forty-fifth with grace and dignity.

Josey looked unconvinced. "Is she there for you now that you've got all these problems?"

"She will be," I said, meaning, this too shall pass.

"Yeah, I hope so. She sure goes through your booze. So this guy who died in your bed. He's that crazy poet who hangs out at the Britannia, right? Everybody in St. Aubaine is talking about it. How did you get involved?"

Good question. I damn well didn't know the answer. But it was time for me to stop being distracted by Liz's midlife misery and Josey's travel plans and find out.

*   *   *

After Liz left, I took the phone off the hook, put on some soothing Chopin waltzes, made a fire and curled up with Hélène's papers.

Two hundred and fifty thousand dollars! That was more than the International Dublin IMPAC prize. It made the Giller and the Governor General's awards look picayune. How the hell did Benedict get his mitts on that? Looked like I wasn't the only one surprised by the choice. The Toronto and Montreal papers dusted their write-ups with faint praise like "travesty" and "garbage".

The only poem of Benedict's I could even bring to mind was a seasonal favourite entitled "Turkey Farts". The critics must have read that one too.

Despite a grudging agreement that his latest book of poetry, *While Weeping for the Wicked*, was unlike anything else he'd ever written, the papers were united in their shockedness and appalledness. The major French-language dailies fumed about French-Canadian poets being passed over for a Quebec literary plum. I couldn't say I blamed them.

The weekly *St. Aubaine Argot* was alone in its enthusiasm.

The Flambeau Foundation Prize for Literature

This prestigious literary honor is awarded at the discretion of Mme Velda Flambeau, reclusive widow of the late mining magnate, Alphonse Flambeau. The Flambeau, which has not been awarded in the five years since it was established, is estimated to have an accrued value of $250,000, and this year will honour our own local son, the poet Benedict Kelly.

According to the Flambeau Foundation, Kelly's poetry is tender, emotive, deep and touching in its pure, soaring spirit.

We rejoice with St. Aubaine's well-known, favourite poet as he finally receives the recognition he deserves.

The *Argot* didn't mention that the so-called favourite poet was best known locally for cadging drinks and mooching other people's fries at the Britannia.

As usual, the St. Aubaine French-language weekly, *L'Impératif*, went too far in the opposite direction, bleating about the insult to Marc-André Paradis, a mechanic who was also a poet. Apparently, this Marc-André Paradis was pretty hot stuff. Every French paper mentioned him as a far more deserving recipient of the Flambeau than the late you-know-who. Come to think of it, most of the English ones named him, too.

I'd never heard of him.

L'Impératif had a special reason to bleat. Didn't Marc-André Paradis turn out to be another local boy.

*   *   *

At the best of times, it's hard enough cranking out three novels a year. Especially if they're romances and your own life is one hundred per cent romance-free. Add an intimate little murder, and just watch those adjectives shrivel. But since my bank account had sunk even lower than my spirits, I had no option.

I spent the rest of the evening trying to entice my fictional would-be lovebirds, the twittery Cayla and the accident-prone Brandon, as far as the bearskin rug in front of the roaring blaze in the fireplace at Brandon's remote log cabin.

> *"Cayla, Cayla, I've waited so long for this..."*
> *"Oh darling, I can't believe it's finally really happening."*
> *"Cayla!"*
> *"Brandon!"*
> *Thunk.*
> *"Brandon? What happened, darling? Did you hit your head on the sharp stone at the edge of the...? Brandon? Brandon?!! Oh God, speak to me! Oh God, no. Help him! Somebody help him!"*
> *Deep, wrenching sobs shook the lonely, log...*

I crumpled the printout and threw it in the wastepaper basket. That's what really bugged me. How the hell did Benedict, a boozed-up, undisciplined skirt-hound, capture one of Canada's most prestigious literary prizes while I couldn't even pump out a decent piece of genre fiction?

Five

The next morning, Tolstoy regarded me with sympathy and concern. Although I may have misinterpreted his expression, as he had the Frisbee in his mouth.

I'd tossed on the lumpy sofa all night trying to figure out what was going on. Why Benedict? Why me? Even with the herd of reporters thinning and the phone unplugged and Josey Thring hired to take Tolstoy for his outings, I couldn't relax, and I couldn't work. And I couldn't eat, because I had no food in the house. A drink would have been nice, but Liz had polished off the Courvoisier.

Plus, I had an urgent need to visit the dry cleaner as a result of spills received during dinner at Les Nuances. With my one good outfit badly stained, if I had a social engagement, such as an arraignment, I'd have to wear jeans and a tee.

I had no choice but to head into St. Aubaine, gossip capital of the Western World. Fine, I decided, in and out as soon as possible. I grabbed my cheque book, my credit card and my dirty clothes.

Of course, if you've been touched by scandal in any way, a trip into St. Aubaine would feel like wearing a neon KICK ME sign. The kicking started in the driveway, when the engine of my old Skylark failed to take flight. Cars are not my best thing. On the bright side, the reporters were haring off after someone else. The coast was clear.

Remorquage Bye-Bye, my local towing service, cheerfully informed me that they were having a busy, busy day and it would be roughly an hour and a half before I might expect to see them.

I chose Option B.

Tolstoy and I were perched on the porch, out of the drizzle, enjoying the view of the Gatineau river and the absence of media, when Cyril Hemphill's cab pulled up ten minutes later. Tolstoy perked up immediately. Not me. I was spending a lot more time in Cyril's cab than I wanted to. The advance from my unfinished novel was earmarked to purchase a newer car and beam me out of Cyril's life for ever.

"Nice doggie." Cyril opened the front door for Tolstoy and patted the seat.

I hoped Cyril and Tolstoy would keep each other busy while I sat in the back clutching my cleaning and quietly obsessing about Benedict. No such luck. For once Cyril didn't want to talk about the weather.

"Boys, oh boys, Miz Silk, that dead guy in your bed sure did get the whole village buzzin'."

"I bet it did."

"The police even talked to me about it. Lucky for you, Miz Silk, old Cyril here's got a one hundred per cent memory."

We barreled through the puddles on Chemin des Cèdres with no regard for the speed limit. I can always tell we're going too fast when the yellow *Citizen* and red *Le Droit* newspaper boxes blur.

"What do you mean?" I clung to the armrest as Cyril whipped past the *ARRÊT* sign and onto *Autoroute* 105.

"They were triple-checkin' your story about you and Doctor Prentiss being picked up at Les Nuances high as kites and having to practically get poured through your front door by yours truly."

"They were triple-checking?"

"You don't think they'll take your word about your own whereabouts in a murder case, do you?"

Silly me.

"I told them you sure didn't kill the guy, because at the time in question you and Dr. Prentiss were both pretty well hammered."

"Thank you, Cyril."

"Dr. Prentiss even waved her bare feet out the window. First time that ever happened in this old cab."

Cyril's moon face glowed at me from the rear-view mirror.

"So everyone thinks I was deranged enough to kill Benedict Kelly in my own bed?"

"Oh, no, ma'am, we all know you were pissed as a newt, pardon my French."

First stop, food.

We rocketed down Rue Principale and squealed to a halt in front of L'Épicerie 1759. Cyril offered to wait for me. His smile dipped a bit when I reminded him to shut off his meter.

"Of course, Miz Silk, I would of done it anyways."

L'Épicerie 1759 was formerly known as Woody's Health Foods, before the Quebec language police made Woody take down the English sign. Woody insists the 1759 in the new name refers to the serial number on his first cash register, since discarded, and not to the year of Wolfe's victory over Montcalm in the Battle of the Plains of Abraham.

Woody gets his kicks trying to see how much tourists will pay for his "pure" maple syrup and "homemade" bakery products.

I left Cyril at the front of L'Épicerie humming along with the sitar music. I picked up whole wheat pita bread, some hummus and a large bag of organic dog biscuits. With Tolstoy at my side, I pushed my way past the tofu, pesticide-free leeks and giant brown bottles of beta carotene and headed to the rear of the store. The signs in the store say *INTERDIT AUX CHIENS*. Tolstoy doesn't read French.

Woody lurked in the back storeroom washing down a chili dog with a can of Jolt. The Grateful Dead boomed out from all four speakers on his CD player. His grey braid drooped freely, no hair net in sight. Somehow the people who write the tourist guides never seem to sniff out the real Woody.

"Weh-hell," he said, reeling a bit in his wheelchair, "if it isn't the divinely dangerous Fiona. Way to go."

"It's not that great. Trust me."

"You kidding? It's fabulous. You've been on all the networks. That shot of you and Tolstoy slamming the door, that's freakin' terrific. You ask me, they'll pick it up on CNN."

Only one day after the big event, and already Woody had taped the headlines and cutlines from the local papers on the wall.

FLAMBEAU FATALITY: Foul play suspected as Canada's greatest poet found dead in bed of estranged wife of prominent West Quebec lawyer.

LOVE NEST ENDING FOR ROMANTIC RHYMER: Poet dies alone in four-poster as girlfriend parties in exclusive restaurant.

Canada's greatest poet, my fanny.

Prominent West Quebec lawyer, that would be Philip. No doubt some kind soul had already faxed him copies of the articles.

Girlfriend turned out to be me. Apparently I hadn't shut the door quite fast enough. If you were searching for a poster girl to illustrate guilt, this might do. My hair looked like it was exploding, which would account for the wild gleam in my eyes. Tolstoy might have been a white pit bull from his snarl.

"They must doctor those photos."

"Hey, think what this kind of publicity can do for your book sales." Woody twirled with glee.

"Oh, absolutely."

No one mentioned Krazy Glue or that Benedict had been naked. I was grateful to Sarrazin. I wondered if Dr. Lise Duhamel had leaked the bit about the four-poster.

"Kiddo, you sure give people lots to talk about." The wheeze was Woody's equivalent of a fond chuckle. Sometimes, it's not easy being the only person in the world Woody really, really likes.

I sighed. "Let's hear what they're saying."

"First, your former husband." Woody never says Philip's name. "Lots of people think he might have done it."

"Lots of people who never met him, I imagine."

"Some say maybe your latest boyfriend did it because he went ballistic when Benedict crawled back into your life, and he planted the body to teach you not to fool around on him. Heeheehee."

At this point, I helped myself to a Diet Coke. I wondered aloud who my latest boyfriend was.

"Don't get tense, kiddo. I'm only giving you the scuttlebutt."

"Try not to enjoy it quite so much."

"My personal favourite is you killed the guy somewhere else, transported him to your place and made a lot of public noise with Liz Prentiss to throw the police off the scent. Hahaha."

Even I chortled at this one. "So what was my motivation?"

"Stay tuned for the final details. It'll get juicier," he said, happily.

"I don't suppose you heard any good and useful reports about Benedict lately?"

"Benedict? Nah. Not recently. Just that poetry thing. And now this dead thing. So, what you got in that bag?"

"Your homemade hummus, some pita and stuff."

He lit a cigarette. "Don't know how you can eat that shit, kiddo."

When I left him in the back room, I felt worse than when I'd arrived. For one thing, Woody was in for a major letdown when the world realized I had nothing to do with Benedict's death.

Cyril Hemphill had heard all the same gossip plus more in the short time we'd been in the village. The best story featured a complex mix of international terrorism and home-grown passion.

"And those are only the English rumours—who knows what the French are saying." Cyril shook his head.

"What about Benedict? Any good poop about him?"

"Benedict? No. He's been minding his Ps and Qs this last couple of years."

Right.

I'd written a cheque for my purchases at Woody's plus fifty dollars to snag a bottle of Courvoisier at the Régie d'Alcool and an extra ten to hire Josey to pick up on any worthwhile rumours about Benedict.

Courvoisier is always appropriate for those occasions when you can't even set foot outside your house without people pointing and suggesting you killed your lover because he refused to settle your gambling debts, or whatever.

* * *

All conversation stopped in the Nettoyeur Le Quikie when I dropped in my periwinkle silk blouse and matching suede skirt for cleaning.

The girl behind the counter stared. "What are those stains?"

At least ten eyes zeroed in on my dirty clothes.

"Chocolate mousse."

She shrugged, Frenchly. "It will take about a week."

"A week?" I squeaked. This is the problem with spilling dessert on your one good outfit, and then sleeping on the floor. You're up the creek if you get an interesting offer. Not that I'd had an interesting offer for seven or eight years.

"Nothing I can do about it, *madame*. And we cannot guarantee suede. You must acknowledge that you understand this. Sign here."

With everyone still watching, I signed, grabbed my receipt and hightailed it out the door and through the puddles, eyes front.

I got more looks in the Régie.

After that, I headed straight for Cyril's cab, giving the Pâtisserie a miss, although I could have done with a half-dozen *mille-feuilles*. I decided this was not the perfect time to drop into the library and do a little research on the Flambeau. I couldn't even face the Chez Charlie for a cheap lunch.

"Do you mind if I swing by the Marina way?" Cyril asked, innocence painted on his face like rouge.

Oh, sure. Cyril had probably found a way to make a buck driving me along a parade route, past the shops and restaurants near the Marina, where I might have been pointed out as the latest tourist attraction in St. Aubaine, with tourists tossing loonies into Cyril's outstretched palms.

I didn't give a flying fig about Cyril's plans. Whatever else happened, I couldn't risk coming face to face with Benedict's girlfriend, Bridget Gallagher.

"Straight home and burn rubber, Cyril."

Six

The early evening light gave a soft focus to the memorial gathering in Bridget's renovated Victorian home on the hill above the Marina.

"Who is Miz Gallagher, again?" Josey Thring asked as we circulated.

"Bridget? Oh, she's an, um, old friend of Benedict's."

"Just that her name never came up when I was inquiring around like you asked me to about Mr. Kelly. Of course, ten bucks doesn't buy all that much information these days."

I wasn't surprised no one had mentioned Bridget. As Benedict's longest surviving lover, she was well past the news flash stage. I didn't point that out. Good thing I didn't, because Bridget took that moment to hobble over for a chat.

"What happened to your foot, Bridget?" I blurted.

"Oh, that. I slipped on my friend Rachel's stupid stairs on the way to our bridge game. Anyway, I broke my ankle."

"That's all you need right now. It must be painful."

"They can give you stuff to kill that kind of pain. And this is as good a time as any to have a fried brain."

No kidding. "Oh, Bridget, I'm so sorry."

"Not your fault, dear." She leaned her delicate body on her crutch and issued me a soft, forgiving smile. "I'm sure there's a perfectly reasonable explanation for everything."

I thought so too. Bridget and I have never been close, a

holdover from my slight entanglement with Benedict. But since I hadn't known about Bridget at the time, and since I broke it off when I found out and since she knew that, she's always been cordial. Even after Benedict's death, Bridget didn't hold a grudge.

"If I can do anything to help, anything at all," I said. It was awkward standing at my former not-quite lover's not-quite wake with his not-quite widow, seeking the appropriate commiserative phrase.

We stood apart from the mourners gathered there to remember Benedict, to read from his poems and more voluminously from their own.

Josey, who had never been to a memorial gathering for a poet, circulated happily. Of course, Josey had never met Benedict. But she had been repairing the upholstery on my wingback chair when Bridget called to invite me. Being Josey, she'd taken the initiative of answering the phone and graciously accepting on my behalf. And seeing the poet's memorial as fitting in nicely with her Grade Nine Creative Writing Class, she'd angled an invitation for herself, despite the close-friends-only nature of the event.

I suppose it was good. In a village this size, I couldn't have avoided Bridget forever.

Josey approached respectability with the skirt she keeps for court appearances and her cowlicks dampened down. She looked better than I did. I was stuffed into my ancient, one-size-fits-none navy dress, desperately hoping the buttons didn't fly across the room and blind some grieving poet. You never have a periwinkle silk blouse and matching suede skirt when you really need them.

Bridget took my arm, and we turned and limped into the dining room, away from the clusters of poets, fellow drinkers, plus Benedict's former and more recent lovers. We stood by the huge oak table decked out with smoked salmon canapés, vegetables and pâté, shortbread cookies, Nanaimo bars, maple mousse, scones, four kinds of jam and an immense earthenware pot of tea. Too bad I'd lost my appetite. I couldn't even look at food. I stared out the window instead. I watched a bevy of damp reporters, at least one forlorn street person and the now familiar burly form of Sarrazin taking shelter under a tree. I wouldn't have been surprised to see the coroner out there batting her eyelashes at him. But then again, the rain would have ruined her hairdo.

Wait a minute. A street person? Since when did we have street people in St. Aubaine? Particularly on a hill with only houses? Puzzling about that was a welcome diversion from thinking about the police dogging my footsteps. I was distracted from my distraction when Bridget started to cry. Of course, on her, crying looked good.

The tears couldn't diminish her pale, Irish prettiness. The copper waves, the warm blue eyes, the dusting of freckles, the pointed cheekbones, all that still worked well. Bridget was designed to wear black. If she had dewlaps, they weren't showing.

"Anything at all. Just name it," I said. Bridget brought out my latent guilt. She'd stuck by Benedict for years, drying him out, paying his bills. Not like me, putting him out of my mind and getting on with my life. Not even giving him a call on St. Patrick's Day.

She squeezed my hand. "Don't worry. Some day we'll find out who killed him and dumped him in your…"

I certainly hoped so. I'd already charged a new mattress and bedding to the tune of nine hundred smackers. Not to mention how the discovery of Benedict's body had polluted my social life and caused the police to regard me with bearlike eyes. Worse, my wonderful little house no longer felt secure.

Bridget turned to me and took a deep, fluttery breath.

"Do you think it could have been your ex-husband?"

"I'm sorry, Bridget. You'd have to know Philip. He might murder someone, but he'd never touch a dead body. He won't even empty a wastepaper basket without putting on rubber gloves."

"Maybe he wore rubber gloves."

"No, no," My voice rose. "He's in Vancouver on business. Anyway, Philip never even knew Benedict."

"Maybe he found out. People can criss-cross the country in less than a day. Surely, you must want to know who killed him."

"Of course I do. Although I already know Philip didn't."

"But who else would have wanted to kill him?"

Just about anyone, but only if they knew him. I couldn't say that, so I didn't say anything.

"What about your current boyfriend?"

Again with the boyfriend. "From the unlikely to the non-existent." Perhaps I was a bit snappish.

Bridget teetered a bit. "Forgive me, I know it must be dreadful for you. Everyone thinking that either you did it or..."

"I was with Liz in full view of the world."

Bridget's best friend, Rachel, edged into our space, blinking behind her owl glasses and gently took Bridget's arm. Bridget allowed herself to be led away.

"I particularly like all the poets," Josey said, sidling up to me the second Bridget hobbled off.

I liked all the poets, too. Especially since they'd accepted my explanation that I simply had no idea *how* he'd ended up in my bed.

The poets were remembering the time Benedict got roaring

drunk and tried to scale the Centre Block of the Parliament Buildings in the buff, aiming for the Peace Tower. Opinion was divided on whether or not Benedict had been tossed naked into the clink after that or dragged down, wrapped in a blanket and saved by his loyal followers. I wasn't sure which version I preferred.

"Is Bridget a poet?" Josey popped back into question mode.

"At one time. But she felt the need to make a living. She has the wonderful Irish shop at the Marina, Forty Shades of Green. Remember those gorgeous Irish coffee glasses I treated myself to for my birthday? Bridget special-ordered them for me from Dublin. Of course, that was when I still had money in the bank."

Josey whipped her head around. "She needed to make a living? Don't poets make a living?"

"They have day jobs. They're teachers and bureaucrats and carpenters and librarians. And...accountants."

I knew it was all being tallied in Josey's head. We hadn't heard the end of this poetry business. "So you know all these people?"

"Hmm, it's been a long time since I spent any time with Benedict, but I recognize the faces. The men were all part of what we used to call Benedict's O'Mafia."

"And the lady with the big eyes and the brush cut?"

"Abby Lake. She's another old friend."

"And the chunky one?" I felt a bit disloyal recognizing Rachel immediately. In fact, except that her body was shorter and her hair a bit longer, and she had a pale moustache instead of a five o'clock shadow, she looked like Sarrazin with glasses.

"Rachel Kilmartin. An old friend of Bridget's."

"She a poet?"

"No, she runs L'Auberge des Rêves, that nice bed and

breakfast by the river. And she's a caterer. She made all this wonderful food."

"Bed and Breakfast? And catering." New sidelines and career possibilities always appeal to Josey. It took a while before she directed her attention back to the lady poets.

"What about the lady with the long red braid and all the silver bracelets?"

"Zoë Finestone. A poet and a sculptor."

"Wow. She looks like a witch. A big beautiful witch."

She did.

"She's sure giving you the evil eye," Josey said.

Right again.

"I wouldn't want her mad at me, that's all I can say."

Absolutely.

"Okay, so these people were Benedict's real good friends."

I couldn't tell Josey every woman there, with the likely exception of Rachel, at one time or another had been one of Benedict's lovers. Especially Zoë and Abby. From what I'd heard, Abby was very, very close to Benedict right until his death.

"And what about you? Were you another old friend?"

"About eight years ago, I was his student in a writing class." There'd been a lot more, but nothing suitable for her slightly protruding ears.

"Jeez," Josey said, "is Bridget all right?"

Bridget slumped against a wall, white as toothpaste. I rushed to catch her before she collapsed.

"It's okay. I'm fine now." Her hand gripped mine.

People milled around us, munching on the food, chatting, laughing and crying. Sometimes all at once.

Bridget breathed deeply and started to relax. Until Abby Lake reached out and touched her.

When Abby hugged Bridget, she had to bend to do it.

Abby hadn't changed in all the time I'd known her. Lean and strong, with long bones and a dancer's body, she showed distinct signs of weight training and had only the barest suggestion of pale hair. The hairless look accentuated her huge green eyes and peach skin. The eyes swam with tears. And her nose glowed the tiniest bit red.

"Thank you, Bridget." She didn't acknowledge my presence.

The knot in Bridget's jaw stayed after Abby left. Her nails practically perforated my arm. "I'm sorry. But that woman really gets up my nose."

"This is too much for you."

"Oh, no. I love all these people. Except *her*, of course. And that Finestone creature. The rest were Benedict's special friends." If her nails dug any deeper, I was going to need stitches.

I scanned the room full of gentle, laughing, crying people. One of the O'Mafia tuned a fiddle. A smaller balding man beside him sported an accordion.

"Benedict had a lot of good friends." The better friends had been expatriate Irish, like Benedict always pretended to be himself, only with class and morals.

The room hummed with music. Even people with tears in their eyes tapped their toes.

"He had hundreds of friends," Bridget said. "Everyone loved him. He had no enemies."

He'd had at least one. "No one you can think of who would have...?"

"Poor Benedict. It's so unfair. Things were finally going so well for him."

"You mean with the Flambeau and all? All that money."

"Mmmm. Too bad he never got it, he would have been in hog heaven. Think of that party." Bridget couldn't stop herself from grinning. The grin became a chuckle and grew to a laugh.

I found myself joining her. A quarter of a million dollars. That would have been a party all right. I pictured champagne corks popping and streamers floating over St. Aubaine and giggling, naked girls being chased into the bushes.

"He didn't get the money?"

Bridget's grin slipped off her face. "The announcement was made, but the official presentation of the cheque and the award was scheduled for October 1st in Montreal."

"So what happens to the money?"

"Back to the Flambeau fund, they tell me."

"That's too bad."

"Sure is. By the way, did I ever tell you how Benedict always called you the lost love of his life? The one that got away," Bridget whispered with a strange smile.

I hadn't known. And I didn't want to know. I was amazed she could smile, even strangely, if she believed this bit of Benedict's foolishness.

I didn't smile back. "It sounds like the kind of thing Benedict said about a dozen different women. Not meaning a thing."

"But he only said it about you. 'The lost love of his life.' You were someone special to him. And now he's dead, and it's driving me crazy not knowing what happened to him."

It was driving me crazy too. Benedict had been cunningly, artfully, decoratively laid out in my bed. *Playfully.* No one wanted to know who the killer was more than I did. "We'll know soon. The police are working on it."

"The St. Aubaine police? Those clowns? They can't even track down shoplifters. I know that the hard way. They always get the wrong person."

People started to clap and cheer for the musicians. One of the poets, still wearing his raincoat, sang "The Wild Colonial

Boy", backed by the fiddle, the accordion and the clapping of guests. Bridget and I were the only two not singing along.

It made a heart-warming picture, except for one small problem. The killer knew that Benedict and I had a history. And except for my best buddy Liz, the only people in the world who had known anything about that history were right there in Bridget's beautiful home, singing.

Seven

"I can't believe you took her to Bridget's place. What were you thinking of?" Liz tipped my virgin bottle of Courvoisier over her snifter. "*I* didn't even get an invitation."

"Don't pucker your face that way. You'll get more wrinkles." While Liz was gasping, I added, "You couldn't stand him."

"So what? I know Bridget. I like her."

"But it was only close, close friends of Benedict."

"Perfect. Such as Josey Thring, who never even laid eyes on Benedict. You let that girl wrap you around her little finger."

"Do not."

"Do so," Liz said.

Josey's life is a struggle to survive despite her criminal, alcoholic and demented relatives. Why shouldn't I help her out when I can?

"Anyway, she prodded all the guests for gossip about Benedict." I didn't mention the ten dollars or the fact that she didn't come up with any useful tidbits.

"I don't want to talk about it any more. I want to give you a bit of advice about your novel."

"What advice?"

"Yes, well, I think your problems can be explained by sex."

"What sex?"

"Exactly. That's what I'm trying to tell you. There's no sex in your life and never has been, so that's why..."

"No sex in my life? Never? May I point out I was married for twenty-three, count 'em, twenty-three years to you-know-who."

"I rest my case. Get that look off your face. I'm only trying to help you out. That's what friends are for. Get some sex in your life. Change your attitude. Fix yourself up a bit. Work from your strengths."

"I have strengths?"

"Sure. Your hair colour. Men like that ashy blonde. And it doesn't show the grey. I'm sure if you made any kind of an effort at all, you could keep the curl under control."

"Wait a minute..."

"Let me finish. You know what your best feature is?"

"Dewlaps?"

"Very funny. Eyes. Your eyes are your best feature. People pay good money to get that blue-violet colour in contact lenses. Try makeup. Play them up a bit."

"I don't think..."

"That's right. You don't think. Now the main thing is to lop off a few pounds. Get from a size fourteen back to a size eight."

"Are you crazy? It's easier for a camel to get through the eye of a needle than it is to get from a size fourteen to an eight."

"This is a serious business, Fiona. Give it some thought. Anyway, I can't sit around talking forever. I have a life." She flung herself out of the beanbag chair and slipped her skinny little feet into her open-toed shoes. "Remember. Sex. That's the secret."

Like I was in the mood.

*   *   *

If the door-answering system had existed, I might not have had to face Papa Bear Sarrazin looking like someone had eaten all his porridge. I was a bit long in the tooth for Goldilocks, but I had that weak-kneed feeling of being caught on the spot.

Tolstoy, on the other hand, was tickled by the visit.

Sarrazin seemed to feel quite at home. Why wouldn't he? The man had actually seen the contents of my underwear drawer. He casually wedged himself in the kitchen chair and narrowed his eyes. To add insult to injury, Tolstoy snuggled up to him and dropped the Frisbee at his feet.

Sarrazin wanted to talk about my relationship with Benedict. In case I had it wrong about not being involved for nearly eight years. He also wanted details of my activities for the past week.

"Are you sure you hadn't seen him recently?"

I was.

"And you haven't been in touch with him, *madame*?"

"Right."

"Do you know what kind of car he drives?"

A trick question. The police would certainly know that. "The last time I saw him was about..."

"Yeah, yeah."

"...he was driving along in some kind of antique MG convertible. I saw it from a distance."

"Have you seen that car anywhere?"

"No, not for the last..."

"That's starting to get on my nerves."

"What do I have to do? Write it in blood?"

"Which reminds me, the dry cleaners called us about your clothing."

"That was chocolate mousse, and you know it. Your technicians already checked everything." I couldn't afford to have my only decent outfit disappear into the St. Aubaine Sûreté's evidence room.

But this went beyond a wardrobe problem. I had the distinct impression nothing would suit F.X. Sarrazin quite so much as tidying the loose ends on this case by tossing me into the slammer. Which would explain why he was spending a perfectly good Sunday asking questions in my kitchen.

"I imagine I'll be back." He left without smiling.

*   *   *

"I'm sorry, Phillip, that you have to call from San Francisco to express your disapproval. It's too bad you're embarrassed by the body in my boudoir, as you so amusingly call it. Imagine how I feel." I'd learned much earlier to hold the receiver away from my ear. I should have learned not to pick up the phone.

"No, I did not have a long and passionate and incredibly sleazy affair with Benedict while we were married."

Of course, the truth wasn't far from that. I'd had a long and passionate series of fantasies matched by frequent offers from Benedict, but when it came time for action, I'd wimped out. I'd turned down Benedict's last proposal to pinch Philip's new Audi and his credit cards and head for Montreal for a dirty weekend. Instead I'd applied myself to the task of making my marriage work. Go figure.

"No, I will not pick up the cost of your calls. If you don't want to pay, don't play." I hung up in the middle of his response and went back to my cognac. Liz was examining her elbows in the living room mirror. I hoped she wouldn't sprain her neck.

"That's just Phillip trying to wear me down so he can offer me a reduced settlement."

"Got to hand it to the man. He's a world class tightwad," Liz said.

"Agreed, but Phillip doesn't really matter." Only two people really mattered. F.X. Sarrazin, for the wrong reasons, such as his powers of arrest and his apparent belief that a corpse in the bedroom should lead to a quick slam of the jailhouse doors, and Bridget, who was definitely entitled to an explanation.

"Don't let him get to you."

"I suppose I could get the telephone disconnected, although it might be handy to have in an emergency."

"Funny. Now pay attention. Elbows. Take a gander."

I peered at Liz's elbows. I didn't see anything unusual.

"What about them?"

"What about them? They're one of the sure signs of age, that's all. You can hide a lot of stuff with clothes or make-up or you can get surgery. But what the hell are you going to do about elbows that resemble miniature bloodhounds hanging off your arms?"

I could not recall having a single elbow thought in my life.

"Well?" she said. "How bad are they?"

What could I say? They fell short of the miniature bloodhound description, but they did have a certain shrivelled droopiness.

"Don't be such a coward. How many times have you spotted elbows like these and figured some woman was at least ten years older than she pretended?"

"Never." For one thing, I didn't really care how old people were and whether they were pretending to be some other age. For another, all my life I've had enough trouble maintaining my beauty rituals of flossing my teeth, keeping my hair from exploding and hunting under my bed for my only tube of lipstick. This elbow thing sounded like a real nuisance.

"I'm doing something about them," Liz said. "And the dewlaps."

"Me, too." Meaning I would, from that point on, never check my elbows. Which wouldn't present a problem. Avoiding the dewlaps might be a little trickier, since you could see them in the mirror. Unless you viewed the mirror dead straight on. Whatever works.

Liz helped herself to another cognac, perhaps in the belief the liver is not a barometer of beauty.

I had a coffee. I needed a clear head to make my plans to rid myself of the bothersome unknowns surrounding the Benedict-in-my-bed problem. I didn't want the conversation to drift back to some other deteriorating body part, so I changed topics.

"I can't believe he won that award. Can you?"

Liz shrugged. She picked up her cognac and headed back to the mirror to have another frown at her elbows.

"Who cares, Fiona? You know those things are always rigged."

Rigged? Literary prizes are always rigged? I was stunned. Like so often in my life, once Liz left, her conversational droppings stayed around to smell up the atmosphere for hours.

Rigged? The Flambeau?

*   *   *

With a note of triumph, Montreal Directory Assistance informed me that Mme Velda Flambeau's home telephone number was unlisted. The Flambeau Foundation number was not.

The Flambeau Foundation responded to my request for more information about Benedict's win by asking me to state my name, the date and time and a brief yet meaningful message after the beep.

*　　*　　*

I stuck my head out the door and, spotting no media, made the trek a quarter mile down Chemin des Cèdres to the Lamontagnes'. Tolstoy came along for the walk, and I took the Frisbee. I tire of the Frisbee long before Tolstoy does, but there were other distractions for him. He likes to piddle his way up the long, elegant driveway leading to the two-storey grey stone building that tells you Jean-Claude Lamontagne has a shitload of money and isn't afraid to show it. Since Jean-Claude is never home in the day and rarely in the night, I felt I could visit without running into him and having to deflect yet another offer to purchase my property.

Hélène was a bit surprised when Tolstoy and I returned her recycled newspapers. "I hope they were useful."

"Not as useful as you'll be. You know everything that goes on with the ritzy and glitzy. What's the real story on the Flambeau? Could it have been rigged?"

She lowered her voice although we were alone in the six-thousand square foot house. "*Oh là là*, Fiona. They are saying Mme Flambeau must have slept with Benedict Kelly to make such a crazy decision."

"Slept with him? Ha ha. Isn't she about eighty?"

"*Oui*, that's what they're saying. *Et non*, she's not even sixty."

"Have you never met her?" Sooner or later, Jean-Claude and Hélène meet everybody who is anybody in Quebec.

"No. But I hear from people who know that she is really *spéciale*."

Meaning bizarre.

"I hope this doesn't upset you," Hélène broke in.

"No, no, I hadn't seen him for seven years. Eight really."

"And you seem so *dérangée* and after all..."

"Of course, I'm bothered. Benedict was murdered. You should hear the rumours about me. And I'm getting framed. Come to think of it, maybe Mme Flambeau was framed."

"*Oh là là.*"

"Hélène. I'd like to talk to Mme Flambeau. Any idea of how to reach her?"

"No."

"Perhaps you could...?"

"I would love to help, but I am very busy lining up volunteers to sell tickets to the One Act Play Competition. As soon as that's over, I will have time to make a few extra calls."

"Right, well, you could put me down to sell a few tickets."

"Ten?"

"Absolutely." Ten is a lot of tickets when you think about it, especially if you're trying to unload them to my friends. "While I'm here, you know anything about this local poet Marc-André Paradis?"

"He is supposed to be very good. Very *émotif.* He has a car repair shop somewhere on *Autoroute* 105, but that is all I know."

I lit up. "Car repair? Excellent."

Eight

I could understand why Mme Velma Flambeau, keeper of the Flambeau fortune, might want an unlisted number, but it seemed an unusual thing for a mechanic to have one. I was on my tenth attempt to find a telephone number for Marc-André Paradis when I decided on another strategy. I slipped into my old jean jacket, tucked my hair under a Blue Jays cap and started up the Skylark.

Five minutes later, I pulled into Auto Service Tom et Jerry, formerly Tom and Jerry's Service Station. I filled up the tank, although I wondered if that was an unwise investment considering the Skylark's terminal condition. Inside, I used my credit card to finance the unwise investment.

As soon as Tom recognized me, he swept a couple of newspapers underneath the counter and pulled out his spray container of Windex.

"Oh, hi, Fiona," he said, "what's new?"

"Nothing at all."

He blinked. Furtiveness did not become him.

"Tell me," I said, "you guys ever hear of someone named Marc-André Paradis? Supposed to run a repair shop up the highway a bit."

"Paradis? Yeah, he does high-end imports only." He flicked a glance toward the Skylark.

"Not for me, of course. I'm happy with you guys. Naturally."

Not that my car runs right or anything.

"Not for you?"

"A friend was asking. She has a...Saab."

"Really?"

"Yes."

"She should try the Saab dealer then. Paradis only takes people on referral." Tom's tone indicated he thought this was a pretty good idea. You could get a higher grade of customer. Not one driving a Skylark, for instance.

*   *   *

Sarrazin made me nervous. Not just because he was in my living room at nine in the evening when you'd think a rural detective should be off duty. Not just because it hadn't been all that long since his last visit. Not just because he seemed to have spent the day trying to tie me closer to Benedict's death, if that was possible. He also made me nervous because he was a one-man crowd.

He shook off his umbrella and headed straight into my living room, cutting off my suggestion we talk in the kitchen.

I hated that. My living room is where I relax with my dog in front of the fireplace, where I read, where I lose at Scrabble, where I laugh with my friends. I didn't want it contaminated by a bear with the power to arrest me.

At least I had support; Liz had dropped in for a drink for the third time that day. She took one look at Sarrazin and headed straight for the front door.

"Time for me to make my house call," she said.

Since when did Liz make house calls? "Where are you going?" I whispered. "Stay put."

Talk about feeling betrayed. Maybe Liz was my alibi, but if

she hadn't insisted on tying one on for her forty-fifth, I would have been curled up in bed in my flannel pjs that night and, assuming no one would have killed Benedict before my astonished eyes, I wouldn't have needed an alibi in the first place. All to say, the least she could do was hang around when the police pulled out the rubber hoses.

"You know, this is getting serious, Fiona. It might be time for you to get a lawyer," she said, closing the door in my face.

Sarrazin glared at the Scrabble game as he lowered himself onto the Queen Anne chair. Naturally. The larger the man, the more likely he will be to sit on the only small, delicate chair in the room. I took my place in the wingback.

Tolstoy greeted Sarrazin with a wagging tail. I did not suggest coffee this time. There are limits.

Sarrazin loosened his size seventeen collar and cleared his throat before frog-marching me through every minute of the night of Benedict's death. One more time. Exquisite attention to detail. Had I gone to the Ladies' Room in Les Nuances? How long had I been gone? Had Liz gone anywhere? Had we seen anyone we knew?

What made me nervous were the questions backing into the afternoon of the same day. Where had I been? Who had I seen? When? What about my note they found in his cabin?

Here. There. Nobody. Who knows? And, damn, what note?

"I don't know anything about a note."

"Funny, it has your signature."

"It can't have my signature."

"You sure?"

"Of course, I'm sure. I hadn't been in touch with him for…" I was distracted by his bearlike smirk. "What does it say?"

"You tell me."

"I've *told* you… Wait a minute. Maybe it was an old note."

"Nice try. Too bad it was dated March 14th. This year. Not seven years ago. Not eight either."

I felt my head swim as the implication sank in. Benedict hadn't been the only target of this murder. Someone *wanted* me in the role of murderer. And the police thought that was just ducky.

I managed to say, "I believe I have a right to know what was in this alleged note."

"Sure, why not? It said, Many thanks for all your trouble, xoxoxo, Fiona."

Not what you'd call romantic. In fact it was just like a thousand thank you notes I have written in my life, although not a single one of them would have been to Benedict. So what was that about?

When Sarrazin left, he took a sample of my handwriting and signature. "You understand why I'm interested," he said on his way out.

* * *

I tried working to get my mind off the prospect of getting arrested.

A seductive rivulet of rain snaked sensuously down Cayla's capacious cleavage. Her hair was plastered against her head, her lips parted. Around her the storm raged.

"Darling," Brandon gasped, "at last I'm out of that damned neck brace. I'm longing to..."

Cayla arched. A shudder ran through her. Her eyes closed, her nose seemed to pinch. She opened her mouth.

"GEEYAAAAACH," she sneezed.

"Bless you." Brandon wiped himself off. "Are you...?"

"CHEESH, CHEESH, CHEESH," she sneezed.

"...coming down with a cold?"

"Ub course. I'b cubing dowd wid a code," she snarled. "Why else would I be sdeezig?"

Oh dear, Brandon thought, turning away bitterly. Sneezing did not become her.

You jerk, Cayla thought. If I could stick by you when you were in that hospital trussed up like a Christmas turkey and snivelling at the nurses for pain killers, you'd better be able to...

Despair slunk through my being. My novel was crap. The only positive thing I could think about it was that those two world class whiners, Cayla and Brandon, did not exist outside of the manuscript, and at least I could be rid of them once I completed the cursed thing. If I hadn't desperately needed the advance to purchase a replacement for the Skylark, I would have deleted the two of them from the hard disk with a smile on my face.

"What's the matter, don't you like writing?"

I jumped. Josey! I hadn't even realized she was in the house.

"Of course, I love it." Not strictly speaking true, since my latest incoming cheque had been a royalty cheque for $12.62, and with every word I typed I asked myself if the world was trying to tell me something.

"I wondered, because your mouth gets all shrivelled, and your eyes get kind of slitted. And I heard you hissing."

"How did you get in?" My heart was still thumping.

"You always ask me that. Anyone could open that lock."

Right. Get the geedee lock changed, I reminded myself.

"Can't you see I'm working?" I have to admit this was mean-spirited of me since Josey was soaking wet and showing a definite slump in her shoulders.

She gave me a look that could slice and dice. I felt a jab in my conscience. After all, I wasn't the only person in the world. Just the most miserable.

"Sorry, Josey." But I was talking to her back.

"You should do something soon about this lock before someone comes in and kills you too." The door slammed behind her.

I caught up to her at the end of the driveway, just as she was getting on her bike. I talked her back into the house. I made a fire, some cocoa and a couple of grilled cheese sandwiches. I endorsed the cheque for $12.62 and lent her some dry clothing and a squall jacket before sending her off to dig up all that was fit to print about the totally unavailable Mme Flambeau.

I felt better after that. Which only meant I was psychologically unprepared for my next visitor.

*   *   *

The news that Benedict's body had been released to Bridget and expeditiously cremated was only exceeded in awfulness by her idea of the subsequent step.

"You can't be serious, Bridget." I was so stunned I forgot that it's not nice to leave visitors teetering in the rain while you reel in dismay.

She swayed on her crutches at my front door, clutching a plastic bag from Forty Shades of Green. Her skin was so pale, you could practically see her skinny little bones.

"Of course, I'm serious. Rachel took care of the whole shebang. I couldn't handle it myself."

"I don't mean the cremation. I mean the, um, other thing."

"Oh, I'm sorry. But didn't you ask me if you could do anything?"

Anything at all, I'd said. And meant it at the time. Anything but this.

Bridget teetered. She started to cry, which wasn't immediately obvious with the rain dripping off her nose. Not the first time she'd been crying that night either.

"No, I'm sorry. You'd better come in. You need coffee. Maybe a bit of Irish coffee. That's what you need. I'll have to use Courvoisier, if that's all right." That would give me a chance to use the Irish coffee glasses I'd splurged on and ordered through her.

"Thanks. I could use a bit of a treat. Courvoisier's fine. Aren't we all part of a global village now?" She hobbled toward the living room. "The police finally let me get access to Benedict's place. I sure need something."

Tolstoy rubbed himself against Bridget's leg, in case that was what she needed.

Bridget settled into the wingback chair. Her cast stuck straight out on the footstool. I sat on the floor. That way I wouldn't have to fall off something if Bridget had any more surprises, such as knowing something about the note Sarrazin claimed had been found in Benedict's cabin.

She clutched her glass. Two Irish coffees and two handkerchiefs later, she said: "Isn't it terrible? What kind of a measure of a life is this? All those years, and he hardly left a thing of substance. Nothing tangible. Just these little things, souvenirs he wanted given to old friends." She blew her nose. "I'm sorry. I was okay until I tried to clean out his little cabin. Oh, God, get a load of me, will you, I'm shaking. He meant so much to me. Now I have nothing left."

"You cleaned out his cabin?"

"Rachel did all the physical stuff. I sat blubbering and making decisions I'll probably regret. Oh, listen to me whining. You've been through a lot too. It must be terrible having all that stuff in the papers."

Seeing Bridget, nose like a fire hydrant, made me feel sadder for her than for Benedict. "Don't worry about what he didn't leave. Benedict didn't care about things, except for books, booze and buddies."

"And bimbos," she said.

"Um, and women, certainly." I was unwilling to put either Bridget or myself into the bimbo category.

Bridget smiled. "At any rate, you said you wanted to help, so I'm hoping you won't mind delivering these few bequests while you're doing the other thing. He left a list of people he wanted to have special little trinkets. I don't think I can do it without breaking down. Maybe in six months, but not now." She fished small wrapped parcels out of the green bag.

I gawked at her. I hadn't wanted anything to do with Benedict for more than seven years, and that went double now. Of course, I couldn't say that out loud. But if Bridget could take the location of Benedict's death with such grace, who was I to refuse her this small but incredibly irritating set of errands?

"No problem. But about that other thing..."

She was ready for me. "It was his last wish, Fiona." She was busily arranging a pile of slim books next to the parcels.

"What do you mean? He didn't have a last wish. He didn't know he was going to die." My voice broke on a squeaky note.

"And these books," Bridget said. "*While Weeping for the Wicked*. It's his latest volume of poetry. Probably what won him the Flambeau. I have just a few. So very good friends only. One for you, of course, and I have a list of who else gets books and mementoes. I hope I haven't missed anyone. It's very hard for me to think clearly."

"About this last wish thing..."

"You know, it's funny," Bridget said, soothing as cough syrup, "Benedict might not have had a will, but on several occasions he specifically mentioned he wanted to be scattered over the river. And who are we to argue?"

Unable to argue, I found myself sputtering. "But you can't seriously expect me to scatter them and give a speech."

"He would have wanted it. Well, maybe not the speech. I know you aren't all that outgoing. But creating a memorial event that will be a testament to his spirit. You're the only one I can ask."

"But, don't you want to do it yourself?"

"Oh, no, I can't stand the thought of it. In fact, I can't stand period." She pointed to the cast. "My doctor says it will be another two months before I resume normal activities." Bridget's voice wobbled, reminding me she was close to the edge.

"What about Rachel? She handled things for the Memorial and the cremation."

Tolstoy pricked up his ears. He hates it when I wail.

"No way. Poor Rachel has her hands full with the Bed and Breakfast. It's not easy running a business on your own."

It wasn't easy writing romances on your own either, especially when you had no sex life and were stuck with Cayla and Brandon as ingredients. But before I could say that, Bridget added, "*Rachel* never cared for Benedict."

Unlike me. Having someone else's lover found dead *in flagrante* on your best sheets landed you in major psychological debt.

"In fact, she really couldn't stand him."

"Fine. What about someone who could stand him? One of his many grieving friends? One of the lady poets perhaps?"

Bridget's lips tightened.

"All those 'lady poets' have glamorous jobs to keep them in

designer clothes while they're pretending to sacrifice over their poetry. They're much too busy."

Bridget would have chug-a-lugged hemlock before she would have turned over Benedict's last rites to Abby or Zoë. Stupid of me to even suggest it.

"Oh. Wait a minute. What about all his drinking buddies? One of the O'Mafia? They're perfect. They can't possibly be employed. I mean, they'd know what would be important for Benedict."

Important for Benedict. As if he were still alive. Of course, when I considered the amount of aggravation he could still generate, it was as if he'd never died.

"You must be kidding. Those idiots? What do you think is the likelihood of Benedict's ashes ending up in the right place? And, anyway, hard as it is to believe, they all have jobs too."

"Wait a minute, so what if they have jobs? How much time can it take to arrange this scattering?"

"Precisely. It's not a matter of time. It's a matter of having it handled properly. It has to be somebody who has brains and flexibility, and a bit of time on their hands, such as yourself. It has to be somebody I could trust to do the job properly. As Benedict would have wanted it. That would be you."

Deep sadness backlit her smile. And it crossed my mind that Bridget loved Benedict even more dead than she had when he was alive. No wonder. Dead Benedict didn't provide on-going irritations in the way of unpaid bills, brushes with authority and the tendency to leave socks and young women lying around. So I figured Bridget might not like to hear that disposing of Benedict's ashes in *exactly the way he wanted* wasn't such a big deal. Even allowing for the prospect of everlasting life, Benedict would be too busy dealing with the heat wave to worry about the ashes-to-ashes part.

I played my last card. "I have a deadline for my new romance novel. That's my job. A big project would throw me off."

A stubborn little crease appeared between Bridget's eyebrows. I could see why she was a success in the competitive world of retail. "It won't take long. Then you can concentrate."

I hardly got any work done when things were going well. Imagine the phone calls a scattering would generate. Ducky, just ducky. Panicky thoughts danced in my brain as I searched for one last excuse. The panic must have seeped onto my face.

Bridget drew a conclusion. "Oh, Fiona, Fiona, don't worry about the cost. Benedict's estate will reimburse you."

"What estate, for God's sake? Benedict didn't have an estate. He was up to his ears in debt all the time, and we both know it. You'll be lucky if you don't get stuck with a lot of loans you foolishly co-signed instead of having the cash to have a big party with a..."

"With an urn. And quite a nice one." Bridget smiled the smile she probably reserved for bankers about the overdraft. "There's enough money."

"Come on, Bridget. Pull the other one."

"It's true. Benedict had an old term insurance policy. And I'm the beneficiary, since I've been paying the premiums for fifteen years, mainly so I wouldn't get stuck with those debts you mentioned I'd foolishly co-signed for. I wasn't born yesterday."

"Oh."

"The point is, after the loans and things are paid, I have enough to send him off in style. With a party. So select your date and make your arrangements."

I cast around for more objections. Bridget reached into the green bag and produced a squarish object in a burgundy velvet bag. Behind the successful businesswoman exterior, I sensed

Bridget's emotional protection crumbling. She slipped the velvet bag off the object which I had already figured contained Benedict's ashes. She ran her fingers over the sleek mahogany box containing the urn. A couple of tears dripped onto it.

Fine. I know when I'm beaten. "I guess I could do it."

Bridget stood up and hobbled toward the fireplace. She got her balance long enough to place the urn in the centre of the mantel. "Thank you. You know, I came to ask you to do these things, but the thing is, I really wanted to talk to someone who knew and appreciated him."

I bit my tongue.

She talked. And appreciated. Two hours later, I decided to call Cyril Hemphill to pour Bridget home.

The urn remained.

Now I couldn't even look at my fireplace.

Nine

Another trip to the village. No way to avoid it. I was out of dog biscuits again and, trust me, life wasn't worth living without them.

Plus Phillip had called twice (Los Angeles and Denver). Even Tolstoy didn't care for the increasingly hostile tone of his messages, which was another reason to get out of the house, but the real problem was that I couldn't take my mind off this scattering thing. How the hell was I ever going to reclaim my home with that miserable urn squatting on the mantelpiece?

On the bright side, the microscopic cheque I found in my mailbox meant a little of the green stuff to spread around.

It was raining too hard to walk. The Skylark responded with a click of the key in the ignition, the engine turned over and went back to bed. The good news was that at least I'd paid my Canadian Automobile Association premium, and it still had a month to run. For once, it was a slow day for Remorquage Bye-Bye. Tolstoy and I dashed through the downpour as the tow-truck pulled up.

"Can you take it to Marc-André Paradis' garage?"

"Where's that?"

"Up Highway 105, um, somewhere." Water dripped off my nose.

"Never heard of it. You want to pay me to drive around and look for it? Extra eighty bucks an hour."

Everybody's an entrepreneur. The guy probably had a sex life too. "No thanks. Just haul it to Tom and Jerry's."

Tolstoy and I spent the next hour sulking to the tune of the "Water Music". But sulk or no sulk, I needed to get around. I bit my lip for a long time before I called Cyril Hemphill. At least Cyril was happy about it. He and Tolstoy grinned dopily at each other in the front seat. I sat in the back enveloped in fog and bad feelings.

Cyril twisted right around to chat with me. "Don't you worry, Miz Silk, I'm setting people straight about that murder."

Tolstoy regarded Cyril with admiration.

"Yep, I told them no way a woman like you could beat a man to death. Leastways, not when you were..."

"Watch the road, please," I said.

Cyril swivelled. "...shit-faced, ma'am, pardon my French."

Something must have told Cyril this might be a good time to change the topic. "So they finally nailed old Mike Thring, eh?"

"Mike Thring? Who nailed him? For what?"

"St. Aubaine cops caught him dealing smuggled cigarettes. He's supposed to be back in court today. I might head on over to the Palais de Justice in Hull to catch that show. That Mike Thring cuts quite the figure whenever he gets in front of a judge."

I was stunned. I'd always thought Josey's Uncle Mike was a harmless drunk. It had never occurred to me he could stand steady long enough to commit an actual crime.

Poor Josey. How embarrassing for her. On the other hand, maybe she'd feel good that Uncle Mike had been sober enough to pull off a creative bit of smuggling. You could never tell how Josey would react to things. Then I remembered her mood the day before when she'd stomped out of my house. Clearly, she hadn't felt good about Uncle Mike's latest hijinks.

"I hadn't realized he was in jail again."

"Jail nothing. Got to hand it to the old geezer. He got out on bail right away." Like all St. Aubaineers, Cyril had a high tolerance for anything that deprived the government of revenue.

"On bail? You must be kidding." Where on earth would Mike Thring get bail money?

*　　*　　*

First thing, Tolstoy and I ambled off to the Caisse Populaire to deposit the cheque. Maybe I just imagined the raised eyebrows and the nudges and the nods around me.

Gisèle beamed from behind the counter. She likes to see me deposit money. She didn't know about the repairs to the Skylark yet. I smiled back. A joyful moment. Tolstoy barked and wagged his tail. Gisèle and I craned to see what he'd barked at.

Josey Thring struggled along through the downpour holding the leashes of not one but four dogs. I had forgotten about that. Dog walking was another lucrative sideline for THE THRING TO DO.

"At this rate," I said to Gisèle, "the GNP of France should rise nicely after her visit."

Gisèle leaned forward and whispered, "Oh, dear, I guess you haven't heard yet."

"Heard what?"

Gisèle lowered her voice more. I strained to hear. "She took out all her savings to bail out that drunk old uncle of hers."

Poor Josey. I was glad to find out about her problem before

I put my foot in it again, and equally glad to learn you couldn't trust Gisèle with any secrets.

Tolstoy and I took our second last fifty dollars from the Caisse and hit the road.

*   *   *

Next stop, L'Épicerie. You could hear the zing of spinning heads as I raced for the back.

Woody was in the storeroom rolling a joint. He found the whole situation most amusing. He twirled in his wheelchair, chortling. Tolstoy barked in approval.

Visiting Woody was even more of a pain than usual. By now, I regretted sticking my nose out of my burrow to forage for food and car repairs. I leaned against a stack of whole wheat flour bags and waited him out. I tried not to acknowledge that Woody had updated the front pages featuring my own personal story on three of the four walls. I averted my eyes, but not before I caught the headlines.

WHEN RHYME TURNS TO CRIME was the easy one. THE FATAL FOUR-POSTER had a certain flair. Not to mention: LAUGH? I THOUGHT I'D DIE: NAKED POET FOUND WEARING KRAZY GLUE SMILE.

"Just gets better," Woody said. "It's like money in the bank. You ask me, you should get in touch with your agent." He took a long drag.

My agent was already leaving strangled gasps on my machine. I helped myself to a Diet Coke from Woody's private stock. "No wonder people's heads are spinning," I whined. "I didn't think the police would give out information like that."

Woody had to exhale before he could comment. "Time to grow up, kiddo."

"You haven't heard the latest. Now I have to arrange to scatter Benedict's ashes."

"Oh now, that is rich. How'd that happen?"

"Bridget begged me, and I felt too guilty to say no."

"You? Scattering the ashes?" He put down the joint, but only so he could rub his hands together. "So when will it be? At midnight?"

Midnight? "Of course not. Why would it be at midnight?"

He spun. "Sort of fits in with some of the local theories."

I refused to ask.

Woody doesn't need to be asked. "Specifically, the ones about moonlit occult rituals and the late Mr. Kelly's part in them."

"Unhuh. I can see where it would fit nicely, Woody, but I'm afraid it will be garden variety daytime ash-tossing. Very ho hum."

"Too bad. Because the midnight thing would go well with the Satanism theory. You're the talk of the town, kiddo."

I drained my Diet Coke and remembered pressing business elsewhere. As I reached the front door, Woody careened down the aisle waving a container of organic peanut butter and a tin of maple syrup. He thrust the containers at me.

I tried to thrust them back. "Can't. I'm broke."

"On the house. Half the village has been in here, hoping to get a peek. You're a boost for business. I gotta love ya, kiddo."

I imagine everyone in L'Épicerie got a good long gawk as I made a run for it.

I had a seriously furtive look about me as I spotted Sarrazin heading into the Bistro Bijou shoulder to shoulder with coroner Lise Duhamel. Very cozy. She looked at him like a kid looks at an unattended rack of KitKat bars. He looked at me like I already had bars in front of my face. The other kind.

*　　*　　*

Even though Tom and Jerry are usually pretty gentle with their charges, the new battery for the Skylark made another dent in my credit card. But at least I was mobile again without Cyril and his meter. Forty-five minutes later, I tracked down Josey, dogless by now but drenched, outside McDonald's. I offered to buy lunch.

"So what's new?" I said to Josey, who sat on the other side of the booth, slumping. It was not like Josey to slump. Especially not when she had a large *McPoulet* plus a *grande frite* plus a *lait frappé chocolat*. I saved my *frites* for Tolstoy.

I had to pretend not to know about Uncle Mike's bail money.

"Nothing." Her eyes were flat and grey.

"Right. It turns out, I have a bit of a problem. My garden really does need cleaning out. If the ground's not too soggy."

She shrugged to let me know she wouldn't do cartwheels. Josey has her pride. But I spotted a bit of the old sparkle in her eyes.

"Is that special still on?"

"The wet weather garden clean-up special? Fifty bucks."

I could have managed that before lunch. "Make it forty."

The eyes got flatter and grayer.

"What is it, Josey?" I said.

I'd chewed up all Tolstoy's fries before she let it out. "I'm not going to France."

"But you've been saving..."

"I had to put up bail money for my Uncle Mike."

"Oh, Josey, did you have to?" I blurted.

"I can't believe you'd say that, Miz Silk. Uncle Mike's my family. I can't let him rot in jail."

Why not? Maybe it would teach him not to smuggle. Of course, it's easy to talk tough when it's someone else's relatives. "But don't tell me his bail took all your money?"

"Not all, but most of it. I don't have time to raise enough. I have to get the ticket next week."

"How much are you short?"

"Seven hundred and ten. *After* your garden."

I was near the bottom of the barrel. My credit cards were already stretching their limits. Even my emergency roll wouldn't do the trick. I decided to kick it in if she got within fifty dollars of the seven hundred. You never know with Josey.

"Any chance he'll be...whatever they are, released or whatever, in time for you to get your money back for the trip?"

"I don't think so. I'll get the money back, but too late for the ticket deadline. If I can't get the difference together, I'm going to have to pull out of the trip before I lose my deposit."

What could I say? "But you'll have other trips."

"Yeah. Right. Whatever."

"I'm sure we can find some fascinating things to do here." Visions of educational experiences danced in my head. "Remember when Dr. Prentiss was talking about all the wonderful things right in this area?"

"I know everything there is to know about St. Aubaine."

"No doubt you do, but the National Capital Region's not that far. We could visit the Museum of Civilization in Hull..."

I babbled out promises. Anything to take her mind off the lost trip to France and to take mine off the urn on my mantelpiece.

"Oh, yeah," she said at the end, "by the way, I got that information for you."

*　　*　　*

Defence lawyers are scarce in St. Aubaine. Except for a bit of cigarette and liquor smuggling centering around the Britannia Pub, a few low-level drug dealers, and the racing of pick-up trucks on Rue Principale after midnight, we're a pretty law-abiding community. The combination of my annuity, my house and my occasional writing windfalls pushed me past the eligibility point for legal aid, so Liz was looking after my interests. Later that evening, she ushered a lawyer whose name sounded like Natalie into my living room and popped her into the wingback. Liz plopped herself into the bean-bag chair. Apparently, Liz knew this lawyer from the golf club. Or maybe the tennis club. Somewhere.

I sat cross-legged on the floor and eyed the woman warily. And I eyed Liz too. When she found out about the scattering, was she going to drop the lawyer and send for a psychiatrist?

Liz discounted my whispered protests. "Of course, you need a lawyer. Anyone who might get charged with a murder needs a lawyer. Got any of that Courvoisier left?"

"No."

"In the cupboard?"

"No." Let Liz guess the spot. No way was I volunteering.

"Anyway, our friend here can give you an idea of your rights."

"I'm in corporate, not criminal," the lawyer said. She was as wiry as a whippet and looked as though she were planning to sprint through the front door as soon as opportunity permitted.

"Fine with me. I'm not a criminal. I don't think I need a lawyer." I wondered exactly what dirt Liz had on this woman to compel her to offer this quasi-expertise.

Liz got between us. "Natalie and I think if someone dumps a dead man in your bed and leaves you to explain it to the police, that makes you a victim in your own right."

Natalie made a face. Perhaps it didn't seem that way to her. Insufficiently corporate perhaps.

Tolstoy got up and left the room.

Liz rattled on. "And now this note thing just ratchets up the problem. But Natalie says you should be free to come and go as you want and you should ask to have legal counsel with you when the police harass you with questions."

Natalie must have been working out her irritation, swinging her long, thin legs. "I'll help you out in an emergency until you find someone fairly competent."

"Let's hope they have a sale on."

"So I can testify she was nowhere near here at the key times," Liz said. "Right? And that note in Benedict's cabin, the one the police were hassling her about? We could prove that was planted."

Natalie made another face, worse than the first one.

I said, "It's been quite a while, and in spite of all the talk, there's no sign of them arresting me."

Natalie burst our bubble. "Don't count on it. This is a small force, and they have to wait for results from the Montreal lab. That note thing? If they want to nail you for this murder, and they give you that kind of information, they're just trying to trip you up. That's why you need a lawyer."

"You heard Liz. I have an alibi."

"That alibi's only good if the autopsy results didn't indicate this guy was killed earlier—or later. Maybe someone stuck him in a refrigerator or a warming oven or something to throw off the time of death calculations. That Sarrazin may look asleep, but he logged plenty of time in Serious Crimes on the Montreal force. He knows what he's doing. He won't take a chance on screwing up a case like this. Don't be fooled."

I was awfully glad I'd hidden the rest of my Courvoisier in the washing machine.

*   *   *

After they left, I took advantage of the sudden peace and quiet to examine the fat package of clippings, complete with citations, obtained by Josey and dropped off for a small consideration. I carried the package out to the porch swing and made myself comfortable.

If there was a fact in print about Mme Flambeau, Josey had found it in La Bibliothèque Municipale de St. Aubaine and photocopied it. She'd purchased a copy of the latest *Maclean's*, where Benedict's face beamed from the cover along with the banner HAS THE FLAMBEAU FLIPPED?

I stuck my nose in the *Maclean's*, discovering the literary community was making not-too-subtle suggestions that the reclusive Mme Flambeau was overdue for a reality check.

I couldn't imagine what the next week's cover might hold. A picture of my four-poster perhaps? With me in it? If I could find the price of a ticket, perhaps I could migrate to one of the lesser known South American countries until the fuss died down.

Mme Flambeau had homes in Montreal, Palm Springs and Nice, which was nice, but there were no addresses or telephone numbers for her homes and absolutely no indication where Madame might spend her time.

Josey had added a note in her neat penmanship: Marc-André Paradis' car repair business was about eight kilometres north of St. Aubaine. He specialized in European cars and was not accepting new clients at the moment.

Ten

What I want most in life is to be alone. Alone in my own little house with my dog, my fireplace, my books, and even my writing, when the writing is going well. What I want least is to be the focus of salacious gossip in my community and to have regular visits from police, lawyers and people with urnfuls of dead poets.

I started another day, staring at the blank screen, hoping for a romantic thought. It struck me that the balance in my life was wrong. Do something, I told myself. Everyone else is trying to take charge of your life. Sarrazin, Liz and Josey. And now Bridget in a major way.

I wasn't even sure what needed doing. Okay, there had been a dead man in my bed, and I hadn't killed him. But on the other hand, twice a year since I'd moved back to St. Aubaine, I practically sold my soul to pay the taxes on my two unserviced acres. So wasn't that supposed to buy me police protection? Weren't the police supposed to be part of the solution instead of part of the problem?

Apparently not.

Then there was the thing about needing a lawyer. That was a worry, even if Natalie was more or less on the case. Sort of.

And I was worried about Josey. Well, I could probably deal with Josey. Like me, she was sort of an innocent bystander.

The only thing to do was to try and figure it all out. And

the sooner the better. So, who had killed Benedict? Who had planted him in my bed? Why? How could a note from me have ended up in his cabin?

I sharpened my pencil and sat down to put my ideas on paper.

If I'd been Bridget, I sure would have wanted to kill Benedict, and I probably wouldn't have waited all those years. But Bridget couldn't have lugged Benedict's body into my place, even if she'd wanted to. Even with a crane, never mind her broken ankle. More to the point, Bridget couldn't have beaten Benedict to death with her tiny fists, even if he'd been unconscious at the time. And logic would tell you Bridget would have plunked the old philanderer in the bed of one of his recent and more blatant lovers. Say Abby Lake. Or even better, Zoë Finestone.

I shivered when I remembered the evil glance Zoë had shot me at Benedict's little memorial. *She* was a really good candidate. Sure, she'd been pretty cut up about Benedict, but after all, hadn't he dumped her for some other woman? I couldn't even remember who came after her in the line-up. And she'd have the physical strength and stamina to lift him. Under certain circumstances, she could probably have beaten him. I tried to remember what her hands were like. I thought they might have been rather hamlike. On the other hand, why would Zoë display Benedict in my bed? Zoë wouldn't even have known where I lived. More likely she would have dumped him on her challenger. Dozens of other women were closer to Benedict than I had been. Many had succeeded me. There had to be a reason. Had Benedict said that stupid thing about me being the lost love of his life to Zoë? No doubt about it, she was a possibility.

But only one of many.

Logic also told me I didn't know enough about Benedict and his recent doings, his friends, his new loves and his rivals. It seemed to me it was worth finding out what had been going in his life.

Speaking of rivals, the other thing that nagged and bothered me was the whole business with the Flambeau. Considering that Benedict was dead less than two weeks after the announcement, it made you wonder if there wasn't a connection.

If I delivered those damn parcels Bridget had left throbbing in the corner of my living room, I stood to learn a lot. After all, they were to be given to people who knew Benedict, cared about him and would no doubt be prepared to blather on for hours about his doings.

Plus, with any luck, I could sell some of those One Act Play Competition tickets for Hélène so I wouldn't have to buy all ten myself. Time to get moving. Let's just say it would beat sitting home brooding about the urn and waiting to be arrested.

*   *   *

The next stage began with a plan. Not my favourite way to work up to lunch but then, it wasn't my plan.

My plan had been to visit Rachel, the most sensible person in the world, at L'Auberge des Rêves and pick her brain.

Easy. Fast. Efficient. She'd stayed close to Benedict and to Bridget. She knew the O'Mafia, plus the O'Girlfriends, Zoë and Abby. She knew everyone. She might know what Benedict had been up to recently and even how to get a line on the phantom poet, Marc-André Paradis. No one else did. It would be time well invested in piecing together what had happened.

Plus I could pick up some sensible advice on how to minimize the aggro brought on by the scattering plans. I'd be home again quickly, leaving just enough time to nudge Cayla and Brandon closer to physical union and out of my life forever.

Rachel was friendly, reasonable, helpful when I called. Delighted to have a chat and assist in any way possible. She even invited me to join her for dinner. As I made the arrangements, Josey was gluing and clamping the legs on the little Queen Anne chair.

"Did you say you were going into Hull?" she asked.

"No. Definitely not."

"It would be great if you were, because we could go to the Museum of Civilization in Hull. I love that building, it's like a big sand dune. Did you know it was designed by..."

"We could not go to the Museum of Civilization for several reasons, such as today being a school day and you being AWOL."

"Didn't I tell you school got cancelled this afternoon because of a malfunctioning fire alarm? "

I didn't want to think about what might have triggered that.

"And anyway," she said, "how come it didn't bother you that I wasn't in school when I offered to fix your chair?"

I said, "St. Aubaine is an hour away from the Museum of Civilization. Rachel lives in St. Aubaine."

"Yeah, sure, but at the end that's closest to Hull."

I ignored that. "I promised you these trips, and we agreed on the weekend, didn't we? We're all set for Saturday, which is not a school day. Right?"

Josey shrugged. "You have a funny attitude. For one thing, a visit to the museum is an educational experience. Don't you remember Dr. Prentiss talking about that? Better than school. I can get a note from my Uncle Mike. Not a problem."

Well, of course, it wouldn't be a problem getting a note from your uncle if you'd recently bailed him out of the local clink.

"Absolutely not." I sounded like I meant it.

*   *   *

The Skylark cooperated long enough to get us all the way to Hull and the Museum of Civilization. My mood lightened as Josey made her careful way through every exhibit in the building, not missing a detail, touching what could be touched, reading each plaque, craning her neck to check the totem poles. Josey was an exhibit designer's dream audience.

"Jeez, that was excellent, Ms. Silk," she said as we left. "Very educational."

"Glad you liked it," I said, as we prepared to cross the street and walk the three blocks to where I'd found free street parking.

"I hate to leave here. What a wicked building," she said, pausing to look back at it. "I love all those curves. It's like a big sand dune."

What the hell, if the kid couldn't go to France, why not spend the afternoon giving her a rare good time?

"And the lunch. That was a pretty elegant restaurant."

"Yes."

"Thanks a lot."

I was thankful myself because the bill squeaked through on my overworked and underpaid card, and I hadn't had to plunder my emergency cash roll. Although I'd had it with me, in case.

"And those exhibits. Jeez."

"Indeed."

"I like the native stuff. Those totem poles. That's an experience."

"For me, too." I was concentrating on Josey, and I almost careened into a large, shambling street person on the edge of the sidewalk. He stuck out his hand.

Without thinking too much, I fished out a loonie and dropped it into his waiting palm. The loonie vanished. Its new owner whipped around and headed rapidly away from us without so much as a thank you. I was left thinking sad thoughts about the impersonality of modern life, where all street people seemed to be identical. And where they appeared to have production quotas.

Josey curled her lip. "What did you do that for?"

"Why not? It's good to help other people out if you can."

"He doesn't have to beg, you know. They've all got welfare, but they take the tourists for suckers. I don't feel sorry for them. They have a choice. Especially that one."

Her small freckled face hardened. Josey had fought her way out of a legacy of poverty, ignorance and alcoholism. She didn't feel sorry for anyone she figured had volunteered for the downward spiral. She was halfway across the street when I caught up, puffing.

"What do you mean, especially that one?"

Josey stood still, her saucer-sized freckles on full alert.

"Don't you remember? He was the one outside Bridget's house when she had the memorial for Benedict."

"What? In St. Aubaine? That's an hour from here." I craned my neck. "It couldn't be the same one." But the shambling man had trotted briskly across the street. I stepped back onto the road to see better. I heard the roar of an engine.

"Look out!" Josey grabbed my arm and yanked hard.

The thunk of metal against my leg blanked my mind. I

collapsed on the sidewalk. Everything vanished except the pain surging through my body. I focussed just enough to make out Josey leaning over me, her eyes the size of salad plates.

"Did you see that?" Outrage made her voice tremble. "Jeez, Miz Silk, he didn't even stop."

"I didn't see him," I bleated. I'd felt it though.

"He gunned his engine and knocked you over, and then he took off. Are you okay?" If I hadn't known better, I'd have sworn those were tears in her eyes.

I sat up and rubbed my left leg. Two women in business suits put down their briefcases and offered help.

"Should we notify the police? Do you need an ambulance?"

"Yes," Josey said.

"No. I'll be fine."

People stopped to watch and make useless suggestions. Fuzzy words drifted around my ears. I couldn't concentrate enough to follow the conversation in French. The pain in my leg subsided to a dull throb.

At least the rain had stopped, although I was lying in a puddle. I apologized to the spectators, now in a ring, three deep. "I'm not used to being in the city. It's my own fault."

Josey said, "Are you kidding? That guy aimed right for you."

Eleven

Rachel started fussing almost the minute the Skylark shuffled up to the rambling Victorian frontage of L'Auberge des Rêves. She dropped her clipping shears into the day lilies and sprinted in our direction. Maybe because I was limping and Josey was helping me along, in spite of my protests.

"Good lord," Rachel said, blinking behind her glasses. "What happened to you?"

"Not me, it's Miz Silk. She got smucked by a car."

"Smucked...?"

"An accident."

"It wasn't any accident," Josey said.

"It was," I said.

"I saw how that guy was driving, Miz Silk."

Rachel said. "You look awful, Fiona."

"Mostly because I fell in a puddle. I'm fine. I managed to walk back to the car. For the last time, Josey, stop fussing. It was an accident."

Rachel said, "Didn't he see you?"

Josey shook her head. "He saw her all right. And he aimed right for her."

"My God," Rachel's hand tightened on the garden clippers. "Did you get a good look at him?"

"No," I said.

"Yes," said Josey, "he was a little skinny guy wearing

sunglasses and a baseball cap and driving a white Jetta."

Rachel's hand loosened.

"Did you call the police?"

I took a deep breath. "I've had way too much of police lately, and the last thing I want is another so-called interview with them or, worse, to waste a couple of hours hanging around yet another police station filling out forms. For nothing. I'm sure it really was an accident. Who would want to harm me? And, even on the off chance it was some kind of random road rage attack, which it wasn't, I'll never see the guy again."

Behind the glint of her glasses, Rachel looked worried.

"But, this is serious, Fiona, you've been injured."

"I'll be fine if I lie down for bit."

"But you're white as a sheet. You have to see a doctor. Listen, I'd better drive you to Emergency."

Josey rolled her eyes. "Miz Silk didn't want to."

"She didn't want to?" Rachel turned to me, "Fiona, really, what are you thinking of? I insist. At least let me call Liz."

I felt so dizzy I just wanted to crawl under a comforter without talking to anybody. Especially Liz. "Really, I'm fine. I have to get home to take Tolstoy for his walk."

"Maybe. You rest for a while, and we'll keep an eye on you."

Josey nodded in agreement.

"First sign of serious shock or concussion and you're off to the hospital, like it or not," Rachel said.

"You can't get a concussion in your leg," I said in an attempt to exert some control over what happened next. Still, I let myself be steered into a beautiful room with a bay window, a tumbling river view and a canopy bed. I hardly noticed. The violet-sprigged comforter seemed just right though.

"I'll just close my eyes for a couple of minutes," I said, "and then it's right home."

I fell asleep with the help of herbal tea, although I would have preferred Courvoisier. Even the herbal tea didn't prevent Sarrazin sneaking into my mind, whispering sweet nothings about probable cause in a bear-like yet seductive voice. Funny, I hadn't noticed he was sexy before. Must have been something in the tea.

In my dreams, I raced along a violet-strewn road while Natalie pursued me in a tow-truck until she successfully squashed me against the side of the Museum of Civilization, which was holding a special exhibit entitled "Splash". In a suitably moving follow-up ceremony, which Woody called "Ash", Philip scattered my charred remains over the lasagna in the Chez Charlie. Sarrazin ate honey from a pot, and Josey charged admission.

*   *   *

When I woke up, Rachel led me deep into the heart of L'Auberge des Rêves, her own private area. She was relaxed and smiling in her jeans and a well-worn flannel shirt.

Josey seemed to enjoy my surprise at seeing Tolstoy curled up under the table. "Rachel drove me over, and we picked him up. He likes it here. He's been fed and everything. I even had a game of Frisbee with him in the garden. We thought you wouldn't be able to relax if you were worried."

Now, instead of worrying about my dog, I could worry about how people could continue to get into my house without a key. Of course, the meal took my mind off all that.

We tucked ourselves around an antique pine table roughly the size of my study but loaded with food. Rachel set up a footstool so I could stretch out my leg, now swollen, red and throbbing.

Rachel was a first class caterer. We enjoyed pork chops with orange and rosemary. Not to mention brown and wild rice, homemade rolls, green beans drenched in butter and a salad with thick, creamy dressing. Then peaches baked in cream and maple syrup. My arteries were slamming shut, but at least I would die with a smile on my face.

Best of all, Rachel, for all her kindness and loyalty and wonderful hospitality, was not above trashing the late Benedict. I had a second glass of wine and really began to enjoy myself.

"...right under her nose, all the time," Rachel was saying, shaking her head. "Really, he led her such a merry chase. All those women, and he was so flagrant about it. So public. It's a miracle she didn't kill him. I would have."

"You don't think she...?"

Rachel laughed. "No, I must be projecting my own feelings onto her. That was the night she broke her ankle. The bridge club spent the entire evening at the Regional Hospital. We played right there in Emergency."

"That was a shame."

"Not really. It worked out well for Bridget, at least it gave her an alibi. That grumpy policeman was breathing down her neck. Seriously."

"I know the feeling."

"He even interviewed the hospital staff and the rest of the bridge group twice, trying to mess up our stories."

"He did the same thing to Liz and to me. I guess in a way Bridget was lucky."

"She doesn't see it that way. She was crazy about Benedict."

I said, "You know, I'm a bit worried about Bridget. First these gifts from Benedict to all these people. Then this thing with scattering the ashes. Did you know she even gave me the urn? What next? You think she's having a breakdown?"

Rachel rubbed her nose. "I don't know. I'm worried too. She's so fragile. All those years with Benedict, you can imagine. On the other hand, she really is overdoing it. I could have brought you those ashes."

"I didn't really want them, no matter who delivered them."

"Who would? How about Irish coffee? You want that?"

"Can we take it in the garden?" Josey asked.

"No problem. It's my favourite spot. And if you don't mind, I need to do a little deadheading before it rains again."

"I'll help," Josey said.

I sat on the steps, next to two huge pots of red salvia and vinca, admired the expanse of garden and sniffed the damp but fragrant air. I sipped my Irish coffee and continued to ask questions as Rachel clipped and Josey snipped.

"Was Abby the worst of the girlfriends? The most public?"

"Nah. Not by a longshot. That thing with Zoë Finestone was public passion at its height. I was always afraid their chairs might catch fire. And she had two flings with Benedict, remember?"

How could I forget?

"Zoë had the nerve to show up uninvited to the memorial. Bridget was frothing at the mouth over that. Bridget and Benedict had come close to splitting up over Zoë. Zoë did everything she could to drive them apart. She was determined to get Benedict."

"What was she striving for? A lifetime of debt and drudgery?"

"No accounting for taste."

Maybe if I hadn't broken off with Benedict, that kind of lunacy could have overtaken me.

"Anyway, one day Zoë issued an ultimatum, and that did

the trick. She got a split, but not the one she was angling for."

"But Abby Lake showed up too. Was that relationship still going strong?"

Rachel shrugged. "I think so. Who knows how long it would have lasted. Benedict was about to start his fall creative writing classes, and that always brought new, shall we say, opportunities."

Ouch. I'd been one of those opportunities eight years earlier. "Maybe Abby was newly dumped and feeling a bit murderous?"

Rachel made a face. "No sign of dumping that I knew of."

Night settled over the garden as I pondered Abby and Zoë as very satisfactory suspects. Rachel and Josey worked happily over the basil and mint.

When a muffled yell drifted into the garden, Rachel snapped her head up and away from the herbs. A rumpled hulk of a man with matted bleached blonde hair and a bottle in his hand lurched toward the garden.

Rachel stood rigid, clutching her shears. "Get out of here. Before I call the police!"

"Oh Jeez, police, again," said Josey. "Just what we need."

"Please, no police," I said. Where the police gathered, could reporters be far behind?

The man stopped, swayed and staggered off toward the street.

Rachel wiped her forehead. "Damned tramps. Harder than the devil to get rid of."

"They're everywhere," Josey said.

Even in St. Aubaine. And what's more, they were all beginning to look alike.

* * *

Another thing I had liked about L'Auberge des Rêves: although the phone rang often, I had no responsibility for it. No incessant, pressing calls. No messages to return or ignore. For the first time in seven days, I'd enjoyed a carefree phoneless evening without the cloud of Benedict's death.

My own phone was ringing as I limped through the door.

"Fiona?"

I hesitated.

"Fiona, is that you?"

Bridget.

"That big, cranky policeman was here again asking questions about Benedict and you."

"Oh." I hoped the big cranky policeman hadn't dropped a bomb about the note.

"You know, it's actually bothering me more now to talk about Benedict's death than it did before. Now the initial shock is over, I find myself dwelling on how strange it seems."

"Mmmm," I said.

"I keep asking myself why."

I certainly knew about the why question. "You know, there was nothing between me and Benedict. All of that was over years ago, before I even knew you, and it wasn't a real affair. We never actually..."

"I know that, Fiona. But I keep asking myself why he was moved to your place. And all that awful stuff we're reading in the papers. What does it mean? Who's setting that up? Is that the key to it or something to throw the police off the scent of the real people who are involved?"

"I wouldn't mind finding out that myself."

"It must be driving you crazy."

"No kidding." I hated the whole idea of Sarrazin with his glowering dark looks intimidating my old friends and

Benedict's into making damaging statements about me. I particularly hated the idea that Sarrazin might tell Bridget about the note.

"They even asked if he had any underworld connections."

"Benedict? Oh, no, that sounds too much like work."

It felt good to hear Bridget laugh.

"That's what I've been telling him. This Sarrazin's a very serious kind of guy. He has trouble understanding what made Benedict tick."

I couldn't figure out what made either one of them tick. "It is nice to think of Benedict leaving a legacy of perplexity," I said.

"You're right, and now that you mention it, that cheers me. Thanks, Fiona. I'll keep it in mind when I talk to the police."

For a long time after I hung up, I stood in the hall, pondering the state of my precarious legal position, throbbing left leg, empty bank account and ruined writing.

That reminded me, I had to fix my novel before Cayla and Brandon went past the point where editing could straighten them out. Since, as Liz pointed out, I had no sex life to give me inspiration, I needed to buckle down and work hard.

But how the hell could I concentrate?

Twelve

"Absolutely not," I said to Josey the next morning. She showed no sign of getting out of the car. "I am going to deliver these parcels, and you are not coming along."

"Don't be miserable, Miz Silk. You need me. You don't know your way around this area like I do. You have a lot of people to locate. It'll be much easier with me to help you deliver the stuff. There's your leg to think about. And if this car breaks down again, who do you think could get a tow-truck here faster, you or me?"

She had a point. "It doesn't matter. You're going to school."

"No, I'm not. It's Founders' Day."

"Founders' Day? There's no such thing."

"Better call the school board and tell them."

"You're absolutely sure this is Founders' Day?" Now that my painkillers had kicked in, I could think more clearly about the school thing. I think the tow-truck argument tipped the balance.

The back roads of St. Aubaine and surrounding hamlets presented many challenges. For one thing, the so-called roads were about six inches wider than two small cars. For another, the ones I needed were not paved. The locals barrelled their pickup trucks along at an alarming velocity, passing in the face of on-coming traffic. And, of course, none of the roads would appear on any map. It would be very handy to have Josey along.

Josey had a fine time. So did Tolstoy. "Look at how beautiful it is," she said. "Even through the rain, you can see the river and the mountains. And the trees are starting to change already. If this keeps up, we'll have the best fall colours in years."

She was right, but she still didn't fool me. It was a perfect day to play hooky. I was contributing to the delinquency of a minor, and this would add to my growing stature in the community.

A pickup truck flashed by us on the other side of the road, close enough for us to smell the driver's breath mints.

"They drive kinda fast around here, don't they?" Josey said, with a hint of admiration.

I clutched the steering wheel and peered through the sloshing wipers. The sooner I tracked down these poets and found out what Benedict had been up to, the sooner Josey could get back to school and I could get back to work.

"You know, maybe Dr. Prentiss was right about the Findlay Falls," Josey said.

"No falls," I said, feeling my leg get worse.

"Miz Kilmartin had some nice brochures on stuff, and they were mentioned. She said you might enjoy it when your leg is better."

Fine, maybe my leg was never going to be better.

Eventually we found Mary Morrison's small pink symmetrical bungalow nestled not more than two feet off the roadway. Late-blooming roses grew up both sides of the front door. I felt a wash of relief at having survived the drive.

Tolstoy stayed in the car with the windows rolled down one-quarter. Just enough so he could breathe, and the seats could get wet. We took our rain jackets.

"They must be rain roses," I complained.

"The rain is good. Keeps things green," Josey said.

Things were not supposed to be green. They were supposed to be starting to turn red and orange and bright yellow and gold. We were supposed to have warm, sunny days and crisp, cool, dry nights. That's what fall in the Gatineau is about. As far as I was concerned, she could keep the rain. I made this point.

"It's not fall until September 21st, and the leaves never change colour this early. What's the matter with you, Miz Silk? You should be glad it's still summery."

It would have been about the only thing I had to be glad about.

I thumped on the door. We stepped back in surprise when it opened. The fragrance of fresh apple pie drifted out and mingled with the roses. A delicate creature with pink scalp showing through soft curling white hair greeted us with the confidence of someone who could make apple pie and knew her way around roses.

"Oh, sorry, we were looking for Mary Morrison," I said.

"I'm Mary Morrison."

I'd been expecting one of Benedict's lady poet projects. Someone with cleavage or endless legs or recently enhanced lips.

"My name is Fiona Silk and this is Josey Thring. I'd like to talk to you about Benedict Kelly."

"Benedict." She lit up even more. "Oh, yes. Please do come in."

Josey gave me a sideways glance that said, great, and now we get to tell this sweet little old lady he was found you-know-what and you-know-where.

There'd be no talk of you-know-where, I decided.

The doll-sized parlour was furnished with a faded brocade sofa, two large armchairs and a stack of large-print library books. No sign of a television set or a newspaper. No sound of a radio. Good. Excellent.

At least forty framed photos hung on the walls. Dozens of photo albums sat in stacks. More photos spilled out of boxes.

We perched on the sofa and waited. Miss Mary Morrison bustled to get us tea, rejecting our offers of help. I could feel my heart thudding at the idea of stifling that luminous smile.

She set out a tray with a china pot of tea, cups and a plate each of still warm pie. "Tell me, how is that rascal, Benedict?"

Naturally. She was the one person in the Western World who hadn't heard the news, and I had to be the one to break it to her. Josey gazed at the photos on the wall with interest. I examined the pie. "I'm afraid ..."

"Oh. Has something happened to him?"

Josey exhaled. I took a deep breath.

"Yes," said Josey.

"Umm," I said.

"Dead, is he?"

I coughed in surprise. "I'm afraid so," I said.

"What a shame. But you get used to it, you know."

"Used to it?"

"Death." She lifted her tea cup. "Everyone's been dying."

Surprise, surprise.

"I'm the only one left of my brothers and sisters. All my friends are dead. The ones in their seventies are starting. Imagine. No staying power. But as I said, you do get used to it. And now Benedict. It's a shame, even so."

I nodded. Things were looking up. I might not have to explain what happened to Benedict. I let my shoulders relax.

"What happened to him?" she asked.

I could feel Josey's eyes on me.

"He broke his neck. No one is quite sure how."

"Oh, well, murdered, I imagine," she said.

My jaw plummeted in astonishment. The truth, of course, but exactly what I'd been hoping to spare this fine and delicate old lady.

After a pause, I admitted it was murder.

"Oh, dear, poor Benedict. But he would get mixed up in things he shouldn't, wouldn't he?"

A shiver rippled up my back. "He would," I said. What things, I wondered.

"He was always like that. Even as a boy. I knew someday it would all catch up with him. Still, it's sad." She clutched the pink china cup with her tiny faded fingers. "I taught him, you know, when he was a little boy. Back in the St. Aubaine Elementary School. Always into trouble and never having to deal with the results. Some other little boy would get punished for something Benedict had done. Oh, and he could lie like a rug. Charm a snake. You knew it couldn't last forever."

Miss Mary Morrison had understood Benedict very well.

"He wanted you to have some things to remember him by."

She chuckled, "As if I could forget the scamp."

I rustled in my carryall. And fished out two packages Bridget had wrapped in white tissue paper. Mary Morrison opened the first package and took out a gold Saint Christopher medal.

The unspoken thought hung in the room. Saint Christopher must have been on vacation when Benedict needed him.

"Allow a little old lady a bit of rudeness and tell me, were you Benedict's..." she hesitated, "...special friend?"

Josey exuded interest.

"Absolutely not," I said, with more emphasis than I intended. I switched to a softer tone. "We were good friends years ago. Seven or possibly even eight."

"I only asked because it was just month or so ago that he visited here with a lovely young lady."

"Oh?" This in itself shouldn't have surprised anyone.

"Yes. He was very excited. Things were going very well for him at last. He said he was about to come into some 'serious dollars'."

Benedict talking about coming into serious dollars? What a con artist! He couldn't have known he'd win the Flambeau before it was announced.

"A young lady? What was her name?"

Mary Morrison quivered. "Oh, dear, I can't remember. It's a lot easier to remember people from forty years ago than last week."

"I understand completely. Do you remember if Benedict said where this serious money would come from?"

"Indeed no, I took it for another bit of his malarkey." Before I could frame another question, Mary continued with her own. "So Benedict asked you to deliver these objects?"

"Um, no, Bridget Gallagher asked me. Do you know Bridget?"

"Of course, I taught her in St. Aubaine too. Always crazy about Benedict, even when she was a small girl. I would love to see Bridget. Why didn't she come herself?"

"I'm sure she would have, but she has trouble getting around. She broke her ankle."

"A shame."

"Also, she was quite worried about her emotional reaction telling people the news of Benedict's death."

"Understandable. Still she's been doing well with all of her businesses, hasn't she? Much better than Benedict was, I imagine. Still, I'm sure Benedict's passing would be hard for her. When she's my age, she'll be used to it. You can pass that on from me."

I thought I might not.

The second parcel held a miniature water-colour of the river, soft and moody. I was pretty sure some old girlfriend of Benedict's had painted it, or else Bridget would have kept it, since it was so lovely.

Mary Morrison's eyes filled with tears. We sat in silence. After a while, she wiped her eyes and managed another smile.

"But here, take a peek at Benedict before you go."

Benedict rated more than one photo. A graduation shot. A casual smiling Benedict, leaning against the hood of a car.

Josey pointed at a picture of a class of school children, taken maybe thirty-five years earlier. Benedict's good looks and charm dominated the photo. "Look, and this must be Bridget. You could tell her anywhere. Look at her beautiful red ringlets."

"And there's Rachel." I pointed to a square-faced, solemn child staring beefily at the camera.

The children's expressions ranged from toe-turned shyness to bold confidence. An old collection of young faces, most familiar. But I'd probably seen them all around St. Aubaine. They were all in their mid-forties now. At least one was dead.

I said, "And before we go, Miss Morrison, I'd like you to have Benedict's latest book of poetry."

"Humph," she said, holding back a smile. "I hope that scamp finally learned to spell."

Absolutely.

Things got better. Miss Morrison was more than happy to buy two tickets to the One Act Play Competition and equally pleased to engage Josey to paint her kitchen cupboards as soon as Uncle Mike could drive her out for the day.

Mary Morrison snapped a nice photo of us both framed by the cottage door as we left. We waved as we dashed to the car, rain slashing in sheets, sharp enough to sting. We pulled our jackets over our heads. The Skylark sputtered and reluctantly started.

"Boy, how come I never had a teacher like that?" Josey said. Mary Morrison had passed the test.

Tolstoy licked our ears, indicating we had passed his test.

The entire trip had passed my test. I now knew Benedict had visited his old teacher not so long before with a lovely young lady, all excited about some serious money.

Well, well.

Now just what the hell was that all about?

Thirteen

Kostas O'Carolan was next on the list. Bridget had written "poet" next to his name. What else would he be with a name like that? A Greco-Celtic bard to round out Benedict's collection. When we rolled to a stop in front of what was supposed to be Kostas O'Carolan's house, I shook my head.

"It can't be here. This looks like an abandoned barn or something."

As I spoke, a border collie strolled over and relieved itself on my left front tire. The door of the house opened. Santa Claus rolled out.

We edged ourselves out to meet Santa, leaving Tolstoy, who was not too happy about this Border Collie business, in the car.

Josey scrutinized Kostas O'Carolan's round rosy cheeks, his round rosy nose and his round blue eyes.

He beamed at us. "Ladies, ladies. Come in. Come in." There was that Irish accent again. How the hell many expatriate Irish could be living in our region, I wondered. And was I going to have to meet every damned one of them, as I represented the ghost of the poet past?

The place looked like a death trap, with a deep sag in the roof and more than one window covered with cardboard. I didn't care for the tilt of the chimney either.

Josey scampered through the door, no doubt expecting a sack full of gifts and a turkey dinner waiting on the other side.

I inched in and tried not to wrinkle my nose at the combined essence of raw wool, old dog, musty paper, booze and sweat. What the room lacked in furniture, it made up for in stacks of books. Five or six baskets containing half-finished knitting projects perched on top of books and on the floor. Knitting needles stuck out of the baskets.

I checked around for other signs of Mrs. Claus, but found none.

"Now then." Kostas O'Carolan rubbed his hands. "Now then."

"Right," I began, trying not to breathe too deeply.

"Exactly, exactly, exactly. My dear ladies, what do yis say to a jar of something?" He pointed to a bottle of Jameson.

Josey blinked.

"Bit early for me," I said.

He tsked. "Past lunch."

"In that case," I said, sinking onto a stool.

Josey perched on a chair and shook her head.

"Oh, dear," he said, sorrowfully. "Tea, perhaps?"

"Yes, please. That would be nice," Josey said, in a way that would make any mother in the world proud. "Why don't I make it? Miz Silk can tell you why we're here."

I hoped she'd check the cups for mould. I decided not to peer too closely into the glass of Jameson he thrust at me.

"Miz Silk?" Kostas O'Carolan said.

"Fiona." We hadn't introduced ourselves or given any indication why we were there. Not that it seemed to make a difference.

"Lovely name. Here's to yer health, Fiona Silk," he said, lifting his glass with a graceful smoothness.

"And this is Josey Thring," I added.

He bowed in Josey's direction without lowering the glass.

"Certainly, you may make the tea, if it will make you happy."

"It will," she muttered.

"She'll be a Virgo, I imagine," Kostas O'Carolan said. "I like to have a Virgo drop in every now and again."

From the look of the room, no Virgos had dropped in for the past couple of years.

"You must be wondering why we're here," I said before taking a sip of the whiskey.

"Not at all," he said. "Visitors are always welcome here at Evening's End. I'll be glad to show yis the sweaters."

I ignored this strange remark. I was fretting about how to introduce the Benedict situation without mortifying myself. I would have been happier in the kitchen, scouring crockery with Josey.

I finally said, "So, as to the purpose of our visit..."

"And a very pleasant one it is." He obviously had the opposite reaction to a knock on the door than I had. Here was someone who welcomed the uninvited with open arms and a glass of good whiskey. Excellent. Maybe I could redirect the bulk of my visitors here. I wondered how he felt about phone calls.

"As you know," I continued, "the poet, Benedict Kelly, who I believe was a good friend of yours, has been killed."

The twinkle faded behind the glasses. "Indeed. The poor boy's killed. That's tarrible. And he'd won that big prize too. To think I was too under the weather to attend his tiny, pathetic memorial." He slumped into a chair and took a steadying gulp.

I had a steadying gulp of my own.

"Can you tell me what happened to the lad?" he said.

Someone else didn't own a television or read the papers.

"The police believe he was murdered." That was it. That was the way to get people thinking and talking. Tell them the truth.

"In cold blood?"

He had me there. Had it been in cold blood? I had no way of knowing. I considered the Krazy Glue. "Yes. Definitely."

"Dear me. Poor Benedict, murdered in cold blood. And yis have come all the way up here to..."

"Ah, yes. I have been appointed by Benedict's estate..."

"Benedict's estate! Who would have thought our lad would have an estate. Life is full of surprises, isn't it, Ms. Silk?"

It certainly was. "Benedict left some special possessions to certain of his friends. So, in addition to, um, some other tasks, I've been asked to deliver them." I hoped the bitterness I felt didn't infect my voice.

"I just can't get over our Benedict having an estate." Kostas O'Carolan peered at me shrewdly over his reading glasses. "Imagine the poor boy knowing he was going to die and leaving instructions about his possessions. Very strange. Do you follow me?"

I did. "I take your point. But..."

Kostas slapped his forehead, without spilling his drink. "Ah, what am I thinking of? Oh course! The prize money."

Now there was an opening. "Um, no. It's just this package. I'm afraid he never got a chance to get the prize money. He died too soon." Of course, I was wondering if some other poet might not have made that happen.

"No. Doubly tragic, don't you think?"

I didn't know what to think any more.

He picked up the book and blinked at it, shaking his head. "*While Weeping for the Wicked*," he said.

I wondered why he continued to shake his head longer than one might consider absolutely normal.

"It's the latest collection of Benedict's poems."

"I know, dear lady, I know." He sipped morosely and

fingered the binding of *While Weeping for the Wicked.*

Josey took that moment to re-enter the room with her tea in a cracked but clean mug.

"I imagine it could be worth a lot before long," I said.

"Pardon me?"

"*While Weeping for the Wicked.* Bridget said only a small number were printed, and with Benedict winning the Flambeau and, um, dying so soon after, they would be, wouldn't they?"

Now there was a thought. Would anybody kill a poet on the off chance his books would instantly accrue in value? No, too weird.

"Excuse me," said Josey, who'd been quiet for too long.

"My dear?" he twinkled at her.

"Who is doing all of this knitting? Your wife?"

"Certainly not," he said, sitting straighter and puffing out his already puffy chest. "Ladies, you are gazing at, in the flesh, the proprietor of Evening's End Hand Knit Wool Originals. Kostas O'Carolan, artist-in-wool. Every stitch perfection. Every design unique. Only available in St. Aubaine at La Tricoterie, the best knitting shop in the region. And written up, might I mention, in major shopping guides for tourists. I made the Marci Glickman guide this year."

"Really?" I said.

"You mean, men can knit?" Josey said.

"Certainly, ladies. The proceeds come in handy."

"There's money in it?" Josey liked that idea.

Kostas puffed up another size. "If you're good."

"Isn't that something, Miz Silk?"

"Oh, absolutely."

"I know about these. They're famous sweaters," Josey said. "Tourists fight over them."

Kostas blushed. "It's a good cause, my dear ladies. I don't need a lot, but a few extra dollars keeps the books in supply."

And the Jameson.

He must have read my mind. "My dear lady, let me top that up for you and, since it's stopped raining, will you join me in the garden? You'll see why I choose to live in this lovely spot."

Josey's eyebrow went up. "I was wondering," she said.

Stepping through the rear entrance, I averted my eyes from the things that didn't bear close examination in the kitchen.

The river view stretched away for miles. We were near enough to smell the water. Kostas dried off the wooden garden furniture. That was in far better condition than anything inside the cottage.

"When is your birthday, dear girl?" Kostas beamed at Josey.

"September 18th."

"Ah. Indeed," he said. "I should have known."

September 18th? Less than two weeks. None of the Thrings fussed over Josey, even when they weren't in jail. Her mother, who'd stepped out to get a package of cigarettes eleven years earlier and was now widely rumoured to be shacked up somewhere with a biker, didn't even send Josey a package at Christmas.

Everything she owned, from her neat, faded jeans to her equally faded blue T-shirt, she earned by cleaning gardens, fixing roofs, selling junk at the flea market and other activities I probably was better off not knowing about. And this was the year she'd missed out on her trip to France. I decided I really should make her fifteenth birthday something special.

Except for some mental arithmetic about how long it takes to metabolize each ounce of Jameson, the most complicated thought I entertained for the rest of the afternoon was what to get Josey for her birthday.

Kostas had no problem with what to give people. By the time we left, Josey had instructions in the basics of knitting, a collection of needles and some wool to practice with.

I had a headache.

"Poor, poor Benedict," Kostas hiccoughed much later, getting us back to the purpose of our visit as I got ready to leave. "Now tell me, my dear lady, when and where do yis plan to be holding the poor, dear boy's final departure ritual?"

"Um."

"We have to do it properly."

"Oh, we will," Josey said, getting in the spirit. "Miz Silk's in charge of the scattering."

"Shhh." I didn't want that getting around.

"Of his ashes," she clarified.

Kostas shot from his lawn chair without spilling a drop and held his glass high. "To the Successful Scattering of the Ashes of our Friend, the Late Poet, Benedict Kelly."

Successful? Did scatterings have degrees of success?

"I haven't really given a lot of thought to the details." I'd thought of the scattering as just another ordeal, like finding out who killed Benedict and finishing my novel. Which reminded me, Kostas was a poet, a backslapper, and he did live in the area. Here was a fine opportunity to make a little progress on another front. I hoped he didn't see the light going on over my head.

I sighed. "I really can't get started until I get my car fixed. It's very unreliable, and I'm pretty well stranded without it."

He didn't spot any gaps in logic. "Dear lady, you don't have a good mechanic?"

I shook my head.

"Indeed, indeed, ladies. I can recommend a first-rate mechanic. A poet too. Marc-André Paradis. You've heard of him?"

"Naturally."

So he did exist after all.

"He doesn't take new customers, but he might if I explained the importance and urgency of the matter," Kostas O'Carolan said.

Bingo.

*   *   *

I struggled to keep my mind on the road and not on the new development. What would I learn from meeting Marc-André Paradis, poet-mechanic, once Kostas vouched for me? It was bound to be better than knocking on his door and asking how he'd felt having the Flambeau snatched by the late lounge lizard, Benedict Kelly.

I was yanked out of deep thought by Josey, who'd been extraordinarily quiet following our longish afternoon with Kostas.

"It's too bad we never did get binoculars."

"Binoculars? What for?"

"Well, this car's been following us for an awful long time, even when we took those wrong turns and doubled back."

"Are you sure it's the same one?"

"Sure, I'm sure, Miz Silk. Jeez."

I checked in the rear-view mirror. All I saw was a long tunnel of green coming to a point in the distance.

"He'll show up again. Just wait," Josey said.

Over the next hill, I spotted the entrance to a dirt road. I zipped in and angled the car to get the best possible view of whoever was following us. It didn't take long.

A sleek black Acura whipped over the hill and swooped past the spot where we were tucked. I got a good look at the driver's broad cheekbones and black, slightly downward slanted eyes. A face of strong, but not good, character.

"He looks familiar. I know I've seen him before. I wonder where. There's something creepy about him. Josey, could that be the same man you said tried to run me down near the Museum? You got a good look at him, didn't you?"

"Naw, that was a little guy with a baseball cap."

Hard to believe, but I was the focus of interest for not one but two men who didn't seem to represent the Welcome Wagon.

Fourteen

I was tired and edgy, and my leg still ached. Even worse, I was back in the Britannia Pub after nearly eight years, trying to look like I belonged there. It hadn't been easy shedding Josey, but since the police had a nasty habit of dropping into the Britannia and giving the proprietors a hard time, no one underage slid through the doors. I would have been happy not to slide through the doors either, but it was time to have a chat with the regulars.

First, I checked the surrounding parking areas on the off chance that Benedict's MG was sitting there. It wasn't. My plan was to saunter inside and settle in with the local poets, but for some reason, maybe that dead-in-the-bed thing, I felt bashful enough to want a beer first. Lucky for me, I'd found twenty bucks in the pocket of my camel hair blazer, the seventeenth place I'd checked. Of course, I'd had lots of time to find it. Nobody shows up at the Britannia before nine p.m., when the music usually starts. I had enough cash to do a little overdue snooping. I started with a soft drink in order to conserve my twenty for softening up the poets. Too bad I had forgotten that it's much more expensive to drink soft drinks than beer at the Britannia.

"Never mind," I said, "make that a Blue."

I sat by myself at a battered table with a good view of the bar and checked out the scene. I nursed a plate of the

Britannia's famous fries. They reminded me of sitting in the same space shoulder to shoulder with Benedict, indulging his passion for fries. Come to think of it, I'd always paid for those fries too.

The regulars were there, and not just the poets. The roundup included dealers, drunks, sluts, college kids, pool players and a variety of underemployed artists and musicians. I spotted among the regulars Cuddily Cuddihy, the world's nastiest stand-up comic. Only the college kids had changed over the years.

Josey's Uncle Mike supported himself with the wall. Three men in jeans and leather jackets sat at the bar, cellphones in easy reach. A fourth man, wearing the jacket to one suit and the pants to another, joined them and sat with his back to me.

In the corner, a pair of twentysomething women in backwards baseball caps defended the pool tables against all comers.

I was distracted from the pool players when the warning buzzer went off in my head. Something about the man in the mismatched suit was disturbingly familiar. I took a look in the bar mirror, and I met his eyes. Goose bumps jitterbugged on my arms.

I was squinting in disbelief when a roar of greeting rose from the assembled poets. If I hadn't turned my head, I would have missed the arrival of a clump of O'Mafia.

I glanced back toward the bar in time to see the mismatched suit heading out the door. I glimpsed enough to confirm my suspicions. No doubt about it, the same distinctive broad cheekbones and dark slanted eyes. The man we'd seen in the Acura.

By the time I'd raced through the door, the tail lights of the black Acura were fishtailing through the rain.

The Skylark, which can be counted on not to be counted on, refused to give chase.

Naturally.

When I returned to the Britannia, rain funnelled down the back of my neck. My table had been cleared. Blue and fries were history.

I reordered the Blue part and joined the poets. My wet clothes made me irritable enough not to care what they thought about where Benedict's dead body had been found.

Of course, as you can imagine, the poets were no help at all. Some of them recognized me. I recognized some of them. None of them admitted to recognizing the man in the mismatched suit. They all admitted to being thirsty.

Even though I was good enough to spring for a pitcher of beer and switch to water myself, not one of them uttered a single useful piece of information about Benedict throughout the evening, although they talked non-stop when they weren't waving for refills or failing to stop belches. No one recalled having read *While Weeping for the Wicked*, although someone remembered Benedict had once written "An Ode to Yellow Snow". No one remembered the words, but everyone thought the idea showed brilliance.

At midnight, I called Cyril Hemphill and offered him an IOU for fifteen bucks to ferry me home. He added a ten dollar after-hours fee.

*   *   *

Back on Chemin des Cèdres, having declined Cyril's kind offer to save me the price of a new car by being permanently on retainer as my driver (money under the table, of course), I reflected on what I had accomplished to date. Not that much.

My total achievement was two small gifts delivered to one retired teacher and one book of poetry delivered to one poet and artist-in-wool. Unfinished business included not knowing who was following me and where I had seen him before, not knowing if I'd really been run down on purpose and by whom, not knowing who'd killed Benedict and why, and not knowing much of anything else.

"So much for taking action," I said to Tolstoy. But Tolstoy was zonked out on the rug, snoring.

I slipped my new Sue Foley CD into the player.

After a quick trip to the washing machine, I leaned back in my wingback chair and felt comforted by the nice booze and the nice boozy music. Between that and the hectic day and the throb in my leg, I should have been out cold, but I found myself too revved to sleep. I sat there stirring a slow-simmering idea about planting Cayla and Brandon in a small pink cottage with roses and border collies and teaching her to make fries. This might tie up the book for me. I picked up my glass and trotted towards my study to fiddle with my story. Tolstoy declined to follow. Perhaps he was miffed about not getting to enjoy the fun at the Britannia.

I settled down to work when it hit me like a water bomb. My desk was not the way I'd left it. Who had touched things? Not Josey. She was the type to add to order, not subtract from it. But piles of paper had been shifted, files moved. Not a lot, but enough.

A chill replaced the feelings of warmth and comfort.

What about the police? Would they have shifted things? No. I'd logged a lot of time at my desk since the police left. A quick inspection in the other rooms, and I was sure. The small signs were there. The sleeves of a sweater refolded too neatly. A book upside down. Someone had done a thorough search.

But not a single thing appeared to be missing.

The Colville, which was the only item of real value I own—if you don't count the Queen Anne chair, my Aunt Kit's Spode, the silver and the antique brandy snifters which made up the rest of my inheritance, along with my small annuity—was still hanging on the wall.

My drop-dead emergency roll was still stuffed in a shoe with a pair of socks pushed in over it. Now the socks were stuffed in backwards. Whoever had searched my house wasn't after my fifty bucks or my piece of highly desirable Canadian art. And someone didn't want me to know they'd been there.

I sat back, chilled. The man in the bar. He'd had plenty of time to search the place while I was wasting hours with the poets.

Did I have enough to call the police? I tried to imagine informing F.X.Sarrazin that someone had rearranged my desk. Either he wouldn't take it seriously, in which case I'd be a two-time loser, stupid as well as violated; or he would take it seriously, in which case the police would be back to disrupt my fragile privacy again. Talk about a no-win situation.

That kind of decision just screams "make me in the morning". I took my Courvoisier and my useless watchdog and went to bed.

*   *   *

The next morning, Sarrazin was not at his desk when I called. Probably busy ferreting out ways to shake my unshakeable alibi. On the upside, the Skylark responded to the jump start from Cyril Hemphill, on credit, naturally. Further upside, our new buddy Kostas O'Carolan had finagled an appointment with the poet, Marc-André Paradis.

On the downside were the locks on my doors. "Easy enough to get in here, everyone can see that," Josey reminded me before I'd finished my first cup of coffee.

Josey was right. Why hadn't I had the locks changed yet? Because this Benedict thing had really fried my brain, that's why. I decided not to leave Tolstoy alone in the house until the lock problem was fixed.

By the time we'd collected Kostas and driven along Highway 105 to see Marc-André Paradis, the Skylark was hot, dusty, smelly and too small for the crowd. Josey and Kostas and Tolstoy were dressed for the chill morning drizzle instead of the noon-time sun. The smell of warm dog and raw wool was making me feel the heat even more. Not to mention my concern about getting punctured by flying knitting needles if we were rear-ended. At least Kostas put away his knitting once the temperature in the tin can reached the slow simmer.

Josey sat in the back, allegedly to give Kostas the comfort of the front. I suspected it guaranteed a strategic position for comments on my driving and suggestions for alternate routes.

"We're here now." Kostas wiped his brow with a red handkerchief. "And you'll see, it'll be well worth the trip."

"Excellent. We're lucky this lemon made it to the mechanic."

"And an excellent mechanic he is. He's brought me own vehicle back from the brink of Hades more than once, dear lady."

I chose not to mention that Kostas's ancient car was on blocks in his front yard. It didn't matter. It wasn't Marc-André Paradis, the mechanic, who interested me. It was Marc-André Paradis, the poet.

"Marc-André was a great friend of our Benedict's. Odd our Benedict didn't leave a package of something for Marc-André."

It was odd. "Perhaps he hadn't worked out all his bequests. Not expecting to die so soon."

"Perhaps, perhaps." I could tell Kostas didn't really believe it. "Sure now, he even took the other young lady over to see Marc-André not two months a..." I think he bit his tongue closing his mouth that fast, so it was a while before he reached over and touched my hand. "I am so sorry, dear lady, does this bring you pain?"

"Just the usual headache," I said.

He blinked, and I saw my opportunity. "Who was the young lady?"

Kostas squirmed. "Can't say I remember her name."

"Fine. Forget her, then. Was Benedict driving the red MG?"

He quivered with relief. "Indeed he was, dear lady."

"Did he seem excited about anything?"

"He was that, my dear lady, he was."

"Hmm. Do you know anything about it?"

"He told me he was about to strike gold. And he'd be buying the rounds for years to come. We both liked the sound o'that."

Naturally, they would have.

Fifteen

The first time I saw Marc-André Paradis, I tried not to stare. I peered around the small aluminum pre-fab garage instead of gawking at the man inside it. *Spécialisé en voitures européennes,* the sign said. Two Mercedes, an old Beemer and a green Jaguar were parked by the side. Classy company for the Skylark.

I'd imagined Marc-André Paradis to be scrawny and covered with grease, chain-smoking Gauloises, with a stubby pencil behind his ear and a demented poetic light in his eye. I wasn't expecting the man we found, and I sure wasn't expecting the effect he had on me.

I tried to look casual. I twisted my head to examine an old 10W40 poster on the inside of the door. What colour were his eyes? I'd never seen eyes that colour before, but I remembered the shade from the paint chips Josey had presented when she'd wanted to change the colour in my living room. Peacock Blue. The Peacock Blue had sounded wonderful, like floating in a vast calm lake. Josey had favoured Midnight to add drama. We'd settled on French Vanilla. You could get that same calm water feeling by falling into those eyes. Not that I *could* let myself look into them.

I heard Josey mutter something to me.

Kostas slapped Marc-André Paradis on the back. "This lovely lady here is Miz Fiona Silk from St. Aubaine, and her charming companion is Miss Josey Thring, also from the same place."

Josey radiated pleasure. It's not often she gets called charming. I tried to manage "lovely" but failed, partly because I could feel myself flushing. I hate flushing. I always turn an extreme shade of puce. The official colour of false pretenses. I figured this time would be no different.

"Good morning." Josey held out her hand to shake Marc-André Paradis'. "Nice of you to see us." From Josey's glance, I got the message loud and clear to smarten up.

Why was I wearing my oldest denims and a faded turtleneck the one time in my life when my clothes might have made a difference? Where was periwinkle when you really needed it?

I reached out my own hand, trying not to make eye contact with the blazing blue eyes or even to dwell on his forearm, tan and well-muscled with a sexy touch of grease.

If he thought it strange that Santa brought him a freckled teenager, a panting Samoyed and a tongue-tied goof with dewlaps, he didn't let on. My only hope to regain my equilibrium was if, when he finally spoke, his voice came out high-pitched or quivery or nasal.

I focused on the gravel. I imagined streams of pheromones, doing triple spins past the garage sign. You are foolish in the extreme, I chided myself. All you are supposed to do is find out whether this man held any murderous, yet playful, resentment toward Benedict.

"You see, Mr. Paradis," Josey smiled brightly, "Miz Silk's beat-up old car is practically dead, and she's a writer, so she doesn't have two cents to rub together. So we were hoping..."

"A writer of romances," Kostas said, wiggling his eyebrows. "And, of course, a *great* friend of the late Benedict Kelly."

Everything but the nudge-nudge wink-wink.

I whipped up my head in time to see Marc-André Paradis rub his chin in speculation. "It was a sad thing about Benedict's death, *madame*. And some controversy, I believe." His voice flowed smoother than Kostas's Jameson. My knees wobbled.

"You're aware he was murdered?" Josey said.

I would have kicked her if she hadn't been a bit too far away.

"A tarrible thing. Tarrible. Tarrible," said Kostas. "Of course, poor aould Benedict always lived *such* a life."

Marc-André Paradis ran his hands through his cropped silver hair. "Of course. We all knew about that." He didn't mention my bed, but I figured we all knew about that too.

A brief silence broke out. It was hard to ignore the revolting miasma of dusty, doggy, woolly sweat we brought with us.

One good thing: this Marc-André Paradis might have won the lottery in the looks department, but he was not the original personality kid. So I figured it wouldn't take more than a couple of minutes to recover from the unfortunate and irrational effect he had on my knees and other selected areas.

I smirked at the prospect of my coming recovery before I noticed Josey watching me with a peculiar expression.

"Are you all right, Miz Silk?" she whispered.

"I'm fine. Fine. Fine. Fine." I gave a shrill little laugh to illustrate my fineness.

She must have felt the need of a distraction. She pointed to the window. "That's sure some view here."

Marc-André nodded.

"You far from the Findlay Falls?" Her cowlicks stood on alert.

"The trail starts about two miles up the road, *mademoiselle*," Marc-André said.

Josey liked that mademoiselle thing. "You been up the trail?"

"Oh yes, it is beautiful."

"Would you say it's an educational experience?"

"Certainly. Especially the next day."

"Miz Silk and I are thinking about going up it."

We were thinking of no such thing.

Kostas gulped. "Dear lady, dear lady, don't even dream about it. That's a long, hard climb."

"Right," I said. I hoped there'd be no more talk of the Falls.

Kostas said, "Benedict was a fine friend. We'll miss him."

I chose not to add anything to this, since Benedict had been and continued to be even after his death nothing but a crafty nuisance and an all round bother to his friends and former friends and to me in particular. Marc-André Paradis made a grunting sound that may have been meant to echo Kostas's sentiments or even my own.

No one added anything to the conversation, and for a long minute all you could hear in the room was the faint sounds of traffic from Route 105. And, of course, my own breathing.

"They haven't found who did it?" Marc-André asked.

"No." I didn't mention I probably topped the list of suspects, although I had been hoping to trade places with him.

"I see." He leaned back against the wall.

We lapsed into silence again, until both Kostas and Josey started to twitch.

"Now then, I hope you'll be around for Benedict's scattering, which we three are in the midst of planning," Kostas said.

"Scattering? You mean his...?"

"Certainly, my boy, certainly, that's the modern way. No maggots and that sort of thing. The way he wanted it." Kostas kept nodding his head to emphasize his own words.

"Maggots. Yuck," Josey said.

My head reeled.

"Benedict always said he wanted to have his ashes scattered over the water, the only place he ever felt truly happy," Kostas said.

"Did he?" said Marc-André.

"Indeed. And this lovely lady will be managing the whole thing, since she was a very, very, very good friend of Benedict's."

Just when I thought my puce blush had subsided, it surged back over my face and neck at this point. I was afraid my ears would catch fire.

"Actually, I hadn't seen him for seven or eight..."

No one paid attention.

"Tell me, *madame*, when is this scattering?"

"Sometime within the next few weeks. When I can get my car fixed and after that whenever we find a...a suitable place. On the water."

"And how will everyone find out about the ceremony?"

"A simple scattering is all it's supposed to be," I said. With the exception of bodies in my bed, I probably hate ceremonies more than anything else.

"It should be on a Saturday so people can come," Josey said.

I wasn't sure we wanted to encourage people to attend. I imagined everyone who knew Benedict would want to be there. That could mean every second woman in West Quebec.

"Saturday, it is. The twenty-first." Kostas slapped his plump thighs and bellowed. "And, I know just the spot. Benedict loved it. A bit out of the way, but worth it. I'll do a map."

"I think we need a program," said Josey, "with music and

poetry. Do you know any musicians, Mr. Paradis?"

"I'll be in charge of the musicians, my girl," Kostas said.

"And I will advise the poets," Marc-André said.

By the time we left Marc-André Paradis' garage, we were well on the way to launching the most spectacular scattering in the history of Western Quebec.

Marc-André stuck his head in the window of the Skylark as I turned the key. "Can you bring your car by tomorrow afternoon? About three?"

"Absolutely," I breathed.

For the first time since I'd owned it, the Skylark surged forward energetically and bounded towards the 105. I'd been so overwhelmed I'd forgotten all about trying to flog those One-Act Play event tickets to Kostas and Marc-André. But tomorrow at three I'd get another chance. More importantly, I could use the opportunity to find out if the very dishy Marc-André Paradis had been consumed with murderous rage over Benedict's scooping the Flambeau from under his well-shaped nose. Of course, now that I'd met Marc-André, I wasn't all that crazy about the idea of him as a killer.

Sixteen

"That oughta do ya." Cyril Hemphill wiped his hands, stepped back and admired the new deadbolt on my front door. "Between this big fella and the one on the back door, I guess it'll keep you safe from just about anything." He glanced at Josey, indicating some things you can't be kept safe from.

"Thank you, Cyril."

"I'll put this on your tab. End of the week'll be okay."

"Boy, you really got hosed on that one," Josey said in a stage whisper. "I could have done it a lot cheaper."

Cyril turned to Josey as he climbed into the car. "Oh, and girlie, say hi to your Uncle Mike. *If* you see him."

Josey hissed.

I didn't even want to know what that was about.

*   *   *

I held my head high and sailed into the Chez Charlie for the first time since Benedict's death. The Chez, as the locals like to call it, never makes the tourist guides, but it makes my list because they take credit cards. They don't phone for authorization under fifty bucks either. The perfume of lasagna and barbecued chicken and *plats chinois* hung heavy in the air, along with the secondhand smoke.

The Chez is like time travel back to a better age, when

cholesterol didn't exist and music came from jukeboxes.

As usual, the place was bulging with locals, baseball caps, plaid jackets, scuffed workboots with loose laces. Over the wail of "That'll Be The Day", I could hear the soft buzz of gossip. I picked a green vinyl booth with a good view of the Chilean cooks preparing shrimp fried rice under the watchful eye of the Lebanese owner. Pierrette gave me her red-lipstick smile and took my order. I decided on *poutine*, the fries, cheese curd and gravy combo we go for in a big way in these parts.

Half of St. Aubaine nudged each other and pointed at me and wiggled their eyebrows salaciously. Through the front window I kept an eye on Tolstoy, hitched to a lamppost outside and working the crowd. A large scruffily dressed man offered him a handful of fries. Fries are right up there with Frisbees in Tolstoy's opinion.

Sarrazin lurked in the far booth. He was part of the décor, like the Matinée clock, the naughahyde seats and the orange light fixtures.

He didn't notice Pierrette making eyes at him. Probably had that coroner on his mind. Like Liz said, everyone had a sex life but me.

He caught me staring at him and narrowed his eyes. I gripped my Blue Light. I gripped it even harder when he picked up his plate and his glass and lumbered down the aisle towards me.

He slid into the other side of my booth. He had *poutine* too.

"So," I thought I could get the upper hand in the conversation. "I guess we won't have to keep telephone tagging."

"Yeah?"

"Yes. I left you a message about a break-in. And you left a message for me and then I left another message for you and then..."

"Why didn't you speak to somebody else? Only a break-in."

"Because I thought it might have something to do with Benedict's murder. Nothing was taken. Not even my money, such as it is. But things had been touched, moved. After the murder, you can imagine it's making me nervous."

"Tell you what's making me nervous. I hear you're stirring things up," he said. "Talking to people."

I blinked. Talking to people? No more than usual. And only when the answering machine was not on. Did this violate some obscure municipal No Talking ordinance? Oh. Maybe he meant Marc-André. And Mary Morrison. And Kostas. Or Rachel. Maybe Bridget. Even one of the many possibilities at the Britannia.

"Yes?" I said. "I hear you've been talking to people too."

"Sure, but that's all right for me, because this is a police investigation. And I'm the police."

"Don't I know it," I said.

"So if you know it, why not keep away from witnesses?"

"It's still a free country. I have things to discuss."

Sarrazin shot me a dangerous, inky look. "Like what?"

"The body's been cremated. We're scattering the ashes."

Sarrazin examined his fingernails as though he'd never seen them before. He wouldn't relax until he found something wrong with the whole idea of the chief suspect tossing the victim's ashes to the wind in a No Talking Zone.

"That Thring girl," he said. "What's she got to do with it?"

"Nothing."

"Then why is she going around with you?"

"I ask myself the same thing."

"That girl's got a lot of problems. Bad family."

"No kidding."

"Her uncle just jumped bail on a smuggling case. She must

119

be on her own up there. Social Services might start asking questions. Put her in foster care."

I didn't stop the gasp in time, but I didn't let on I hadn't known about Uncle Mike's bail jump, and I didn't mention seeing him at the Britannia. This Sarrazin already had the advantage of a lot of information. What else did he know that I didn't?

"You wouldn't do that."

"Sure I would." He picked up his *poutine* and slid out of the booth. "If I had enough trouble in my investigation."

*   *   *

I don't know what I expected to find out by driving all the way to Hull and dropping in on Zoë. Telltale tubes of Krazy Glue protruding from the flower pots?

I went in spite of Sarrazin's warning. Or because of it.

When Zoë opened the door of her apartment, I realized I hadn't exhaled once from the elevator to apartment 1819.

Zoë stared down at me from a distance of five inches. A great big beautiful witch, Josey had called her. I tried not to brush against her as I passed.

She said nothing. If you're six feet tall, have a waist-length red braid, several pounds of silver jewellery, wear only black and have ropey muscles on your arms, you probably never have to say anything.

Most people have living rooms. Zoë had a gallery. The 180° view of the Ottawa River from the eighteenth floor wasn't the most striking aspect, trust me. Nor was the wall of serigraphed Benedict faces, Andy Warhol style.

I saw lots of Benedict, but no furniture.

Oh, well. Why would you need furniture when you had an

entire roomful of Benedicts? Some were papier mâché. Some were metal, reminiscent of Giacometti. Some small, some large. One looked like Plexiglas. Most were marble.

There wasn't a place to stand without a fine view of Benedict's buttocks. Or worse. I must have caught her in the middle of a new project. She had safety goggles, a blowtorch and several chunks of metal on a tarp in the middle of the floor. I hated to think what a therapist would make of that.

Plenty of naughty bits but no chairs. So I drifted toward the open balcony door and attempted to appear riveted by the view. When I turned around, I met Zoë's dangerous gaze.

"You're probably wondering what brings me here. You see, I'm distributing some of Benedict's things..."

She didn't like that. It looked like a thousand volts shot through her braid.

"Not that Benedict and I had anything going."

"Don't flatter yourself. He wasn't interested in you."

"Absolutely." I wilted a bit under her sneer. Since it was eighteen stories to the rain-drenched parking pavement, I slithered away from the balcony.

"...and the estate wanted me to deliver this memento."

I attributed this bizarre intention to the anonymous-sounding estate. Zoë would never believe it of Bridget.

"About time," she said.

"Well, I've been a bit distracted. Anyway, it's a copy of Benedict's latest book. He hadn't had a chance to give them to his friends. Supposed to be the book that won him the Flambeau." Zoë snatched the book from me and flipped the pages rapidly, stopping to read some of the poems.

In case that wasn't dramatic enough, she snapped the book shut, pressed it to her breast and closed her eyes. I couldn't figure out what she murmured as she stroked the binding, though I would have bet my emergency roll this was the first time Zoë Finestone had seen *While Weeping for the Wicked.*

I found her reaction satisfying in a strange way. For one thing, she no longer seemed conscious of my presence. She was back to caressing the cover, with her eyes still closed, as I let myself out of her apartment.

All the way home, I wondered how much those sculptures weighed and what kind of harm those big hands could do.

*   *   *

Okay, time to take stock. On the minus side, the urn still lurked on the mantelpiece, Abby Lake refused to answer her phone or her door, and I had to worry about Josey being on her own now that Uncle Mike had jumped bail. As well, Marc-André was too dishy to make a satisfying suspect. On the plus side, Zoë was promisingly suspicious, the nasty pile of bequests was shrinking, and Stella Iannetti was the next on my list. If I had the address figured right, Stella lived in a converted farmhouse on the east side of the Gatineau River about a twenty minute drive out of St. Aubaine.

Josey knocked on the door just as I was about to leave for Stella's. I saw no reason not to bring her along.

If I had my chronology straight, Stella was Benedict's third flame after me and the one immediately before Zoë's second turn. She was one of the few ex-girlfriends that Bridget could tolerate. Stella had given our poet the toss once she found out about Bridget, and Bridget had always appreciated that. She'd be a piece of cake compared to the menacing Zoë and the absent, red-nosed Abby.

Stella was in high school when the late poet was having his slimy way with her. She was still beautiful. Imagine a Botticelli painting of a woman in faded jeans with a dusting of flour across the nose, and you'd have Stella.

She had moved on to the mommy stage of life. Josey and I were treated to toll-house cookies and s'mores, juice and, in my case, quite a good espresso. Stella asked if we needed to use the facilities and moved six teddy bears to make room on a sofa with shredded arms. She had no problem with Tolstoy, as long as he promised not to eat the cat.

"But then, that cat did wreck my sofa. So even that would be okay." She had the kind of warm smile it would be nice for a child to come home to.

The smell of homemade bread wafted from the kitchen. Squeals and splashes and the occasional boom of a man's voice drifted from the far end of the bungalow. Bath time.

Stella took Tolstoy to the kitchen to get a bowl of water. I overheard her say, "Sure, you can drink out of the cat's dish."

Josey breathed in the ambiance. When we are in other people's houses, she studies the details which might lead to new and profitable sidelines for THE THRING TO DO. But when we find ourselves in a family home, her expression changes.

In this particular case, she was checking out silver-framed school photos of twins, grinning wide despite missing teeth. Her eyes strayed to a picture of the third child held by a lanky man standing next to Stella. And on to the formal wedding shot.

Her glance slid to Stella, heading back with Tolstoy. A mother who cherished her home and loved to share it with others. In that cozy spot, I could recognize Josey as the child she still was.

Stella plunked herself on the sofa, narrowly missing a needle-nosed toy jet. "So. About Benedict. You just had to expect it, didn't you?"

I hadn't expected it. But by now it looked like I was the only one who hadn't.

"He was always his own worst enemy," she added.

"I guess he had an even worse one," I said.

"Sure, but you'll see, it will have been the result of something he did. I know it's not fashionable to blame the victim, but I bet he brought this on himself. Then everyone else gets trapped in the mess. Like you. All that hounding by the media can't be easy."

I really liked this woman. "You're right. It isn't. And you know, I hadn't even seen him for seven or eight years."

She nodded. "Doesn't matter. People in St. Aubaine will never forget it."

"Oh, God," I blurted.

"Trust me," she said. "I didn't even go to the memorial service, because I wanted to wipe out that part of my life. But it takes a long time to shake the residue." She frowned at the small parcel I had placed on the coffee table.

I took a breath. "So, you haven't seen him for a long time?"

"Last Christmas we bumped into him at a party." Her eyes shifted towards the splash and boom end of the house. "Before that, a couple of years. I did my best to avoid him."

Bitterness. You don't expect that in a Botticelli beauty.

"I asked you to see us because he left you a little memento. His estate has asked me to deliver it."

She shivered. "Creepy. It's like Benedict reaching from the grave."

I nudged the small, white parcel. Stella stiffened and stared at it like it was a litter of gift-wrapped snakes. For several longish minutes all you could hear was Josey munching s'mores.

I tried distracting Stella. "That was something, wasn't it? Benedict winning the Flambeau?"

Another snort. "Right, and I wonder how he pulled that

off. Oh well, might as well get this over with."

The package contained a framed photo of Benedict and a much younger Stella. She muttered something in Italian. From the sound of it, I figured eternal damnation and the evil eye might have been involved.

Her expression lifted as two children in teddy bear PJs exploded into the room followed by a toddler wearing nothing but soap bubbles. All three were being chased by a large damp man, grinding his teeth. Stella slipped the photo under the sofa cushion. She got to her feet. "It's well worth shaking that residue."

Time for us to leave. Stella had a happy, secure home, and here I had contaminated it with a nasty bit of Benedict. We were halfway home before I remembered I hadn't given Stella her copy of *While Weeping for the Wicked.*

Seventeen

We didn't discuss the need for Josey to spend the night somewhere else besides her home. That would have meant Josey being disloyal to Uncle Mike. She hadn't mentioned his disappearing act, and I knew she wasn't about to. As they say, you can pick your friends, but you can't pick your relatives. And whatever you could say about the dissolute old smuggler, he was all Josey had by way of family.

But in the car, minus the warmth and security of Stella Iannetti's home, I felt a chill of apprehension. Benedict's residue surrounded us like a hazardous fog.

I had trouble adjusting to the idea that I might be at risk myself, but if Benedict-in-the-bed didn't clue me in, getting hit by the Jetta, being followed by the Acura and having my house broken into did the trick. Then it hit me that if I was a target, so was Josey. If for no other reason than being in the wrong place at the wrong time.

Something very, very bad was going on. So it was all well enough for me to go swanning around with parcels, stirring up the old girlfriends, mooning over the mechanic, and annoying the constabulary. Involving Josey was different. If I got popped off, a middle-aged aspiring divorcée with serious writer's block, who'd give a hoot? But Josey had her whole life ahead of her. We had to make that last.

On the other hand, if I sent her home alone, I wouldn't

have put it past Sarrazin to have Social Services sniffing around. She was too young to be on her own. Who knew what kind of illegal substances or ill-gotten gains the cops could find in the Thring household.

"You know," Josey looked up from a complicated piece of knitting, "we should figure out why this stuff is happening."

"What stuff?" I asked.

"Oh, you know, people smucking you with cars, pawing through your things, following us with their license plates covered in mud, that kind of thing."

I kept my eyes on the road.

"You mean to tell me you never thought about it?" she said.

I shrugged, unwilling to say I'd been thinking about nothing else. I knew Josey well enough to believe that at the first opportunity, she'd be off in pursuit of evildoers with me waddling behind her. And we had enough problems.

"Jeez," said Josey, "I can't believe you're not more upset."

If she only knew. Cutting short her miscellaneous educational experiences would be the price for her safety. Josey would find that price too high, but it was necessary. I thought about Josey in that ramshackle cabin in the woods. Alone. Without the fugitive Uncle Mike. Or worse, with him, probably pursued by gun-toting police. And wild-eyed social workers.

But I could make it up to her. If I ever got Cayla and Brandon off to the publisher, the advance could underwrite a little trip south in the winter. March Break, maybe. Or some other kind of France substitute. And then there was her birthday, what was I going to do about that? What a responsibility.

"But at least we have all our new friends," she said.

I had a sick feeling in my stomach. For all I knew, one of our new friends was the reason why we were in the soup.

"Especially Kostas."

"Right."

"You know, Miz Silk, before I met Kostas, I only knew how to knit and purl. I didn't know about Fair Isle or tension or anything. I can't believe he took all that time to teach me those complicated knitting stitches."

Neither could I.

At ten o'clock, when Josey finally put down her knitting project and dropped off to sleep on the roll-out cot in my study, I crept out to use the phone. If anyone could arrange to get Josey into a safe place on short notice, it was Hélène Lamontagne.

Moonlight filtered through the glass in the front door and scattered stripes over the walls and the phone.

Hélène answered her phone on the second ring. "*Oui, allô?*"

"It's me," I whispered, "and I have a big problem."

"Fiona. What is it?"

I took a deep breath. "There's something strange going on here. It has to do with Benedict."

Hélène gasped. "Something else? What kind of... something?"

"Let's see, I've been hit by a car, someone broke into my house and rummaged through my things. And we're being followed."

"*Oh là là!* Hit by a car. Are you all right?"

"Yes. I have things to do with Benedict's ashes, but Josey's staying at my place because old Uncle Mike is on the run from the police. He took her trip money for bail and now the old buzzard has skipped. I'm worried about her. I can't leave her in this risky situation."

"But Fiona, you must be in danger too."

"Probably."

"I don't know," said Hélène. "Josée won't like having her

visit with you cut short. Especially after she lost her trip money. She loves it at your place." Hélène has a soft spot for Josey and wants her to have a little bit of the good life.

"She won't like having her life cut short either," I said.

"Josée's safety must be the most important thing, *naturellement.*"

"She needs some place to stay," I said. "If we go to the authorities, they might put her in a foster home. Sarrazin's already been hinting at that."

"Oh, no!"

It's always so satisfying talking to Hélène. "Oh, yes. And I can't send her to stay with Liz because...well, because."

"I understand."

Right. Hélène knows Liz.

"And Woody is out of the question."

"*Mon dieu.*"

"Even if Philip were home, I couldn't ask him to do anything, let alone this."

"But of course."

"So I'm getting desperate. You read so many awful things about kids who are wards of the Crown."

"She can stay here."

I'd almost given up hope.

"Oh, Hélène, really? What a wonderful idea. But that's too much to ask. I mean she needs somebody who would make her go to school. Would you mind that?" My long dead aunt would have been proud of me.

Hélène managed a ladylike snort.

I had to laugh. "Am I laying it on too thick?"

"Yes. But I would do the same. It will be nice to have Josée here. Jean-Claude is so busy, and with Marie-Eve away at Laval, I will enjoy her company. And I will make her go to school."

"What a relief. Well, maybe when all this is over, I can find some way to make it up to you."

"I am happy to do it. There will be nothing to make up. Unless you wanted to give us a hand with the Hospital Auxiliary Tea and Sale in October. I'm doing up a roster now."

Oh, couldn't I just chew up a bit of crushed glass instead? "Sure. Absolutely."

"Wonderful. Let me find the right time to tell Jean-Claude about Josée. I will make the arrangements as soon as possible, and I'll call you. Tomorrow morning I hope."

Tomorrow would be fine. More than fine. And October seemed safely in the distance.

"Thank you, thank you," I said.

"*Pas de problème.*"

When I hung up, I jumped at the shadow which moved behind me.

Josey's eyes were slate-coloured in the darkness. For once, no expression showed on her freckled face. Except for the kind of emptiness you might expect from a child whose life had been spent in squalor and whose hope of escape had just evaporated.

She pivoted on her heel and marched back to the study. She closed the door. When I checked on her later, she lay under her covers with her face to the wall.

I hit the laundry room and poured myself four fingers of the finest. I headed for the wingback and slumped there for an hour trying to work things out in my own mind. I had no choice but to send Josey away. The only sensible, adult, moral thing to do. Too bad I felt so rotten.

Why couldn't Josey have had a family like the one in the photos in Stella Iannetti's home? The pretty smiling mother, the tall, shy father, the twin brothers and baby sister, happy and loved. Children whose pictures predicted stable, sensible, confident adults. Just like Mary Morrison's school photo of Benedict and Bridget and Rachel showed children like the adults they grew up to be. I was thinking about that photo when it hit me, like a sock full of nickels.

The man in the bar, the man in the car following us. That face had been in the photo too. The eyes with their tilt, the strong cheekbones, the swarthy skin. I'd seen them before on a resentful childish presence photographed more than thirty years earlier.

Now I had more reasons to spin all night.

*   *   *

The old Josey returned at breakfast, not the silent stranger of the night before. But underneath her good humour and pep, I sensed something different.

"You can come back," I blurted as we dodged the drizzle to get to the car. "We could plan a...a..." I searched for something sufficiently appealing, "...a museum tour. Or something."

She trained her freckles in my direction. She'd believe that when she saw it.

If it hadn't been Saturday, I could have driven her to school and watched her safely through the doors. As it was, I had to decide if she was better off alone in my house or safer coming along for the ride. It's the kind of decision where you know whatever you decide, you should have made the other choice. We rumbled down the driveway and onto Chemin des Cèdres. "I have no alternative. I can't take the chance you'll be hurt. Or worse."

Tolstoy leaned over from the back seat and licked Josey's ear. I got the cold shoulder from both of them. A game of

Frisbee could win back Tolstoy, but what would it take to have Josey trust me again?

*   *   *

Outside the small pink cottage, a handful of dead roses remained on their stems. Josey raised her eyebrow. We could hear Tolstoy whining from the car.

In the few days since we'd seen her, Mary Morrison had aged ten years. Her translucent pink skin had turned grey and opaque, her hair sagged, she leaned on a pair of canes, and she shuffled as if to the grave.

I took a step back in surprise when she opened her door.

"Oh, sorry, Miz Morrison," Josey blurted, "if you're not feeling well, we can come back. It's not real important."

I nodded. I desperately needed the name of the man in the photo, but it could wait until we found out what dreadful thing had happened to Mary Morrison. I couldn't interpret her guarded expression.

"I guess you'd better come in," she said.

We sniffed no delicious smells of fresh baking. Something felt wrong in the tiny room.

"Sit down." Mary Morrison sank into a chair. "I'll get a pot of tea in a minute or two, if you'd like."

Josey and I inhaled simultaneously, alarmed at the idea of her teetering into the kitchen to wait on us.

"No, tha..." I started to say, but Josey stood up first.

"I'm supposed to be learning to do things like that."

"Are you? That's nice." Mary Morrison said, leaning back. "Do you think you can find everything?"

"No problemo," Josey said.

"Use the good china, dear."

"Sure," Josey said, making for the kitchen. "Is there anything else I could do at the same time?"

"Why, yes. There are some lemon squares my neighbour brought me, if you'd like to put a few slices on a plate."

I checked out the room. Dishes and books were piled on the table in the corner. Like a packing job had begun. I couldn't see any of the photos we had come to ask about. What was going on?

Mary Morrison leaned back in her chair with no sign of the light we'd seen in her on our first visit. She waved her hand in the direction of the half-packed objects. Her lower lip trembled.

"They want me to leave my little cottage and move to Toronto with them."

I could hardly imagine such a grim change in one's life.

"Why?" I asked. It came out as a whisper.

Her eyes filled, and the tiny hands shook a bit.

"After you visited me, the same night, someone broke in here and made off with some of my things. Imagine, right here in my little cottage while I slept. You know, we always used to say, safe as houses. And now my nephews are all up in arms and insisting I can't stay alone."

I imagined Mary Morrison transported away from this world of green tunnels and fields and river and mountain and the scent of roses. I imagined her reaction to the dubious advantages of city life. It would be the end of her. I reached out and touched her shaking hand.

Josey chose that moment to arrive from the kitchen with a tray, loaded with teapot, milk and sugar and a flowered plate with precisely arranged squares.

Mary Morrison didn't even notice when Josey set her tray on the small table between us and plunked herself into a chair.

"What did the robbers take?" I asked.

"They stole my past."

Josey sat up and stared. "Your past? How?"

"My pictures, my photographs. All my photographs. Every one, even the boxes from the cupboard." The tears spilled over and trickled down her cheeks. "Why would anybody do that?"

We paid no attention to the tea or the lemon squares. Mary Morrison's loss of a lifetime of memories blotted out everything else.

I thought I knew why. "Tell me, did many people know you had these photographs?"

"Everyone knew. Everyone who's ever been here."

"And no one ever tried to take them before?" Even as the words tumbled out of my mouth, I realized how foolish they sounded.

Mary Morrison didn't react to the foolishness. "No one ever did," she said. "In fact, that's why the police wanted to talk to the two of you."

Josey was less upset by the police wanting to talk to us than by the plan to uproot Mary Morrison. "Toronto is supposed to be a nice place to visit, but you wouldn't be happy living there."

"Thank you, my dear. I know." She reached for a cup of tea.

I wondered how long she would remain alive, if she were yanked from her roses and her view of the river and the mountains.

"I don't think we can let them take you," Josey said.

Mary Morrison perked up, perhaps from the combined effects of the English Breakfast tea and Josey's call to rebellion.

"But my nephews are frightened this robber or some other one will come back, and perhaps this time I'll be hurt or maybe even have a heart attack."

Josey pursed her lips. "It's your life, isn't it? Where do you want to live?" She shot me a look dripping with meaning.

"Here in St. Aubaine," Mary Morrison said, "in this house."

"There's a lot of unemployment around here. Couldn't you make arrangements for some young kid to be here every night, as a protection? Pay them a few dollars, so you don't have to feel obligated. You could get them to help you in the garden."

This gave me new insight into Josey. Maybe instead of a career as a wild-eyed entrepreneur, she would make her mark on the world as a defender of the rights of the downtrodden. She could give Natalie, the lawyer, lessons.

But I needed to get our business accomplished. "Miss Morrison, we came here to ask about one of the children in the school photo with Benedict."

She put her hand to her head and rubbed her temple. "My dears, this robbery is such a terrible thing for me. I can hardly think straight. Usually, I can see the faces of those children as clearly as if they were right here in this room. Now, it's like I've lost my memory."

"Of course, it's the shock." I reached over to pat her hand again. "I'd like you to think about it if you can, and I'll come again when you're feeling more settled."

Mary Morrison opened her mouth to speak when the knock came on the door. She motioned us back into our chairs and teetered over to answer it. She teetered back in, followed by the last man in the world that I wanted to see.

"Oh, dear," she said, "oh, dear."

Sarrazin settled his large frame into Mary Morrison's remaining chair. He smiled affectionately at her. He retracted the smile and focussed his black bear eyes on us.

Eighteen

"Must have been rough, kiddo. That Sarrazin guy? He's a weirdo, all right," Woody said. "Can't stand the sight of him. I don't think he has the brains for the police. Kinda makes you sick, doesn't it."

Our humourless encounter with Sarrazin hadn't bothered Josey much. She comes from a long line of Thrings, all of whom had a lifetime of disagreements with the law. But I found it hard to get used to being suspected of breaking and entering. And theft. At least being suspected of murdering Benedict had a certain passionate grandeur.

Josey and I were in Woody's back storeroom, recovering from our interview. With Woody's help. Tolstoy crunched organic dog biscuits underneath the *INTERDIT AUX CHIENS* sign. Josey snacked on some all-natural sesame bars. I had some sunflower seeds.

Woody passed around cans of Jolt. "You want a burger? We can send out."

"He's a detective. He must have brains," I said.

"You ask me," Woody said, apparently to himself, "he's a lousy detective. Look at his priorities."

Woody had a point. Sarrazin was the senior detective in St. Aubaine. It was strange he'd put a murder investigation on hold to hightail it over to question me about some old photos.

Woody said, "He was just sticking his nose into it because

of Miss Morrison. He'd stand on his head for her. Let's put it this way, my business was burgled. It took him two days to send someone here."

It made me think, which wasn't that easy since Woody never shut up. "No Jolt, kiddo? What about a Diet Coke? Put a little colour in your cheeks?"

Josey was chortling, as only a Thring, hearing disparaging remarks about the constabulary, can chortle.

Woody was on a roll. He basked in Josey's amusement. "Listen, I know about this guy. I remember him from St. Aubaine Elementary. Booted out of class. Getting the strap. Came from a real rough family. Trouble reading and everything. Never did his homework. Got everything bass ackwards. Especially Bs and Ds."

Josey stopped chortling. Much as she disliked the police, her sympathies would always lie with the outcast in the classroom. "That wasn't his fault, was it? He must be forty-five years old, and people still remember every mistake he made in *elementary* school? It's extremely mean, Mr. Quirke."

If Woody was startled when her eyes got to the size of soup bowls and her freckles became three-dimensional, he chose not to mention it. Being Woody, he just kept on talking. "That Miss Morrison? She was the best teacher we ever had at that school. She worked with him and worked with him. I guess it made a difference. He seems to have done all right for himself."

Josey nodded with some satisfaction. She liked stories to end well, even if a teacher played a role.

"I thought he came from Montreal." I said.

"Nah. He went to Montreal. You ask me, he couldn't cut it. Couldn't take the big-time pressure. Hopped home again. Major frog in a minor puddle here, ha ha. Probably going to end up Chief of Police here. Big deal."

"I love a happy ending," I said.

"You were lucky Miss Morrison put in a good word for you. If it hadn't been for her, you might have found yourselves overnighting it in the slammer."

"Humph," said Josey. "It didn't stop him from searching our vehicle and going back and rooting through Miz Silk's house again."

Woody nodded. "Right on, ferreting for loot."

"We had nothing to hide," I said.

"And what did he think we were going to do with a bunch of photos of people we never even knew?" Josey said.

"Hey, I don't read minds. But I think that guy means trouble. He's been talking to a lot of people about your alleged relationship with Benedict. Asking about your about-to-be-ex. That's what I heard from Gisèle at the Caisse. Philip was bad enough when he thought you were as pure as the driven. I can't imagine what he'd be like now that everyone's talking about events in your bed."

"I *am* as pure as the driven," I muttered. Well, I had been fairly pure before I'd spotted a certain mechanic.

"That's the news. Don't worry about it, kiddo. The publicity's dying down, but we can find a way to make this stuff pay off for your career."

"I don't think so, Woody."

I leaned on a bag of whole wheat flour, getting jangled on Jolt and fretting about dyslexic detectives.

Josey grinned. "That Miz Morrison sure has a lot of control over that cop, though."

Woody snickered.

I struggled to keep a straight face but was overcome by the memory of Mary Morrison, armed only with Sarrazin's history of backwards Bs and Ds, chastising the big detective for bothering her guests. He'd been blushing when he backed out of her cottage with our keys to check my house and car for stolen photos.

Even though we were laughing, I figured Woody was right: if we weren't careful, F.X. Sarrazin could mean even more trouble.

*　　*　　*

I volunteered Josey to give Woody a hand while I kept my appointment with Marc-André. Josey bit her lip. She'd already noticed I was wearing my good black jeans and a relatively new black turtleneck and my camelhair blazer, all freshly pressed. She was probably worried about what kind of fool I would make of myself if she left me alone with him. And she'd miss out on being called "*mademoiselle*". On the other hand, helping Woody could mean money. And food. And weird insights into the behavior of the police. Tough one.

I sneaked off while she weighed her options.

Tolstoy stayed with Josey. Maybe it was those organic dog biscuits.

*　　*　　*

I tried to keep my mind on the car engine as Marc-André Paradis performed an assiduous diagnosis. I was more concerned about his effect on my systems than the Skylark's.

I missed the prognosis.

"Thank you," I breathed.

"My pleasure."

I had exhausted my conversational abilities. I tried smiling.

He wiped his hands on a rag. I couldn't take my eyes off them.

"I'm finished for the day," he said.

"Oh."

Silence. I tried to remember what I wanted from him.

"Would you like a cup of coffee?"

"Oh, yes."

I followed the poet-mechanic to the barn next to the garage. The barn turned out to be a home, and a nice one at that. Good, now we'll meet his wife, I thought. That's better. With luck there'll be five kids, and I'll see him in a more sensible light. Just another man worrying about meeting the mortgage payments on the barn and wiping baby food off his shirt after his daily grind of metaphors punctuated with the odd European carburetor.

We entered through a back door. Marc-André Paradis stood back to let me go ahead, and I quivered when I brushed past him. We passed through the u-shaped kitchen. No dirty dishes anywhere, orderly and elegant, with the granite counter and the small table top gleaming. And a *cafetière*, which caught my eye. No toys, no aprons, no fridge magnets holding kid stuff.

"We'll go into the *salon*, okay?" he said, pointing the way.

Except for the kitchen, it was the only room in the downstairs area. He made coffee. I admired the unbroken stretch of hardwood floor. He had few possessions. Aside from the deep leather sofa I sat on and the leather lounge chair across the room, he had a stereo, with stacks of cassettes, LPs and CDs. An antique maple table sat in the middle of the floor, taking advantage of the huge window with the river view. Papers were stacked precisely on the table, and an ergonomic chair was tucked neatly into it. I liked the idea that Marc-André Paradis kept the best river view for his work area.

I don't know much about art, but I knew the abstract

canvas on the wall had set the purchaser back a good ten thousand smackers. The poetry industry might be in recession, but people still needed their Beemers fixed.

A clinking signalled Marc-André and the coffee. I checked if my hair remained in half-decent shape. Too much to hope for.

"Nothing elegant, but it should do," Marc-André Paradis said, putting down a smooth carved maple board holding the mugs. And a bottle of Armagnac. "I don't get a lot a social callers. Good thing Kostas gave me this last Christmas. A little something in yours, *madame*?"

"No, I'd have to let it wear off before I drive home."

"Are you in a rush?"

My head thundered. I wasn't. I managed a tiny "no".

"Then why not let it wear off?"

Marc-André Paradis added a little something to my coffee and his own. He sat on the sofa. I hoped I wouldn't blow an aorta.

We talked about me. We talked about him. We talked about writing poetry. We talked about writing romances. We talked about my-about-to-be-ex-husband. We talked about his late wife. We even talked a bit about Benedict, but we didn't say anything useful.

Marc-André didn't show much grief for the scoundrel who'd scooped nearly a quarter of a million dollars from him.

"How did you feel when he won the Flambeau?" I asked.

"It was a surprise. More than that, a shock. I did not realize he was a serious poet."

No kidding.

"The only poem I ever remember reading of his was called, let me think, oh yes, 'The Effect of Beans Upon the Constitution'."

"A lot of people were surprised you didn't win."

He shrugged.

"And then he died. That must have felt worse," I said

"What difference did it make? Whether he was dead or alive, I didn't win it."

"True, but..."

"And I didn't want it. People don't become poets for prizes. Or money. They often give up money to become poets."

"Right."

"It did not do him any good, did it?"

True enough.

"So," he said, "will I see you again before this scattering?"

"I hope so."

"I'll call you."

"Excellent."

When I finally pulled out on to the highway, Marc-André waved from the driveway. I should have used the time on the drive home to assess his viability as a suspect. Instead I found myself singing. *A sex life a sex life I think I want a sex life.*

*   *   *

Back home on Chemin des Cèdres, things were looking up. Josey, retrieved from Woody's and twenty dollars richer, was curled up on the porch swing, working on her knitting. Tolstoy kept her company, the Frisbee by his side, just in case. Excellent. It was almost like being alone. The deadbolt installed by Cyril Hemphill seemed sturdy and unassailable.

And yet another good thing. My novel rekindled. You see, I had never observed how blue Brandon's eyes were. Blue-green really. Peacock. Cayla sat right up and noticed.

Cayla leaned over and ran her fingers through Brandon's thick, thick silver hair. She marvelled at his eyelashes, sooty frames for those blazing eyes. How had she missed their colour and intensity before? How had she not fallen in love with him the first time she'd seen him? The eyes alone should have done it.

The strength of his well-muscled forearms made her swell with womanly pride. She traced the aristocratic outlines of his ears and mused on how delicious he looked without his shirt.

She felt so lucky. Such a beautiful, beautiful man.

And such a beautiful setting. The moon hung low and serene over the long, ivory beach. Far, far away reggae music drifted out over the sea.

Cayla held her breath as Brandon stared deep into her eyes and reached out to…knock.

Nineteen

Knock?

I jerked myself away from the computer screen. The knocking continued. Some people give up if you don't answer a door after fifteen or twenty tries. Not this knocker.

I was hesitant to open the door in case the media had heard of the great photo robbery and figured I'd look good plastered over the front pages again. *Passionate poet-killer rips off senior citizen.* That kind of thing.

"Who is it?"

"*C'est moi.*"

I opened the door to the smiling face of Hélène Lamontagne.

"I could not get through on the phone, so I wanted to leave a message on your door answering system. But it does not seem to be working."

Normally, I could count on Josey to head visitors off at the pass. But there was no sign of her. No doubt she'd given the knitting a break and headed off to clear out a bit of the brush on the edge of my property. That was just as well, because Josey was the subject of the visit.

Hélène said, "It is too bad, because the news is good. May I speak with you?"

I kissed my writing goodbye.

"Come on in. Let me save my work. Coffee in three minutes."

Before saving my material and switching off the computer, I made a note to replace all previous descriptions of Brandon's eyes. I upgraded the note. Change Brandon, period.

"*Bon*," Hélène said when we settled down over our coffee, "everything is arranged. I have even spoken to the youth services worker, and there is no problem with Josey staying with us for a few weeks until her situation is improved." That is one of the good things about dealing with Hélène in her role of Mrs. Jean-Claude Bigwig. She can even reach Social Services people on the weekend. We're talking influence.

"Perfect," I said. Josey was safe.

"Not entirely," Hélène said. "Mme Flambeau is quite hard to reach. I suppose I could keep trying..."

"Please keep trying," I said.

"It's just that I am so busy now trying to get a committee together for the community carol sing during December. Once I have someone to manage the logistics, then I'll have more time."

If you gave me a choice between a spot on a committee and an urn on the mantelpiece, I'd have a hard time picking the one I liked least. And what the hell are logistics? "Logistics?" I said. "I can do that."

*　　*　　*

Letting Josey know the good news, officially, from Hélène, was the next step in the process. I wasn't altogether sure that Josey's interpretation of good news would dovetail with Hélène's.

Not because of Hélène. Josey likes her. But it was the Jean-Claude part of the package that worried me. Josey always calls him "His Lordship" behind his back. The name suits him, but it made me wonder if she'd be happy camped out in the manor house with St. Aubaine's demon developer.

But it was a lot better than some of the alternatives.

"Don't blame me if they kick the doors in when you're all alone in this house, that's all I can say."

"I'm glad you're taking this with good grace, Josey. If I need you to rescue me, I can always call you at Hélène's."

"Sure. If they don't cut the phone wires."

I refrained from saying if somebody was prepared to cut the phone wires and kick in the doors to do me harm, I would be glad not to have to worry about Josey's safety too. I knew she wouldn't take it well.

A matter of pride.

*   *   *

I spent the rest of the evening alone. I blocked out the sex life song and tried thinking. Mostly variations on the "what the hell is going on" theme. Benedict's death had to have something to do with winning the Flambeau. Or did it? Was it an explosive mix of dangerous women? Who was the man who was following us? Some deranged poet? I asked myself who might recognize the description of the man in the photo if Mary Morrison couldn't help us.

Lucky for me Rachel was home when I called.

"You must be kidding," Rachel said. "I've blanked out every memory of my childhood. I was a pudgy kid with glasses, you know, in a world full of bullies. But let me think. Did he have red horns?"

"No horns."

"Too bad. Up to that point, he sounds like every little devil I remember from grade school. Sorry."

Bridget answered her phone but sounded like she'd been

asleep. Not surprising with the hours she kept at her shop. I apologized.

"Don't be silly, Fiona. I'm glad to help. I have a vague memory of who you mean, but I can't quite put a name on him. Somebody who dropped out early, I think." I could hear her yawning. "I have all those old school pictures here somewhere. I'll go through them. Are you in a rush?"

"No, no." The correct answer was yes, yes. But I didn't want to get pushy. I knew Bridget would come through.

"Okay, give me a day or so to dig them out and sift through them. Is it anything to do with Benedict's death?"

"Absolutely not. Just an idea I have for the scattering."

"Oh, all right. Great. Soon as I can."

Bridget was probably asleep before the phone hit the cradle.

Three times lucky, as they say. But not this time. I got Sarrazin's voice mail.

After the beep, I said, "I can't believe I didn't mention this when you were talking to us about the break-in at Miss Morrison's. I guess I was so stunned at being suspected. I want to let you know that the man who has been following me is in one of the stolen photos. A classmate of Benedict's. Since you went to the same school, maybe you have some idea how to find out who it is."

I hoped Sarrazin didn't think this was so much flim-flam. I also hoped Benedict's classmate wasn't really dangerous. But that's not what kept me awake for the rest of the night. It was good old-fashioned lust. Every time I closed my eyes, I saw Marc-André Paradis' peacock blue eyes. It should come as no surprise I spun like a silkworm until the morning. *A sex life a sex life I think I found a sex life.*

Just before dawn, I finally zonked.

I blinked at the clock in the morning. Ten-thirty! I made myself two cups of killer Colombian roast before even venturing into the shower. I needed to be awake to maintain my new upper hand on Cayla and Brandon.

At eleven, I almost tripped over Josey and Kostas in my living room. Maps and paper covered the floor. Tolstoy was right in there, fraternizing with the enemy.

It surprised me to see Kostas, wedged into my wingback, like he planned to stay for a while. It surprised me even more to see Josey.

"Oh hi, you're up," she said.

"Don't even pretend this isn't a school day. Didn't Mrs. Lamontagne get you on the bus?" Part of me took a certain satisfaction in thinking Hélène might not be able to handle Josey.

"It's Sunday."

I lifted my third cup of coffee and attempted to reconnect my dignity. "I knew that."

Then it hit me. The locks had   d. So...?

"Exactly how did you get in?

"It's easy enough, isn't it?" Jose

"But this is a brand new lock wi   ."

She shrugged. "You just gotta know

I gurgled with annoyance.

"It's been done before, you know," Josey said. "How else do you think Mr. Kelly ended up in your..."

"Good morning, dear lady." Kostas twinkled at me, as if he were oblivious to the acrimony. "Got the aould heap going," he said, pointing through the window to the sagging green car.

"Terrific."

"You want some breakfast?" Josey asked.

Breakfast would require an absence of butterflies in the stomach. I declined.

"Oh, and I brought in the mail. It's been sitting there since Friday. Looks like you got a cheque here, must be from that article you wrote this summer. That's good, isn't it?"

I wasn't sure if it was appropriate to reward the raiding of my mailbox and the checking of my cheques by saying thank you. On the other hand, I'd been too distracted to collect the mail from the end of the week.

"And wait until yis hear our plan of action for the scattering ceremony," Kostas said. "It's grand."

Right. The scattering could not be anything but miserable. But I slumped in the beanbag chair and listened.

The latest idea was to have Miss Mary Morrison say a few words about one of her favourite pupils. "She'll be thrilled. Indeed, it should perk her right up."

I nodded. I knew Mary Morrison would like the ceremony and with any luck would lend it a bit of dignity.

"So," said Josey, "this is what we'd like to see happen. I hope you don't mind, we went ahead and planned it."

I gulped a bit more coffee. "Not in the least," I said.

"Good," Josey said, on her way to the kitchen. "Okay, maybe Kostas can explain what we worked out."

"Certainly, my dear girl, certainly. And let me say you have been of invaluable assistance in helping to plan for the event."

Josey glowed. "We picked the spot. Kostas knows it, and so do I. It's at the top of a grassy hill. You can see the woods, and they'll be beautiful this time of year..."

"If it doesn't rain," I grumped.

"And, dear lady, you can see the river, and yet yer fringed by these wonderful trees. Marc-André used to live near there.

He agrees that's where Benedict would want to be tossed to rest."

I stopped sipping my coffee and started rubbing my temples. Marc-André might be God's gift to romance writers, but since when was he in charge of deciding where Benedict was going to spend his last moments as an entity? It promised to be a rough morning.

It got rougher.

"First, I'll put the word out to everyone to tell them we've decided where to hold this scattering ceremony." His tiny blue eyes managed to be twinkling and sincere at the same time.

I gazed back at him. He didn't slip on either the twinkling or the sincere fronts. I couldn't figure out what the hell he wanted from me. "I'm sure it will be tasteful," I lied. People everywhere, shouting, drinking, crying, spewing poetry. But there was no point in arguing, since everyone who had ever known Benedict most likely had already been informed. Josey would have taken care of filling in St. Aubaine.

"Are you worried about something, dear lady?"

Where to begin? "No, sorry. I can't get used to having an urnful of ashes in my house."

"Indeed, perhaps we can find a..."

"Don't worry. It'll be fine. The scattering plans sound excellent." What the hell.

"Grand, grand. I'm glad you're thinking that way. Marc-André was going to contact the poets. But why don't you ask him if he'd read a bit of his work at the event? He'd never come right out and offer, you know. The request will be better coming from you."

My heart pounded just hearing his name. A sex life is one thing, but I was way way too long in the tooth to have a crush like this.

Josey called out from the kitchen. "We definitely want to have some poetry. It sounded so nice at Miz Gallagher's reception. After all, Mr. Kelly was a poet. And we like Mr. Paradis."

Who could argue? Why did I even want to argue? Benedict needed a ceremony, after all. I just wished it had nothing to do with me.

"Now, the fiddlers are all arranged," Kostas said. "Quite a few French fellas too. It seems everyone wants to play at Benedict's funeral. Or whatever we're calling it. It'll be a lovely shindig, with nearly every fiddler from Quebec to Eastern Ontario and back again."

Josey returned with a plate.

I'd forgotten what I'd said about breakfast, and I slipped a slice of cheese onto the buttered brown bread.

"There's still the matter of the food," Josey said.

Kostas took over the conversation.

"Indeed, we'll have to give them a bite and a jar. There'll be quite a crowd. As Benedict would have wanted."

They both turned to me, obviously expecting objections.

"Absolutely," I said

Rachel had already agreed to do the catering. I wondered how she was with loaves and fishes.

Twenty

"Here you go, dear lady, it's Marc-André." Kostas's surprise might have been more convincing if he, himself, hadn't dialled Marc-André's number and spoken to him for at least five minutes.

Marc-André sounded pleasant and cheerful and sexy enough to make my knees tremble. I sat again and crossed my legs. So what if the left one still ached?

"Hello, Fiona, Kostas says you would like me to read a few words at Benedict's scattering ceremony."

"Yes."

"I'd be happy to."

"Thank you."

Amazing. I probably know umpteen thousand words in the English language and hundreds more in French plus a few in Latin, and where were they all now that I really needed them?

"Do you have any particular poems in mind?" he asked.

"Umm, no." I'd never heard of Marc-André until the Benedict disaster and, for some reason, reading poetry had not been on top of my To Do list since.

"Would you like to get together and go over some of my work? You could pick what you think is suitable."

Words words words think of some words.

"Fiona? Are you there?"

"Uh-huh. Absolutely. Good idea. Excellent. Fine. Right."

"And, Kostas mentioned the urn is bothering you. Is it?"

"Only when I see it or think about it." Oh good, a whole string of words. I hoped I didn't open my mouth again and sing out *A sex life a sex life I think I found a sex life.*

"Of course," he said. "I don't think it would bother me. I might even enjoy it. I could keep it here for you."

"Uh-huh." Wait a minute. "What do you mean for *me?* The urn isn't mine. I hadn't even seen Benedict for..."

"Fiona? I have a job to finish here, and I can't get away this afternoon, but Josey says you are going to the Findlay Falls for a hike today. Would you like to drop the urn at my place afterwards?"

Would I like to get that damn thing out of my house and get to see Marc-André again? Would I *like* it?

"Uh-huh," I said.

Hold everything. What was that about the Findlay Falls?

*   *   *

I wasn't sure what I didn't like about Marc-André looking after the ashes, but something about it seemed weird. What were the moral imperatives about keeping the remains of your former-almost-lover anyway? And more important, what would Bridget think about bouncing Benedict around like the hot potato he had become?

"I think Mr. Paradis was flattered when you asked him to read his poems at the scattering," Josey said.

I tried to hold back the latest puce flush. Luckily, we were passing Nettoyeur Le Quikie at that moment, and I remembered they'd called to say my clothes were ready, earlier than expected. I swerved into their parking section and prepared myself to be the focus of gossip. I figured it would be worth it to get my periwinkle suede skirt and matching silk blouse back.

"How's your leg, Miz Silk?" Josey asked when I got back in the car.

I was grateful she'd changed the subject from Marc-André Paradis. "It's fine now," I said without thinking.

"Good, so we can drop those ashes off," Josey said, staring at my neck, which was already flushed in anticipation of whatever she was going to say, "on our way back from the Findlay Falls. Miz Lamontagne says it's real beautiful there and worth the climb. And with all the people around, we'll be safer there than here."

"No Findlay Falls today." I shot her a Sarrazin glare, which got me exactly nowhere.

"I worked on the maps while you were asleep, and I figured out the route where you can experience the most educational type of things. Outside of France, that is. But I guess I won't get to see that anytime soon."

Right. Full marks to Josey.

*　　*　　*

"It's a good thing Miz Lamontagne packed us this excellent lunch," Josey said from her perch on the rock. "We probably won't get down from here before five-thirty. Didn't it turn out nice today? The trees look really beautiful through the mist."

We were finally at the Falls, or, more accurately, half-way up the steep hiking trail that ran alongside them. One of us was in a really good mood. The other one was me. I couldn't bring myself to agree with Josey's description of a beautiful day.

"Mist? Mist? Could you possibly be referring to this chilly drizzle?"

"Dr. Prentiss was right. It sure would be great to have a pair of binoculars up here, wouldn't it?"

"Would it? I think it would be great if Dr. Prentiss were here, herself, climbing in this sleet." It was easy for Hélène and Liz to approve of this climb. They hadn't legged it up steep slopes for the past three hours. When we'd estimated the climb, it had appeared short and straightforward. Now we squinted down at stamp-sized fields. I wasn't entirely sure how I'd been diverted from the simple task of delivering Benedict's urn to Marc-André Paradis to galloping up what felt like a mountain. But somehow, on the way, I'd found myself pulling into the parking lot by the foot of the Findlay Falls trail.

It seemed like another lifetime when we'd passed the first of the two lookout points where all the tourists with any brains stopped. The ache in my leg muscles reminded me that the extent of my exercise was the regular half hour a day tossing a Frisbee for Tolstoy. And even that was getting short shrift with all the chaos in our lives. On the bright side, I didn't have to lug the urn.

"She's right about binoculars," Josey said.

I flashed her a glance filled with recrimination. She missed it because she was fishing in her knapsack. "Those chicken sandwiches were good. Let's see what else we got."

She produced two nice looking pears and a dozen chocolate chunk shortbread cookies and proceeded to unwrap them.

"I really like this place, don't you? Do you think anyone ever lived in those caves?" She slipped Tolstoy a shortbread cookie.

"No." I reached for one before they all vanished.

"You sure?"

I didn't care for this cave talk. "Yes. Bears maybe."

"Bears? Wow. We should check."

"No. We shouldn't."

"But if they're just ordinary black bears, they usually won't hurt you if you don't get between them and their cubs. Or their food. Or make any loud aggressive noises. Or..."

"I'm going back. Now."

Josey paid no attention. "I like that waterfall," she said.

I would have liked the waterfall a lot myself if it had been closer to civilization, and if it didn't derive from a million little drizzle-fed springs trickling across the terrain we had climbed.

Josey stood and brushed off the crumbs. "You ready to go the rest of the way? Who knows what we'll find."

I gazed up the slope with mistrust. I wasn't expecting to find anything more appealing than bear poop. "No. I'm not ready to go the rest of the way. Remember the tourists we saw around the bottom of the falls? Remember the dozens of cars we saw in the parking lot? Do you notice not one of those people came up this route? They only hike to the second level. There's a good reason for that. Two if you include the bears."

She shrugged.

"Plus, we're vulnerable here. What if one of us, most likely me, sprains an ankle? How would we get help? We're a million miles from anywhere." Worse than that, we were separated from the crowds, and this was not the ideal situation, given earlier events. I noticed a whining tone creeping into my commentary.

"But it's interesting. And this brochure says you can see for miles when you get to the top."

I grumbled. "There are things worth seeing from the top of the Himalayas. But I'm not going to climb them to check it out."

"We don't want to be sheep and only do what other people do."

"I have no problem with being a sheep. You will remember

we passed the sheep some time ago. They're a lot closer to civilization than we are, let me point out. And I'm not going any further. I don't want to argue about it any more."

"See, you're wrong, Miz Silk, here comes someone else now."

Sure enough, a baseball cap peeked out above the vegetation. A lone climber wound his way up the narrow, rocky trail.

I didn't care. I had made up my mind, no more stumbling over bear droppings and slimy rocks.

The lone hiker crunched closer. Tolstoy cocked his head with interest. I opened my mouth to silence whatever preposterous proposal Josey was bleating.

"Miz Silk," she squeaked. "Jeez. Let's get out of here."

"What?"

She stuffed our thermoses and her guidebooks back into the carryall.

"We gotta go," she said.

"I love the idea, but why the hurry?"

"Because," she whispered, "I've seen that hat before. It's what the guy who smucked you with the car wore."

I stayed calm. Josey scrambled over the boulders ahead. Tolstoy bounded after her.

"Hold on," I said to their vanishing backsides, "there must be hundreds of red baseball caps like that. I'm sure that guy couldn't have followed us up here."

I changed my mind when the first bullet whizzed by my head.

Twenty-One

"I told you so," Josey whispered.

Now I believed her. We hunkered in a small, dark, smelly cave. We rolled, tugged and pulled a large rock into the opening.

Outside we could hear the clatter of small stones being thrown. No doubt to cause us to betray our location by a yelp of pain. Or a bark.

Every now and then, in no particular time pattern, a bullet would ricochet off the rocks surrounding us. Josey and I alternated holding Tolstoy's mouth closed.

We sat, racked with shivers, not knowing how long the rock would protect us. Stones rattled at sporadic intervals. It seemed like months. But we knew mere hours had passed, because the sky only darkened once.

Silence and the moon lay outside our cave. We could see slivers of silver through the crack between the rocks. From time to time, small scrambling sounds squashed any idea of leaving the cave. Bears? Rats? Or something much more dangerous?

"If we had a cellphone like everyone else in the world, we could call for help," Josey whispered.

Usually, I hate the idea of anything that gives people one more way to invade your privacy and coerce you into doing things you don't want to do. This time, I could actually see the point of cellphones. Not that either one of us had enough wherewithal to spring for one. As the hours wore on, I could see how I might want to rearrange my spending priorities, such as they were.

We snuggled together, with only our rain jackets and Tolstoy to keep us warm. Lunch was long gone. The dampness from the nearby streams on the hillside seeped into our clothing. We breathed the dank air and tried to ignore the smell of bear.

Josey whispered, "I'm glad there are no bears in here now."

I twisted my head to squint at her and found she'd dozed off in the seconds since she'd made the comment. I had to admire her ability to do that, although it left me alone pondering when the bear was coming back. Was it next in line after the shooter in the baseball cap?

Some primeval survival mechanism chirped in my head: "At least you have lots of time to think."

Right. I thought about Benedict and how certain I'd been that his murder had nothing to do with me. Some debt he owed. Some jealous husband. Some murderous poet. But what other reason could explain everything, including my bed, and not one, but two people stalking me. Who knew about the excursion to the Findlay Falls? Half of St. Aubaine, that's who. One of our stalkers could have followed us for days, waiting to catch us with no traffic, no Kostas, no witnesses, no help. Waiting for what? To kill us or to scare us away?

I was certainly scared away. A discussion with Sarrazin seemed pleasant in comparison. You could count on him to be cranky but predictable, which seemed far superior to holing up in a mountain cave hiding from an armed maniac. How did I get bullied into this?

Beside me, Josey stirred and stretched. "You know what I want if we get out of this place alive?" she said.

"What?"

"Can't you guess?"

"No."

"Hmmph. If we get out of here, the first thing I'd like to do is something I've been thinking about for a while."

Hanging around with Kostas obviously had an effect on Josey. She'd turned beating around the bush into an art form. "And what's that?"

"There's a lot of stuff I never had a chance to do yet. I want to make sure I don't miss a minute."

I already knew what I would do if we got out. I would learn to stick to my guns and do a better job of keeping Josey far from this whole mess until it was safe. Then when things settled down, and only then, I would give her a hand with that not-missing-a-minute stuff, even if it meant more educational experiences, indoor only.

Josey drifted off to sleep again. She made soft, guzzling snoring sounds with her head on my shoulder. Tolstoy made remarkably similar noises. I went back to thinking.

I concentrated on the man I had seen in the photo in Mary Morrison's house. The same person who'd been in the Britannia and who had followed us in the black Acura. Was the killer in the red cap a confederate of the creep with the yellow hair? He must have been. Then it hit me. Yellow hair already seemed familiar when I spotted him at the Britannia.

Why was that?

I had nothing better to do than try to mentally revisit every place I'd been for the last few weeks to see if his face popped up again. Where did I spend my time? The Régie d'alcool, L'Épicerie 1759, the Chez, the Caisse Populaire, Nettoyeur Le Quikie, the post office, Tom and Jerry's service station—until I switched to Marc-André. The thought of Marc-André pushed the man in the black Acura out of my mind, and I concentrated on him for a while. Single. Sexy. A man who worked with words. An artist. An accomplished mechanic. A potential sex life on wheels. But would I live to see him again?

Blessed drowsiness crept over me. Until a new thought flickered, and my eyes shot open. I knew where I'd seen the man who'd been following us. He was the same ominous yellow-haired tramp outside L'Auberge des Rêves. Not only that but except for his bright matted hair, he could have been the twin of the one who hung around outside of Bridget's during the memorial. And he'd also been panhandling outside the Museum of Civilization just before the car hit me. Plus I'd spotted him through the window at the Chez, where he'd had the nerve to feed Tolstoy fries and pat him on the head.

My heart rate rose.

The man with the yellow hair had been spying on us since right after Benedict's death. So what was the grubby panhandler doing driving around in a sleek black Acura sedan?

The other thing I planned to do if we escaped alive was find out who the hell he was. No matter if the photos were gone from Mary Morrison's. If Sarrazin didn't deliver, I could talk to everyone who'd been in Benedict's class. In a nosy locale like St. Aubaine, someone had to recognize his description.

The silver slivers of moonlight disappeared. Nothing but black showed through the rocks. Was something sniffing and grunting? Coming home for dinner? Yes. Coming closer. Fading away. I never thought I'd rejoice at the soft patter of drops.

Rain.

*   *   *

If the half-dozen teenaged hikers found it strange to have two ratty females and a formerly white dog crawl out from behind a rock the next morning, they didn't mention it.

"*Bonjour*," one of the hikers said, as we joined them on their way down.

"Good morning," Josey answered, her spirit undimmed by sleeping sitting up, her back pressed to a cave wall.

Tolstoy issued a joyful bark.

I didn't say anything. My own spirit was seriously dimmed by my wet bum. We hiked through the drizzle for a brisk hour back to the car park. No red baseball caps showed up on the way.

Our new friends disappeared as soon as we limped into the parking lot.

"We'd better call the Quebec Provincial Police," Josey said.

"Absolutely," I said, meaning it for once.

It proved not to be necessary. The first thing we spotted in the parking lot was a pair of uniforms. Two QPP officers stood with their hands on their hips, staring with disapproval at what remained of the Skylark.

And then at us.

*　　*　　*

"Tarrible, tarrible," Kostas said from the back seat of Marc-André Paradis' immaculate ten-year-old Beemer. "Who would have done such a tarrible thing?"

Marc-André Paradis shook his head. "It would be more than that car was worth just to replace all the glass."

Josey said, "And what about all that damage to the body? I think he must have used a hammer. Maybe he jumped on the roof."

"Jazus, Mary and Joseph."

I sat in the front seat, suffused, dripping, flooded, saturated with misery. I smelled of damp earth, sweat, fear, bear dung and unbrushed teeth. I sat next to a man who made my heart race. He was probably going to need his car shampooed to remove the hum. I wanted food, I wanted a bath, I wanted the earth to open up and swallow me.

Why the hell hadn't Liz picked up her phone when we'd called from the pay phone? And where was Cyril Hemphill when you really needed him?

Kostas sputtered on. "I can't believe those damn fools in the QPP didn't take the whole thing more seriously."

In the back seat, next to Tolstoy, Josey spoke with more energy than I ever expected to feel again in my life. "Stupid cops. Since when do vandals shoot at you? They thought we had it coming for leaving the car in the park overnight."

Kostas puffed up like he was on helium. "Isn't it just like the police? Bothering a person all the time over every little thing, and then when yis need them, sure they've better things to do. Vandals, indeed. Since when do vandals chase ladies into caves and besiege them with stones?"

"And bullets," I said.

Josey agreed. "They didn't believe us about the bullets."

"Indeed, and since when do vandals break into vehicles and leave the valuables?" Kostas asked.

I couldn't argue with him, although I wasn't sure I would classify my purse with its twenty dollar bill and its up-to-the-hilt credit cards as valuables. I hadn't even been able to check to see what had been taken.

Kostas exhaled. "My dear lady, what is goin' on?"

I said. "Something to do with Benedict's death."

I met Marc-André Paradis' gaze. His forehead was rumpled, his eyes troubled. Kostas slipped from outrage back into practical mode. Perhaps because I'd slumped with exhaustion and started to shiver again.

"Do you think they found what they were looking for?" I could feel those peacock blue eyes on me as he spoke.

"I don't know. I find it hard to believe someone would follow us and shoot at us and destroy a car to get an urn."

"Why do you suppose they wanted the urn?" Marc-André said.

"I cannot imagine." Of course, that was because I, myself, had really not wanted that urn. Really, really not wanted it. Until it was stolen. As they say, you never appreciate what you have until you lose it.

"But you know, Miz Silk, that urn was in your house when he broke in, and he didn't steal it then. Maybe he's after something else."

"Dear lady, maybe he's just a nut, and there's no way to ever figure out what was going on in his mind."

"Their minds," I said. "There are two of them. Maybe they're after completely different things. Maybe they don't know what they're after." I felt a distinct throbbing in my temple.

Marc-André's forehead rumpled more. On him, it looked good. "Perhaps you are not safe in your house," he said.

"You're telling me," Josey said.

"Dear ladies," said Kostas, "yis are, of course, most welcome to stay with me at Evening's End."

Josey and I gasped in unison. Evening's End was only marginally more comfortable than the cave we'd spent the night in.

"I have a new bottle of Jameson's, and I'm sure with a little tinkering I can get the hot water going again for showers. Marc-André will help me, won't you, me boy?"

I felt tears stinging my eyes at the idea of having to stay in Kostas's smelly old house without even hot water. I tried to think of something to avoid the situation without crushing Kostas. I was willing to take my chances going home.

"They can stay at my place," Marc-André said, with quiet authority. "I have an extra bedroom and lots of hot water and some of your own Armagnac. They can rest as long as they want in peace and quiet, because I'll be in the garage. And if they need any rescuing, I will be three feet away."

"No reason in the world why I couldn't rescue them, me boy."

"Oh, but you already have plenty to do getting ready for the scattering," Josey said.

Brilliant child.

For once, the scattering was convenient for me. I chose not to mention that, with any luck, the missing urn would make the scattering unnecessary.

"Right you are, Josey. Kostas has plenty to do," I said, as firmly as I could considering my teeth were chattering.

*   *   *

I awakened with a start, disoriented. Except for the state of the sheets caused by my spinning and whirling, the room was absolutely monastic.

Half an hour later, clean, warm, dry and dressed in my laundered jeans and sweatshirt, I limped down the stairs. When I entered the *salon*, Josey was squinting at a television program about museums. A knitting project sat on her lap. Tolstoy was curled at her feet. Someone had done a number on him with shampoo, cream rinse and a blowdryer.

She said, "You're alive. It's almost six o'clock."

I was not only alive but smelling nicely of fabric softener and Pears soap. My hair had managed to dry in a not too uncontrolled way. I had it pulled in a high ponytail, and only about a third of it escaped in kinky wisps. I wore lipstick. With subtlety, I hoped.

"Marc-André's gone out to get a bit of dinner."

So a waste of time about the lipstick. "Right," I said, sinking onto the sofa.

Josey ogled me. "Wait a minute. Are you wearing lipstick?"

"Not really."

"You *are*. You don't usually wear lipstick in the house."

"Sure I do," I lied.

"Kostas and Marc-André are getting us a car to use."

Getting a car?

"Your car is only fit for Paulie Pound's scrapyard now. Don't worry though. Marc-André said he'd take care of it for you, no problem. And I could help sell some of the parts. Paulie Pound will probably try to rip you off. You'd be lucky to get seventy-five dollars for it."

It was hard to feel cheerful about this. Much as I disliked the Skylark, I didn't want it crumpled with the other wrecks in Paulie Pound's car graveyard. I wasn't sure it would even fetch seventy-five dollars in the state it was.

"And that Sarrazin guy was here asking questions," Josey said.

"Here? Why didn't you tell me?"

"You were out cold."

"I was sleeping, not in a coma."

She shrugged. "I could tell because you were snoring. I'm guessing people don't snore when they're in comas."

Snoring? Oh just ducky. I hoped I hadn't had an audience. "No one was in my room, were they?"

Her eyes widened. With guilt. "I was trying to help, Miz Silk. Your clothes were pretty bad from the cave."

"You washed them?"

She nodded.

"That's a relief. Thank you." I definitely did not want Marc-André laundering my muddy underwear or hearing me snore.

"Okay, but I'm not sure you should be so relieved."

"Why not?"

"Something else is missing."

"Don't drag this out, please. What's missing?"

"Not just the urn, but all the copies of the book."

It had been hard enough to imagine someone stealing an urn. This really didn't make sense.

"Perhaps they're already becoming valuable," she said.

"Maybe.

"And there's something else, Miz Silk. The guy in the baseball cap sure didn't like you. He ripped your clothes."

"What clothes? He never got near me."

"You know, your dry cleaning."

"Oh no, not my periwinkle silk blouse."

She nodded.

"I loved that blouse. And the skirt?"

Josey, at her most serious, leaned forward and lowered her voice. "It was like he had it in for you. Personally."

I shivered. It took my mind off the fact that I'd cancelled my all-risk coverage on the car. I wondered if my home policy would pay for the contents. If I remembered correctly the deductible was higher than the cost of every piece of clothing in my closet.

The creak of the back door distracted us. A second later, Marc-André came in.

"She's up," Josey said, before I could check the mirror in case my dewlaps were drooping.

"Bonsoir," he said. "You look much better. We were worried. Are you hungry? I found roast chicken and green salad with vinaigrette and a baguette. I hope it will do."

I was starving, a sensation that had taken a back seat to exhaustion, worry, and even lust, until that moment.

I did wonder where you "found" roast chicken and salad until Marc-André confessed he'd had his friend, a poet who worked as a sous-chef at Les Nuances, make it for him.

"I'm sorry I don't have any wine," he said, a bit shyly. "The Régie was closed and the stuff in the *dépanneur...*"

I tried to match his elegant shrug, indicating I wouldn't be caught dead drinking that turpentine.

"Not like we got anything to celebrate," Josey said.

"We're alive." I said.

She grunted.

Marc-André said, "You could celebrate the fact we've been able to get you another car. You can have the car tomorrow whether you're planning to leave then...or some other time."

I loved those little pauses when he spoke. I wasn't anxious to leave a place with sexy pauses and reenter a world crawling with crazed killers in baseball caps.

"Soon though. I really need to get home and finish my novel." Nicely non-committal. No puce blush. Excellent. Things were looking up.

Marc-André shook his head. "You shouldn't run off so soon, after such a shock. *Mademoiselle* too."

That's when it hit me like a slap in the face with a wet fish. I wasn't looking after *mademoiselle*. Hélène was.

Twenty-Two

"Oui, allô?"

"Hélène, I am so sorry. You must have been frantic."

"Think nothing of it. Josée already phoned me. I'm happy you are both all right."

"Now I have some more bad news for you," she said. Was it my imagination or did I feel a tinge of frostbite on my ear?

"What kind of bad news?" I couldn't imagine what would be worse than dodging bears and bullets all night in a cave.

"Jean-Claude is very upset. He wants Josée to leave. He thinks I should not have taken on this level of obligation, with all the stress and worry."

"But none of this is Josey's fault."

"That is not how he sees it. I feel responsible, myself, Fiona. After all, I even packed that lunch. I did not realize you could be in danger."

"Thanks. I hope Jean-Claude will listen to you."

"Well, he's just a bit irritable because we're not having a very good response for volunteers for the Christmas Lights Singalong."

"Ah. Naturally. I'll be glad to help out with that."

"Wonderful. I'll tell him. You're not afraid of heights, are you?"

"What?"

"Anyway, I let the St. Aubaine police know that you are

safe. I had notified them when you didn't return from the outing last night. But did you know they cannot do anything for people missing less than twenty-fours?"

"You mean Sarrazin wouldn't take it seriously?"

"Perhaps *he* would have, but he was not on duty."

I thought, maybe you should have called Dr. Duhamel's place.

Hélène said, "He is taking it seriously now. He wants to talk to you."

Naturally. So what else was new?

"I will try to get Jean-Claude to give Josée another chance. But please, do not count on it. And, by the way, no luck yet with Mme Flambeau."

Once again I felt bewildered, inept and guilty. Not to mention loaded down with volunteer commitments.

Wasn't that the effect that being close to Benedict, even in his ashy state, had on women? Didn't he always cause some kind of mental meltdown?

"Dessert and coffee, *madame*." I jerked back to earth.

Marc-André served the coffee. Josey carried the goodies.

"My wife always found a *pâtisserie* was the best thing when she was depressed. And she was a nurse."

"Good enough for me," said Josey.

Marc-André grinned. His teeth weren't completely straight. A tiny imperfection that only made him sexier.

"Tell me," I said, "when Benedict visited you, he was with a girl. What was her name?"

Marc-André's hand jerked slightly, spilling a couple of drops of coffee on the bird's eye maple table.

"It is difficult to keep wood from getting marked, isn't it?" he said, wiping with energy.

"Yes, it is. Do you remember her name?"

"I'm afraid I do not." He didn't meet my eyes.

"Kostas said they had quite a long visit with you."

"I don't really recall it in detail."

"It's important."

"Fiona, he is dead now, and he wasn't the most faithful man...but you have to move on."

I blinked, my mug of coffee suspended. "Oh. No. You mustn't think..."

Marc-André shook his head. "I know how hard it is to get used to the idea that someone you love is dead. I loved my wife very much. It is not easy, but there are things, habits and attitudes, that make it worse for us."

"You don't understand. I didn't love Benedict. We had a sort of involvement, maybe eight or even nine years ago. I broke it off."

The expression on his face said, perhaps.

"Definitely," I said. "My only reaction to Benedict's demise was relief I wouldn't have to pay someone else's parking tickets in addition to my own." Not strictly true and certainly cold-hearted if it were, but I wanted to squash any idea that Benedict had a place in my heart.

"I see." The peacock-blue eyes watched, sharp and challenging. "Wasn't he found in an intimate situation...?"

I straightened. After all, he did read the papers.

"That's right. And I don't know how he got there. That's why I have to know what's going on. This girl with Benedict might have nothing to do with it, but at the least her name will fill in a piece of the puzzle." I sat back and watched him.

Under close examination, he was even less perfect. Not just the teeth. His nose had a little twist in it. Add that to the scars on his hands, machine shop stuff, and a pair of misshapen knuckles, and he wasn't a screen idol. Just a decent mechanic, missing his dead wife. All right, he was a poet of some note, with nice silver hair, a leather jacket and a fine collection of modern art.

Naturally, I found him more tantalizing than ever.

Josey's head whipped around, and she narrowed her eyes. Could she read my thoughts?

"I guess there's no harm in telling you," Marc-André said.

Josey and I held our breath.

"Abby," he said. "Her name was Abby Lake."

Of course. Abby Lake, with her dancer's body, her pale brush cut, her immense green eyes brimming with tears.

Abby Lake. So, why wasn't Abby racing all over hell and creation lugging Benedict's geedee ashes and posthumous gifts?

The answer was simple.

Bridget would never have stood for it.

*   *   *

Kostas arrived, quivering like a tomato aspic, driving all thoughts of Abby from my head. "Ladies, ladies, step outside for a minute. I have a surprise for yis."

We stepped outside.

Kostas said with pride, "We have succeeded in obtaining an almost exact replica of your recently departed vehicle."

"Oh," I said.

"Jeez," Josey said.

Kostas's face told us he expected more.

"Hmmm," I said.

"Yeah," Josey added.

Kostas inclined his head expectantly.

"How ever did you find it?" I tried to squeeze some level of enthusiasm into my voice without giving myself a hernia.

"My dear ladies, it was not at all easy."

I felt ungrateful. After all, it's not every day your friends find you a car. But did it have to be an exact replica of the one you never liked in the first place?

"Thank you for everything," I glanced from Kostas to Marc-André and back. "I guess it's time for us to go."

"Marc-André and I think, for the next while, you'll be safer with someone around to watch out for yis, don't we, Marc-André? Since you need to be in your own home to prepare for the scattering, we're thinking someone should be with yis. A neighbour woman has graciously offered to care for me dogs, so me time is me own, and that means I'm yer man."

"I would join you myself, but..." Marc-André gestured towards the garage, where a line of upscale imports sat waiting.

"He'll be with us in spirit. And in person if we need him. He's given us his cellphone. Isn't that grand?" Kostas patted his pocket with pride. "First time I've had one of those."

That's when I dropped my bomb.

"There's not going to be a scattering."

"No scattering?" Josey's freckles stood out in sharp relief.

Kostas sputtered. "No scattering, but, my dear lady, why?"

"For one thing, there are no ashes."

"Jeez, right," said Josey. "We have nothing to scatter."

"That is true," Marc-André said, his brow furrowing.

Kostas didn't say anything for at least a minute. Finally he said, "By Jazus, we needn't let a small detail like that hold us back."

"Uh, perhaps you didn't hear me. There are no ashes."

"My dear people, there are two things we must consider. One, half of West Quebec is already coming to this ceremony. Two, these ashes are merely a symbol of Benedict."

"A symbol?" I squawked. "They're more than a symbol. They're him. They're all that's left of him."

"So, Kostas, you're saying the more important thing is the *symbol?*" Josey said.

"Benedict would have really loved the idea of a mob of people giving him a last goodbye, no matter what, dear lady."

"Knowing the man, I would agree," Marc-André said.

I slumped against the exact replica. What nonsense was this? "Won't half of West Quebec notice the lack of ashes?"

"Ashes are ashes, dear lady. And they're not hard to come by. Everyone has a wood-burning stove."

"But that's not at all..." I sputtered.

"In short, we'll get some other ashes and scatter them. Who will know?" Kostas beamed at his new idea.

"Just us and the guy who stole them," Josey said.

"Exactly, dear ladies, exactly."

*   *   *

Our first stop would be Miss Mary Morrison's. With Kostas as our navigator, we zigged across the back country roads in what seemed to me to be a random pattern. Even a skilled tracker would have had trouble tracing us.

Josey sat in the back seat with Tolstoy. It gave her more room to spread out her expanding knitting project. Her needles clicked. Kostas gave her his attention.

"Watch yer tension, me dear, that's the secret of fine knitting. If ya wish to become an artist-in-wool, yer stitches must be smooth and even, showing a serene soul."

Nothing I needed to worry about. I imagined Marc-André and how nice it would be when all this stuff with Benedict was sorted out and we could...

Josey shouted. "Kostas."

Was it a knitting crisis? I kept my eyes on the road.

"I see it again," Josey said.

This time I whirled around. "What? You saw what?"

Josey's face had turned milk-white, her giant freckles on full alert.

"The little car that hit you. The guy with the red baseball cap. The one that shot at us."

I stared back at an empty road. "I can't see anybody."

A white Jetta popped over the hill behind us. I stood on the brakes. "Just a quick look at his face, then we boot it," I said. I knew he had a gun, and he liked to pull the trigger.

I strained to see in the rearview mirror. "Okay, time to make tracks," I said.

I made a 270° turn at the first crossroad. We bounced along a road designed only for the hardier varieties of bear. I raced through the thick overhang which closed behind us like a dripping green curtain.

Josey squinted through the rear window for signs of pursuit. We shot out of the cow path and onto a dirt road. "We lost him!"

I said, "Her. We lost her."

Josey's eyes shone like new hub caps. "What do you mean, her?"

"The cellphone, Kostas," I said.

I keyed in Sarrazin's number. I didn't need to look it up any more.

Josey raised her voice. "We have a right to know who you saw, Miz Silk."

"Right," I said as Sarrazin's voice mail answered. "News flash. The guy in the baseball cap who has been following us is none other than Abby. Abby Lake."

Twenty-Three

She had her colour back and some pep in her step. Mary Morrison didn't let break, enter and theft slow her down for long, particularly since she was no longer being pressured to leave her home. And she seemed glad to see us, even at nine in the evening.

"Come in, come in. You're just in time for a snack." She pointed to a heaping plate of raspberry squares and a pot of tea.

"Neighbours. You were right, of course, they're not about to let me down. The young lads down the road have been taking turns sleeping here. And there's four of them, they won't even wear out soon. Won't take a thing for it either. They're exactly like their father was when I taught him thirty years ago."

"So you're okay?" Josey said.

"Indeed, and you'll be coming to the scattering ceremony we're planning for poor aould Benedict?" Kostas said.

"A ceremony for Benedict? I wouldn't miss it."

"And you won't have to move?" Josey asked.

"I managed to calm the nephews for a wee bit."

"Move? Sweet Jazus," Kostas blurted. "What a shame. To have to leave a lovely house like this, my dear lady, it breaks me heart. And me with me roof falling in. Sure, there must be a way to keep ya here safe enough on a permanent basis."

"Yes," said Josey, stroking her upper lip thoughtfully,

"there must be."

"Miss Morrison," I said, "I hope you won't find this distressing. Do you remember there was someone in one of your stolen photos I wanted to identify? Who else might remember the names of all the boys who went to school with Benedict?" At the back of my mind, I wondered if we should bother to pursue the angle of the large man now that we had Abby Lake fingered.

"Someone who might remember all the boys? Maybe, my dear, maybe it wouldn't even be necessary. My head's a bit clearer now that I don't have to pack up my home. I was in a bit of shock the first time you asked. Which lad was it?"

"In the same class photo as Benedict. A tall, chunky boy with dark eyes, a little downward slant to them and a wide strong face, heavy cheekbones." Probably a waste of time describing someone she'd taught thirty years earlier. What were the chances his name would pop up as a result of my description? "His hair was dark then. But he might bleach it now."

"Oh, dear, that would be Dougie," she said, without hesitation. "Dougie Dolan."

"Dougie Dolan?" Somehow that didn't sound threatening.

"Who else could it be? Look for trouble, and you'll find Dougie. What did he get up to now?"

A truly gratifying reaction. Whatever this Dougie Dolan had morphed into as an adult, it wasn't a pillar of the community.

"Is he another scamp?"

"Much more than a scamp, I'm afraid."

"He appears to be following us. We don't know why."

"Something in it for him, I'd say. Always wanted something for nothing, even as a child. Now he's after the easy money."

"He's always after easy money?"

"Oh, definitely. If Dougie Dolan had spent half the energy

on legitimate activities, like a job, as he did trying to get rich quick, he'd be living in a castle. I'm sure of it."

"Bit of a lad, is he?" asked Kostas.

"A bad hat. Don't you know him, Kostas?"

"Heard of him, of course."

"I'm not surprised."

"And Benedict. Did he stay in touch with Benedict?" I asked.

"I don't believe so, dear. They weren't the best of friends, even as children."

"They didn't like each other?"

"Hated each other. Benedict always made the mischief, and Dougie always took the blame."

"That isn't fair," Josey said.

Mary shrugged. "Dougie Dolan got away with plenty himself."

"Miss Morrison, would Dougie Dolan have known about your photos?" I asked.

"Of course. Everyone knew about them. Why?"

"I think he may have stolen them so we couldn't identify him."

"Oh, good," she said, her eyes lighting up.

"Good?" I almost dropped my raspberry square. "Why good?"

"Because, knowing Dougie, he'll not have destroyed them. He'll hang on to them in case they come in handy sometime. He might even present them back to me and expect a reward or something. Wouldn't be the first time."

"Good. That's a relief. We know who he is now. I was afraid he might be someone dangerous."

Mary Morrison's eyes widened. "Oh, but he is dangerous. Quite dangerous."

*   *   *

We drove the rest of the way home without a sign of Abby. Or Dolan. Josey was stashed at Hélène's place for the night, although the long-term prospects didn't look good. Kostas was tucked in the wingback in front of the fire with the tail end of a bottle of Jameson and a smile on his face.

It had been a while since I'd felt that throb in my leg, so I had a smile on my face too. Tolstoy and I had spent a happy fifteen minutes with the Frisbee in the back yard. I came back in with a clear head and ignored the flashing light on the answering machine (almost certainly more bleating from Phillip). In turn, I left a message about Dougie Dolan for Sarrazin. For good measure, I left another message with the Flambeau Foundation, not that they'd returned my first call. I was going to be much happier when Hélène tracked down the very elusive Mme Flambeau.

I retired to my study to sort out my life with pencil and paper. I felt grateful for the solitude, even though it meant not gazing wistfully at Marc-André Paradis or listening to the finer points of knitting technique.

Tolstoy opted for the fire with Kostas.

I listed the sequence of relevant events in a column:

-Benedict's death.
-His placement in my bed, with his little glued-on smile.
-The attempt to run me down.
-The yellow-haired man, now known as Dougie Dolan, following us in Hull, St. Aubaine and all around West Quebec.
-The break-in at my house.
-The Findlay Falls, where we'd been shot at.
-The Skylark being vandalized. The theft of the books and

Benedict's ashes.
   -The slashing of my clothes.
   -The spotting of Abby in the Jetta.

I examined the column critically. Could Abby Lake have been involved in all those things? What was her motivation?

Time for a bit of logic rather than blanket assumption. Not that logic is my strong point.

First, Benedict's death. Abby had been in love with him, but then so had a lot of people. Had she been jealous enough to kill him over one or more of his numerous infidelities?

Whoever killed Benedict had to have known about our relationship, such as it had been, much earlier. Had that been what tipped Abby into crazed behavior? Or was she pursuing me because she believed I'd killed her lover?

I chewed on the end of my pencil.

Benedict had died of a broken neck. Something that could have occurred by accident, even in an argument with a jealous woman. A few too many drinks, a shouting match, an accidental slam into the furniture, a fall down the stairs. It made sense.

And Abby with her strong, lean body, the product of weight training and years of dancing, would have had the strength to lift him, to dump him in her car, and to deposit him in my bed. She could have done it by herself.

Here the logic collapsed a bit. Two problems: one, would Benedict stand there while Abby beat him? She hadn't looked like she'd been in a fight when I saw her at the Memorial. Two, why would Abby choose my bed?

I doodled a little bit with the pencil.

Unless. Since Benedict had been foolish enough to call me the lost love of his life in front of Bridget, maybe he'd dribbled

180

out something like that to Abby. Knowing Benedict, he could have been foolish enough all right.

Could it have sent her over the edge?

For a woman who'd snapped, what better revenge than to lay her dead lover's body in the bed of the woman he'd dangled in front of her nose. And Krazy Glue a smile on his two-timing slimy face. She'd get the double effect of casting the suspicion as far away as possible—from her to me. Poetic justice.

For insurance, she could fake a little note in what looked like my handwriting and leave it for the police to find in Benedict's cabin. That would ensure no one believed I wasn't in touch with him.

It all hung together. I figured Abby's residual jealousy could have given her a motivation to follow me around waiting for a chance to do a bit more damage. Perhaps she didn't think I was miserable enough, perhaps she was jealous of all the publicity, perhaps she hated the idea that I was the Queen of the Scattering. So why not try to run me over? While I was enjoying nature at the Findlay Falls, why not take a few shots at me? Even if she missed, there'd still be tons of satisfaction. Even if I managed to stay alive, she could always pound the bejesus out of my car and slash my clothes. And reclaim Benedict's ashes.

Yes. I had it figured out. Except for how Abby had duplicated my handwriting and just where Dougie Dolan fit in, but it would all fall into place sooner or later. If I could avoid getting shot, run over or arrested.

Suffused with good feeling over having sorted out the whole mess, I tiptoed past Kostas and Tolstoy, both softly snoring, and headed to the washing machine for a night-cap.

I was smiling into the snifter when I remembered to check my messages. Three waspish calls from Liz with important information about injections for spider veins. A long spew from Philip in which you could practically hear his jaw spasms all the way from Salt Lake City. Normally, it would have bothered me. But perspective is all. I'd been shot at, burgled and corpsed, so dealing with Phillip was a piece of cake. Maybe there was hope for that settlement.

On the down side, I didn't like the tone of Sarrazin's returned message. He didn't out and out say so, but he implied it was certainly convenient for me, prime suspect numero uno, to finger other likely candidates, but I shouldn't seriously expect him to waste five minutes on it. I couldn't wait until he heard the one about Dougie Dolan.

Of course, I may have been projecting. Either way, it was time for Goldilocks to meet Papa Bear again. Not that I was nervous, or clumsy or inept or anything, but Aunt Kit's antique brandy snifter did slip from my hands. The fragrance of Courvoisier filled the house.

Kostas sniffed and opened his eyes.

*   *   *

Cayla stared at Brandon as if she'd never seen him before. She didn't call him darling, chookums, or lambibun. The colour of her face went from chalk white to puce and finally settled on a fishbelly shade of pale green.

"You," she sputtered, "you dope, you ox, you klutz, you bozo, you big, dumb twit. You DOORKNOB."

Brandon raised his chin with dignity. He'd been noticing lately that Cayla had a tendency to let an unappealing little stream of drool dribble down the side of her mouth when she ranted.

"Do you, do you know what you've done? Idiot."

Brandon decided the fishbelly green shade did nothing for

Cayla's complexion, which he'd always considered a bit sallow.

"That snifter belonged to my mother," Cayla shrieked. "It's been in our family for..."

"One generation," Brandon interjected, unwisely as it turned out.

"The least you could do is pay attention to what I'm saying, since you have more or less wrecked my belongings."

Brandon wanted to say it was only a snifter and a profoundly unattractive one, but the moment didn't seem right somehow.

"You know what you are? You know what you are, Brandon?"

He watched her and held his breath. As long as she didn't say it. As long as she didn't say...

"Clumsy," she screamed, "clumsy, clumsy, clumsy."

Brandon jerked in pain. He stayed silent for a full minute, feeling the deep wound. "Most people," he said, finally, "most people would have said movementally challenged. But I see, Cayla, you are not most people."

She stood amid the shattered shards of the snifter, which gleamed sharply in the moonlight. She wished she could take back her words, but it was too late.

Tears stung her eyes, and the back of her throat ached as she watched Brandon walk away, head held high, stumbling only briefly over the ottoman.

I read the words on the screen and shook my head in disbelief. What tripe. That's what you get for trying to write in the middle of the night without a drink in your hand. I shut off the computer, climbed back into bed and flicked off the light, knowing it would mean returning to my dreams.

Dreams in which I had to choose between marrying Marc-André Paradis or being arrested by Sarrazin, both of whom were laid out in fine mahogany coffins, with the white of the *fleur-de-lis* repeating nicely on the blue satin linings. Dreams in which Benedict spouted vile poetry to me from his urn. Dreams in which I used Josey's knitting needles to protect the three of us against a crazed Abby Lake. Dreams from which I jerked awake every ten minutes from three until seven.

*   *   *

At seven I tried closing my eyes again. A troubling idea kept them popping open. Dougie Dolan had already looked familiar in the Acura following us and again when I saw him in the Britannia. He'd been cleaned up, but eventually even I had figured out he was the same big blonde panhandler we'd seen in front of Rachel's bed and breakfast. So that left a problem.

Rachel had looked right at that man. She'd shouted at him to go away. If I'd spotted him after a couple of quick glimpses, no way she wouldn't have recognized him as the boy she went to school with.

Rachel. Our friend. Miss Hospitality. So why hadn't she mentioned Dougie Dolan when I'd asked her about the boy in the picture?

Twenty-Four

Hélène sounded embarrassed. "I am so sorry, Fiona. But Jean-Claude has already called this morning, and he was not pleased to learn Josée spent the night here. We must find another solution. He will be home tonight. And even if he wasn't..."

She didn't have to finish the sentence. Let's just say that Hélène, for all her sterling qualities, had never been known to defy the lord of the manor. And Jean-Claude Lamontagne hadn't squished his competition in real estate development by being cute and cuddly.

"Will you be able to find a good place for her?"

"Of course. Don't worry about it," I said. "I'll think of something." I detected no sign of frostiness in Hélène's voice—that was good. Too bad my Plan B for Josey, Rachel Kilmartin, had slipped badly in the ratings. That reminded me that, while I had no intention of leaving Josey there, I needed to speak to Rachel. For some reason, Rachel wasn't answering her phone. That couldn't be good for business. I left a detailed message. A lot of the detail concerned Dougie Dolan and my opinion of Rachel for keeping him a secret.

Since I was in message mode, I called Montreal again and left my third message with the Flambeau Foundation.

I hung up and faced Kostas's anxious smile.

"You seem so upset, dear lady. I will be more than happy to help in any way I can."

Naturally.

"I have to find another spot for Josey until this is over."

Kostas's face drained of its colour. "Change her living arrangements now? But sure, dear lady, how can we disrupt her when she's not finished her sweater. Can't she stay here?"

I avoided saying the sweater was not a life and death matter. In fact, it was considerably less important than having her attend school. And as for staying with me. Well.

"Abby Lake might try to attack us again before the police begin to take her seriously. I can't take the chance."

"Perhaps Rachel...?"

"No."

Kostas blinked. He mopped his brow with his handkerchief. "I suppose you're right, but she's not going to like it."

"Tell me something I don't already know."

Kostas grumbled, "She's really enjoying this adventure. And you know the dear girl had to cancel her trip to France."

"Absolutely. Josey will be distressed to be dropped from the cross-country, all-star-scattering-plan and dodge-the-murderer-marathon, but no choice and no argument. When this is over, I'll take her on a real vacation. Somewhere she won't get shot at."

"I suppose, dear lady, I suppose."

"We don't want Social Services to discover she's not safe and slap her into a foster home. Imagine how she'd feel about that."

"Indeed, you're right, we must be sensible, but it saddens me. She could have learned so much with a few more days. I'll never find another pupil so willing, so unspoiled by negative concepts of knitting."

My turn to blink. I had to admit the bond between Kostas and Josey had become something strong and special.

"And what about her birthday? We have to do something for that," he said, putting the final nail in the argument.

"Right. But only if we make sure she doesn't get shot or run over because she's standing too close to me."

"But dear lady, you have me now. How much danger can there be with the three of us sticking together?"

*　　*　　*

The sight of Josey, scrubbed and dressed, with her cowlicks at full alert, caused an immediate guilty reaction, shared equally between Kostas and me. Tolstoy barked in greeting and rushed forward to get his ears scratched.

"You *are* going to school today." I barked a bit myself.

"Miz Lamontagne's kind of jumpy this morning, so I'm just waiting here at your place for the school bus. Unless that bothers you."

Kostas and Tolstoy shot twin glances of reproach my way.

"No problem. I just want to ensure you really go." I didn't ask how the school bus would know to stop at my house, particularly with Josey on the inside and out of view.

"Of course," she said. "There's some important stuff going on today. Real important stuff."

"Fine," I said, feeling like I had come off badly in a diplomatic skirmish. "I'll take my coffee and get ready. I have an important day myself." Kostas and Josey were determined to work out a cable stitch. I left them together in the living room, with Tolstoy's chin on Josey's feet.

The three of them more or less ignored me as I polished off the French roast in the largest mug I could find.

"Be on that bus," I called out every now and then.

Of course, I could always drop her off myself.

187

*   *   *

I headed out into the rain for my next task, alone at last.

Bridget had a right to know. I practiced the best way to tell her that crazy Abby Lake had stolen Benedict's ashes and Stella's copy of *While Weeping for the Wicked*. By the time I arrived at Forty Shades of Green, I was pumped up. Too bad the shop was closed. No wonder. It was nine in the morning in a tourist village on a rainy weekday in the early fall.

I hit the Régie first for a bottle to top up the washing machine supply, then sat in the Bistro across the street from Bridget's shop, read the papers and charged cappuccinos at three bucks a pop until I saw Bridget pull up.

I brought her a large cappuccino as an advance peace offering.

Bridget looked ten years older this morning. She whirled as I caught up to her at the front door. A touch of bitterness contaminated her laugh. "I know I look awful. Hope I didn't scare you, Fiona."

"Of course you didn't scare me," I said, following her into Forty Shades of Green. "I'm the one who sneaked up on you."

"True, but you should have seen your face."

The shop looked cluttered and chaotic, boxes and parcels piled up in the aisles, sweaters unfolded and hanging messily from displays, papers strewn across the sales counter. Bridget hadn't tidied up after the previous day's shoppers.

"You should have someone to give you a hand here. How can you manage?" I said.

She shook her wet curls. "You mean give me a foot? I'm sure my staff feel like giving me a boot, I've been such a witch lately. But speaking of hand, is that a cup of cappuccino I see in yours?"

The private, allegedly witchy Bridget faded away, to be

replaced by the familiar funny and charming Bridget.

For a minute, I considered Forty Shades of Green as a place to stash Josey until things simmered down. Josey could help out and go home with Bridget in the evenings. On the other hand, Josey took a bit of getting used to. Bridget probably did too.

Plus, who was to say Abby wouldn't make Bridget her next victim? Josey could still get caught in the crossfire.

Bridget settled in at her antique desk and opened the top of the cappuccino cup with girlish pleasure.

"I don't want to keep you from your work," I said. "I'm sure this is a busy time of the year."

"Busy? I wish. This crappy rain must be washing our customers into the river, because they're sure not coming in here."

"I suppose it must have an effect."

"Worst year we've ever had. Same with everyone in St. Aubaine. I don't mind saying I'm at the end of my rope."

I took a deep breath. "I hate to tell you this when you already have enough troubles but you've got to know. Abby Lake has gone right off the rails. She's shot at Josey and me and trashed my car and..."

The cappuccino slopped onto Bridget's lap. "Don't tell me she's lost it completely. I always thought she was a few sandwiches short of a picnic. Oh, God, what am I doing making silly remarks, Fiona. This must be awful for you."

"It's all right now," I lied. "The police are on to her. So it won't be long until..."

"She gets committed?"

"...they get to the bottom of things."

"Sorry. As I believe I've mentioned, that woman really gets up my nose." A crooked grin crept onto Bridget's pale face. "I'll be glad if she gets hers."

"She hasn't got hers yet. And she might think you should be getting yours. So watch out for a small white Jetta and a guy with a red baseball cap. That's Abby."

"Wait a minute, if they already know who she is, and what she's done, surely even these clowns here on the St. Aubaine police force must be able to handle one dancer." She gasped and held on to her cup. "She must have been the one who killed Benedict. Of course. I should have known she had the strength to..."

She stopped before she had to say, "...beat him to death.".

"Maybe she didn't. There appears to be someone else involved. A man named Dougie Dolan."

"Dougie Dolan?" She slammed the cappuccino cup down on the desk. "Damn, look what I've done now. Maybe I shouldn't have caffeine."

I kept my mouth shut while she mopped up the latest spill. I could have helped her, but being quiet and calm seemed like a better plan.

Finally, she said, "Okay, I'll get a grip on myself. That creep Dougie Dolan? What's he got to do with it?"

"I wish I knew."

"Dougie's always been a complete jerk. And I never would have wanted to run into him in a dark alley, but why do you think he'd be involved? A thing for Abby? They'd be made for each other. A real pair of losers." Two angry red spots had appeared on her pale cheeks.

"A pair of losers, maybe, but possibly dangerous ones. Watch out for him too. He was hanging around outside your house dressed like a bum during Benedict's memorial."

"Don't worry, I'd know that turkey anywhere."

"I guess that's good. Another thing, Bridget. Rachel would know Dougie Dolan, would she?"

"Of course. We were all in the same class. But she would never have anything to do with the likes of him."

"Can you think why she'd let on she didn't know who he was?"

"Rachel? Sure. You know how soft-hearted she is. She's got to be everybody's mother. Probably thought she was bailing him out. She should have more sense. So he was hanging around at her place too. God, what is this all about?"

"I wish I knew."

"Like a nightmare," she said with a shaky little laugh. "I'll give Rachel a call and tell her not to be stupid. And I'll be careful myself. You too, Fiona."

"Absolutely."

"It can't last forever, and we'll be glad when it's all over and the police, such as they are, have figured it out."

I was glad she didn't call them clowns as she usually did. It might have weakened her theory. "Listen," I said, "there's something else I have to tell you."

"And then when Benedict's had his proper ceremony with everything just lovely, we'll all feel better. A perfect end for him. Something to remember." She stared out at the rain running down her storefront window. "You know, I think we'd better have a rain date for that scattering. Maybe even two. We wouldn't want a single thing to ruin it."

So it turned out not to be the ideal time to mention Abby had made off with the urn. Not cowardice on my part, just consideration. I gave a lying, cheating wave and stepped out into the monsoon.

* * *

It was bad enough when I was avoiding the police but now, as far as I could tell, the police were avoiding me. I took my chances and stormed the Sûreté. I sat in the waiting room, fidgeting and wondering what species those molded plastic seats could have been designed for, when Sarrazin loomed into view.

I guess I wasn't the first one to comment on the high level of security in the building—coded passes, bulletproof glass, intercoms. It bordered on the ridiculous, considering it was the police force for a pretty sleepy district. "Well, it does make you wonder how Mike Thring ever managed to break in here. If you can believe that old story," I said.

That only earned a grunt.

This time I didn't end up in an interview room. Sarrazin's post was past the ID camera and fingerprint area. He didn't rate an office, just a desk, one of three, in the middle of an open area. Maybe he was surly because he couldn't get used to working without the excitement of the Montreal police force. Not every police officer takes well to small-town Canada. He didn't look all that domesticated. On the other hand, he did have a flourishing collection of African violets on the left side of his desk. Not a withered leaf among them.

I sat down and decided to try for the upper hand. "Since I've been leaving you messages and haven't been hearing back, I decided to drop in and see how things were going. I'm quite anxious to get my life back in order."

He stayed on his feet and leaned against the desk. His black eyes glittered. Apparently he also preferred to have the upper hand.

"I've been answering your messages, Ms. Silk."

Damn. I hadn't checked my messages that morning. "I'm having a little trouble with that gadget."

"That a fact? You seem to be out a lot. Maybe one of these trips you can get your machine fixed." He inspected the underleaves of the nearest violet.

"Hmmm."

"That reminds me, I've even been around and knocked on the door a few times."

"Have you? Unfortunately, the door answering system is also on the fritz." I didn't really expect him to bite on that one.

"So these messages you've been leaving, listing other suspects we might want to talk to. Are there any more now? Or perhaps you'd like us to investigate everyone in the telephone directory for St. Aubaine? In between interviews, we could call you and keep you posted. It will help to fill our time."

So far our heart-to-heart wasn't going all that well. "Let's just say..." I sounded like a boy soprano. I dropped an octave. "Let's just say that after the body in the bed, I've been hit by a car, my own vehicle has been trashed, my clothing has been slashed, my home has been broken into and I've been shot at. I've called and given you the names of two people who have been seen following me, both of whom were connected with the late Benedict Kelly, and one of whom is an unsavoury character. I don't understand why you don't believe me."

I think I would have been ahead in the debate, except that my voice shot back up to high C somewhere in the last sentence.

"Yeah, well, I can see where you'd want us to finger other people." Was he laughing at me?

"Don't get me wrong, but it is in your interest to look seriously. There have been other witnesses. If something happens to me, you'll have a hard time explaining to the media why you didn't take the appropriate steps." There. I held my voice steady. I was starting to feel like a competent adult when I realized he wasn't laughing. It was more like a smirk.

"Witnesses?"

"Yes."

The smirk turned into a snort. "You mean the Thring girl? And Kostas O'Carolan?"

"Yes," I said with great dignity.

"Yeah, right, they'll be great in court."

"They probably will be. But it shouldn't come to that. Have you questioned Abby Lake? What about Dougie Dolan?"

"We will." The smirk was replaced by an inky stare.

That meant only one thing to me. Sarrazin hadn't talked to Abby Lake or Dougie Dolan yet.

"Whatever your opinion of me, there are other people to consider. Josey could get injured. Or worse. And Bridget Gallagher. Abby's never liked her. God knows what could happen there."

I thought I spotted a little flash in his eyes.

I said, "This woman has a *gun*. A revolver or something. You don't find that somewhat unusual?"

He leaned forward inkily. "We have only your word for that. And the Thring girl's."

"But my car was trashed. You saw it."

"Yeah, yeah. I hear you had a lot of trouble with that car."

"Yes?"

He shrugged. I hate those shrugs. "I hear you're broke."

"And?"

"I ask myself if it could be handy for you to get a hold of bit of cash."

"Cash? The Skylark wasn't worth six hundred dollars, working. I sold it for scrap to Paulie Pound. A hundred and fifty bucks. And I got that much only because Josey found a separate buyer for the tires, the hub caps and the sideview mirror. I didn't even have collision coverage. I think you..."

"You know what I think? I think you should leave it to us."

"I'd be happy to leave if to you if you were doing your job."

I couldn't believe that I, Fiona Silk, semi-professional doormat and all round chickenshit, would speak to the police like that.

Neither could he, judging by the colour his neck turned. He stood up straight and headed towards the exit, indicating our chit-chat was over. "I don't tell you how to write your books, Madame Silk. Don't tell me how to be a police officer. As far as I'm concerned you are still a suspect."

I skedaddled after him. Considering the implications of what he'd just said, this seemed like an excellent time to leave the police station.

Although as a general rule, the reluctant lawyer, Natalie, and Sarrazin were tied for last place in the people-I'd-like-to-spend-time-with category, (excluding murderers). Natalie was looking better by the minute.

*   *   *

I thought I saw a twitch in the plein jour curtains at L'Auberge des Rêves. After ten minutes of banging on the door, I gave up. That was no way to run a bed and breakfast, leaving potential guests standing in the rain. Fine with me. Maybe Rachel would answer the door for Sarrazin when he came knocking.

*   *   *

I barged back into my house, tucked away the new bottle of Courvoisier, and grabbed my own copy of *While Weeping for the Wicked* for Stella. I called out for Tolstoy.

The Irish Rovers were blasting from the stereo. I turned down the sound and left a voice mail for Liz requesting Natalie's number and telling her why.

I had my hand on the door when I stopped, stunned.

Kostas padded down the hallway, wrapped in a towel, his hair tucked under Aunt Kit's pink shower cap, holding a bottle of Jasmine Bubble Bath.

"Lovely afternoon, dear lady."

There was no sign of Tolstoy but, then, there never is at bath time.

I finally said, "Oh, right, absolutely," and dashed for the door. Liberty and equality were doing fine. Privacy still needed work at the Hôtel Chez Moi.

Twenty-Five

By the time I pulled into Stella Iannetti's driveway, I could more or less see the humour in it. I reached for *While Weeping* and headed for the door. Stella answered. Something sticky was clumped in her hair, her blouse was buttoned wrong and lipstick smeared her chin. She said, "Shhh."

"Oh sorry, am I interrupting something?"

"Yup, nap time. Everybody's got the flu, and they're finally down for the count."

"Oh. Stella. I am so embarrassed. When we were here the other night, I forgot the most important thing."

"Shhh. *Sleeping.*" She mouthed the words and pointed towards the far end of the house.

Sleeping. I liked the sound of that.

She beckoned me into the kitchen. We tiptoed.

We both slumped into the chairs by the kitchen table. I, being less experienced, failed to check the seat for the sharp edges of half-built LEGO houses and shot up again quickly.

"You learn," Stella said.

"Right."

"Where's your little friend? Not playing hooky today?"

"Pressing business at school. Couldn't be avoided."

"And the fuzzy white one?"

"Hiding out."

Stella rebuttoned her blouse and fluffed her hair. She

smiled encouragingly at me. She seemed to be waiting for something. I wondered what.

"The most important thing?" she said, after a while.

"Oh, right, right, right. Yes. Here it is. Benedict's own last book of verse. He wanted you to have it."

"Be serious."

"Oh, no, absolutely. He did."

"Who cares? I mean, have you lost your mind? What are you doing lugging that crap of Benedict's around and pretending it's important?"

I couldn't think of what to say. I didn't give a flying fig about Benedict's poems, and I certainly didn't think they were important in any way, and I guess the pretense was obvious.

"Maybe it'll be worth a lot of money some day. I mean, he did win the Flambeau."

"Go figure. So what's this about?"

"Okay. Remember when you said Benedict leaves a residue in your life?"

She nodded. "Plus a major residue in yours lately."

"No kidding. Here's my problem. Abby Lake has been following me, she tried to run me down, she stalked me, she trashed my car and she's still on the loose."

"All part of the Benedict benefit," she said. "So getting back to your story?"

"Did I mention she shot at me? I actually spent the night in a cave to escape."

"Ick."

"Exactly." I liked talking to someone on the same wavelength, which Stella definitely was. "But that's not the worst part."

"It gets worse?"

"Yes. Josey's been there every time."

"My God, she's just a kid."

"I know."

Stella rubbed her upper lip. "I can't believe it, anyone endangering a child like that. So, um, why don't you just make sure Josey stays home?"

"Because she can't go home. Her uncle's just jumped bail, and her grandmother has some form of dementia. Her mother's been gone for eleven years or so. There's no one else."

"Tough one."

"Exactly."

"Don't you have any friends who...?"

Obviously, Stella hadn't met my friends.

"The only one who is suitable can't get her husband to agree. And Bridget's on the verge of a breakdown."

Stella nodded. "What about some kind of home?"

"Out of the question. Josey's terrified of falling into the clutches of Social Services. I'm certain she'd run away."

"For sure."

"So the point is, I feel incredibly responsible."

"That's an amazing story. Abby attacking you."

"Hard to believe, isn't it?"

"Yes. Well, no. She's a flake. Always was. But why you? I could see it if she took off after Bridget or Zoë. She really hates them. Oh yeah, it must have been the place where he was... Yeah, that would do it for Abby. It would be personal."

"It is. She even slashed my clothes."

"Maybe I'm wrong, but I can't see her trying to hurt Josey."

"Probably not, but she does have a gun and doesn't mind firing it. Josey could get caught in the middle."

"That's scary."

"Another thing. Do you know a fellow called Dougie Dolan?"

"I don't think so."

"Big guy, slanty dark eyes. Dresses like a tramp sometimes. He went to school with Benedict."

"Sorry. Why?"

"He's following me."

"Someone else is following you? He must be connected with Abby in some way."

"Right, and I don't know the connection, but he's supposed to be dangerous."

"What about the police? They must be able to do something. Even in St. Aubaine, for God's sake."

"You'd think so."

"Idiots."

"So, the point of all this is, I'm in a real pickle about Josey. Since you two seemed to get along, and since you understand how Benedict can leave a residue in your life, I thought maybe you would be willing to let her stay here for a couple of days. She's extremely helpful. I don't know if she's good with children, but she'd certainly earn her keep. It's a lot to ask and I'd understand, of course, if you say no." The original brook, babbling.

Stella had gone quiet. I wished I were on another planet.

"It couldn't be Josey who's attracting all this violence, could it?"

I felt goosebumps rise on my arms. Josey? "I don't see how it could be."

"I have to think of my own children."

"Naturally. But it's all to do with me, for some reason. Nothing has happened to Josey or at her home."

"All right," she said.

"And if it doesn't work out..." I was still babbling.

"Don't worry, if it doesn't work out, you'll hear from me soon enough."

"Oh, absolutely. When can I bring her by? Do you need to discuss this with your husband?"

"When I tell him someone else might be handling bath time, he'll think he won Lotto 6/49. Let's do it as soon as possible."

Too good to be true. I felt like crying in gratitude. I blew my nose instead. Good thing I stayed dry, because Stella's twin boys took that moment to drag themselves into the room and drape themselves around their mother. They stared at me with sleepy eyes while Stella wiped their noses.

She washed her hands and handed me a small plate with five tollhouse cookies. The twins got one each.

"I can't eat…"

"People who blow their own noses get more cookies," she said.

The twin on the left managed a charming, scamplike grin. The other one matched it.

Then it hit me. I'd seen that scamplike grin before. But not for seven or eight years, if you didn't count the Krazy Glue.

"I can't thank you enough. You have no idea what this will mean for Josey."

"Sure I do. I've been there, a teenager with lots of problems, and no one to look after my wellbeing," Stella said.

"Right."

"And major residue."

"No kidding." Now I knew, and she knew I knew.

"So." I got up to go. "I'm not sure if you'll want to keep this. It's the last available copy of Benedict's last book. The one that won him the Flambeau."

"Oh right. That's the reason you came here, wasn't it."

"Actually, that was a ploy."

"Uh-huh. Don't ever try to get work on the stage."

*   *   *

Liz was pacing in my living room when I walked in. Natalie occupied the seat of honour, looking corporate. Kostas, fresh and fluffy, hovered in the kitchen door, regarding the wingback with longing.

"I couldn't keep them out, dear lady," he said.

Liz shot him a look. He shot one back, defiantly.

"Who could? I thought it was best to give her a key," I said. Nothing could put a dent in my excellent mood. Josey was going to be all right.

"Where'd you put that Courvoisier, Fiona? And no stalling."

"What are you doing here in the middle of the day?" I said. I stall whenever I want to.

"It *is* an emergency."

"It is?"

"That's certainly what your message seemed to imply. The one where you claimed you were about to be arrested. Right at this exact minute, I should be at Dr. Fairooz's office for a consultation on an upper lip dermabrasion. But no, I'm sitting here trying to help you save *your* skin. I dragged Natalie over, and God knows she's a busy woman. What do we find? You gone and Rumplestiltskin here instead. And not a drop to drink."

"Have you tried the kitchen? There's always coffee," I said.

Liz followed me and seemed surprised when I turned on her. "How come Natalie is always available when she doesn't do this kind of work? And doesn't like me."

Liz shrugged. "So what do you have to drink?"

"Water, water everywhere." Except in the washing machine, which I chose not to mention.

"Funny," Liz said as she stalked back into the living room. "Listen, Natalie here doesn't think you should be charging into the cop shop twice a day and getting them all agitated."

"Bad idea," Natalie said. "Really bad. Really really really..."

"Natalie's had a whole lot more experience dealing with the police than you have. Ergo, you'd better listen to her."

"I'm sure she has."

"Don't be snarky. I'm worried about you. Natalie has agreed to represent your interests. Leave everything to her."

Natalie swung her feet.

"Absolutely," I said. "Oh, and while you're at it, Natalie, do you handle divorce work?"

* * *

"Thought they'd never leave." Kostas hustled up, smelling nicely of jasmine.

"Good news. I've found an excellent place for Josey."

"I told yis before, dear lady, she's not going to like it."

"Probably not. But she'll like it a lot better than the alternatives."

"She feels rejected, that young lady. I can tell. I'm a man of some sensitivity, you know."

"You are, Kostas. But it's better all round. And she'll like it at Stella's."

"Stella's? Our Stella's?" I could tell this met with approval. "When does she go?"

"As soon as she gets home from school, I'll take her over."

"Oh, indeed. It's a shame we didn't have the chance to celebrate her birthday first."

"We'll do something later. Really."

"Since it's turning into such a nice day..."

I peered through the window. He was right. I'd been so relieved about Stella's offer, I hadn't even noticed the sun breaking through.

"...why don't we take her over to the Park at the Marina for ice cream, and we'll promise her something special for her birthday and then tell her?"

"Look, Kostas. We don't know where Abby Lake is or Dougie Dolan. The police aren't taking them seriously. I don't want to take Josey to a deserted spot."

"Dear lady, you can hardly call the Marina deserted. There's always a bit of a crowd there. And since it is such a nice day, it'll be jammed."

"I still worry about Abby or Dolan following us." It was one of my major worries. Minor worries included finding something that would look enough like the urn to be substituted during the scattering.

"Leave it to me. I can shake anybody," Kostas said. "Guaranteed, dear lady."

I didn't doubt it.

"And my treat, of course. Just got me pogey. I'm flush."

Tolstoy's tail thumped. He loves the Marina. He had the Frisbee in his mouth. I know when I'm licked.

* * *

The sun beamed as we swung out of Chemin des Cèdres on our way to surprise Josey at the school. I was dressed in shorts and a cotton top to take advantage of the unusually hot weather. I brought an extra T-shirt for Josey and a pair of shorts that were much too small for me and would be much too big for her. The grey indefinable clothes Kostas wore never seemed to be related in any way to the weather. Tolstoy always looks just right in white.

We swung through St. Aubaine on our way. Kostas claimed an urgent need to check up on his consignments at the La Tricoterie. I thought I'd better get cracking and find a birthday gift. I still had no idea what to buy for Josey. I ducked into the Roi du Dollar and found a card and wrapping paper. Whatever I found, it would have to fit into two pieces of maple leaf paper. The mood was not improved by spotting Sarrazin and the glamorous coroner tucked into a corner table of Thé Pour Deux making eyes at each other over a cream tea. I pivoted nicely but not before he looked up.

She smiled the way the cat does after a canary canapé. He smiled the way you might smile at someone you were planning to arrest any minute now. I smiled the way someone who has nothing to smile about smiles.

I went to round up Kostas and Josey. I could trust them.

*　　*　　*

Josey hummed rock tunes in the back seat. The sweater grew longer and Kostas coached from the front.

"Your tension's much improved. That's the secret, you'll be an artist yet."

Tension improved. What kind of tension were we going to experience when Josey found out about her new accommodations?

Shortly after five we pulled into the *stationnement* near the Marina. The waterfront park was full of people. I relaxed. No one, but no one, could have followed us through Kostas's road maze. Even if they had, what could they do in a crowd like this?

The park felt cool and green, with patches of filtered

sunlight visible through the cedars. The air was fresh and wood scented. We picked up ice cream cones in the Marina.

Josey and Kostas selected Rocky Road. I had Mint Chocolate Chip. They discussed techniques for Fair Isle knitting.

First things first. Ten minutes spent tossing the Frisbee to the loyal hound. Then Josey took over, and I listened to the river lapping on the shore and admired its crayon blue colour. I wished I could relax in this wonderful spot as a regular ordinary unpursued visitor. I scanned the environment for signs of something not quite right and kept my back from being exposed. The slightest crack of a twig made me spin around, my heart thumping like a reggae drummer.

Of course, I felt even more guilty about Josey. Rationally, I had no problem placing her with Stella. Josey was a fourteen-year-old girl. I was an adult. I had a responsibility not to get talked into things I knew were wrong. No arguments.

Emotionally, I knew she'd do a number on me. And I always fall for Josey's numbers. What a patsy. For the first time in my nearly forty-five years, I wondered how parents cope.

Josey and Kostas joked and bantered. The ice cream had rekindled our spirits. But the Mint Chocolate Chip wasn't enough to do the trick. Kostas and I practically tripped over each other when we spotted Abby Lake's small white Jetta snuggled next to Skylark Jr.

Even from a distance, you could tell at least two of the Skylark's tires had been slashed. A few cars away, a young couple leaned against a Jeep Cherokee with Manitoba plates.

I felt a rush of rage. She'd managed to track us, when the police should have been watching her. You couldn't trust that Sarrazin as far as you could toss a grizzly.

Abby sat behind the wheel of the Jetta, resting.

"Thank heavens you're here," the young woman by the Jeep said. "We've been waiting for you. And we wrote down her license number, in case she left. I can't imagine why anybody would do such a thing."

"You saw her? You saw her slash our tires?"

She nodded. He said: "When we were coming out of the trail. I guess we should have spoken to her, but she had that knife, so we decided to call the police and wait here, out of her sight."

"And anyway," she broke in, "when we went to the phone booth, a man went over to her car. I think he gave her a piece of his mind for slashing your tires."

I felt a little buzz of anger around my ears. Abby Lake represented the story of my life. My forty-four years and some months of being badgered, bossed and bothered by anyone who felt like pushing me around. My ex-husband-to-be, my friends, my dog. Everyone from country policemen to nosy neighbors, to fourteen-year-old girls. Everyone figured they could tell me what to do, what not to do, how to live my life, where to keep my booze. The fact I found myself in charge of Benedict's scattering was typical of the life of Fiona Silk, prize wuss.

And now, ten feet away sat the deranged woman who had endangered our lives and given me nightmares. Relaxing a bit after destroying my tires. If that's not pushing you around, I don't know what is. I stood totally still, rage washing over me.

Kostas tugged at my arm. I pulled away and barrelled toward the Jetta. I approached the car window. "Miz Silk," Josey yelled. "Don't go, the cops are already on the way."

Oh, right. We just knew how much we could count on them.

It was time to look her right in the eye and say "enough". Of course, I also figured this would be less dangerous than it sounds. Even Abby Lake wouldn't shoot or stab me with four witnesses staring straight at her. Especially with the wail of a siren getting closer.

But Abby Lake didn't pull out any guns. She didn't react. When I stuck my head in the open car window, I could see why.

Abby's dead white hand lay draped over Benedict's urn. A revolver sat propped beside it, on the seat. Abby's head was turned toward the window, a single, perfect bullet hole centred in her forehead.

Twenty-Six

If Sarrazin was a black bear, the officer who took my statement was Winnie the Pooh. Lucky for me he was not only cute and cuddly, but he spoke fluent English. You can't always count on it. My tolerable command of the French language had deserted me along with my normally adequate control over my knees.

For the second time in one day, I found myself behind the door of the Sûreté. It wasn't the kind of place to grow on you, even when Sarrazin was off duty. Five agitated people and one dog garnered stares from the other officers. One by one, we repeated our explanations with carefully selected background bits to the nice Sergeant. This time I took the precaution of calling my lawyer.

Natalie was not available. Why was I not surprised?

The young couple who'd witnessed the shooting found the situation much more dramatically satisfying than I did. Kostas exuded bonhomie throughout, surprising me somewhat, and Josey quivered with suppressed enjoyment. Go figure.

I couldn't erase Abby's final appearance from my mind. The hole in her forehead, the immense green eyes, staring. Her open mouth, bright with fresh red lipstick.

The Sergeant looked like he'd missed his honey at eleven. Such a nuisance finding women shot to death in local picnic areas.

"Let's start at the beginning," he said.

"Absolutely."

By the time I finished talking, he was rubbing his temples. "So there's a strong possibility of suicide while distraught."

"Suicide? I don't think so." Abby might have searched my house and attacked me twice, but someone else had killed her. Whoever killed her, and it sounded like Dolan, hadn't done it for the ashes or for Benedict's books. Abby herself must have been the target.

I felt intense gratitude to the people from Manitoba. They'd seen Abby Lake get into her car. Alive. They'd seen a big man with peroxided hair approach her car, lean over and apparently speak to her and then leave in a black Acura with gold markings and a mud-covered license plate.

We were lucky they'd seen Abby alive while we were in the park. And they were even luckier the killer hadn't seen them.

"And the man you think might be responsible?"

"His name is Dougie Dolan, and he drives a car like the one the witnesses saw. And he's big, and did I say he has bleached yellow hair? First we thought he was following us, but now we figure he was following Abby Lake, and she was following us."

Officer Winnie fiddled with his computer. "Dolan, Dolan," he muttered to himself. "There he is. My my my."

*   *   *

Skylark Junior was finito. What the four slashed tires hadn't accomplished, the sugar in the gas tank had.

Luckily, I knew a good-looking poet.

We were on our way, once again, wedged into Marc-André's BMW, with me in the front and Josey, Kostas and

Tolstoy in the back. I worried about Tolstoy's dirty paws on the spotless upholstery, but on the plus side, at least I didn't smell bad this time.

Josey was in excellent humour. "Now that she's dead, I guess I can go back with you until Uncle Mike gets his situation resolved."

My neck tensed. "Not until they arrest Dolan."

"We're not in any danger from him."

"Guess again. We may not know what he's up to, but we know he killed Abby. That's dangerous in my books. Sorry, Josey, you have to stay with Stella until it's over."

The temperature in the Beemer dropped.

One good thing though, we now knew how Abby had tracked us, despite Kostas's brilliant attempts to evade her. Winnie the Pooh had been thoughtful enough to tell us about the receiver in Abby's car and the transmitter stuck underneath ours. "Easy enough if you know how." It made me wonder if Abby had used the same trick with the original Skylark. At least it was one small part of the mystery cleared up.

On the other hand, we still didn't know how Dolan had kept up with us.

Even if the police did know about Dolan, I had plenty of reason to stick close to Kostas and, with any luck, Marc-André, until everything was sorted out. Things were going to be fine if we could only avoid dangerous men and police officers until this geedee scattering.

Naturally, I'd forgotten about the media.

*   *   *

A convoy of vans blocked my driveway. No way to get in without encountering hand mikes and boom mikes and chipper, hair-gelled interviewers. But at least it was raining heavily again, and they all looked miserable.

Heads whipped towards the Beemer. Noses pressed against windows. Soggy feet hopped.

"Don't even slow down," I said to Marc-André.

Marc-André stepped on the gas, looking grim. Perhaps he could understand my reluctance to deal with the media. Perhaps he was getting claustrophobic with the crowd in the car. Perhaps he was worried about getting stuck with me forever.

I chewed my nails. "Doesn't anything else newsworthy ever happen in this region? Does it always have to be us?"

"I wouldn't mind talking to them," Josey said.

"Indeed, my girl, you're right on the money. Excellent advertising. The best. A picture is worth a thousand words. Dear lady, are you sure you won't reconsider?"

I didn't have the heart to say the fourth estate was not interested in Josey's gardening specials or Kostas's latest sweaters designs. Just the hole in Abby's forehead.

"And I needed to pick up a few things," Josey grumped, as the old Beemer shot onto Route 105.

*   *   *

I explained to Josey, and not for the first time, that Tolstoy and I would be perfectly safe without her in the house. No one was likely to murder us in full view of TV vans.

Still, she gave off a guilt-inducing vibe for the duration of the drive to Stella Iannetti's. Stella was glad to see us. Behind her smile, I sensed quivering energy. "I heard it on the news. I can't believe it. Abby dead. Come on in."

She even gave Josey a hug. Josey, who's not crazy about being touched, submitted. I got a pat on the arm. Tolstoy got

212

one on the head. Kostas got two pecks on the cheeks and Marc-André a frankly speculative appraisal.

We all had cookies. Some with milk. Some with coffee. Some with a bowl of water. Stella's husband, who might understandably have objections to the murder *du jour* crowd dropping in, seemed fine. Of course, bath time was in full swing, and that was now in Josey's job description. Josey relaxed enough to check out her new room.

Perhaps it was the cookies. More likely it was knowing Josey was out of the line of fire. I could feel myself unkink.

Stella dropped her bombshell as we were leaving.

"About *While Weeping for the Wicked*," she whispered.

"What about it?"

"You don't actually believe Benedict wrote those poems."

"What?"

"Didn't you read it?"

"Absolutely." I met her eyes. "Right. Okay, I couldn't bring myself to."

"Can't say I blame you. But you missed some dynamite poetry."

"They're good?"

"Yup."

"And how can you tell Benedict didn't write them?"

"*Because* they're good."

Of course. How blindingly obvious. Maybe if the whole set-up hadn't been so bizarre, I would have figured it out myself. At least, I'd like to think so.

"Abby?"

"No. As a poet she made a good dancer. Here, take the book and check it out. You'll see."

*   *   *

I was distracted in the car, thinking about who might have written those poems. *While Weeping for the Wicked*, a limited edition small press publication, had been good enough to scoop the Flambeau. Why would another poet donate first-rate pieces of writing to benefit a worm like Benedict? It would have to be a poet who was either crazy or not too bright. Like pretty well anyone in the O'Mafia.

Unless the poet had been unaware. Or in love. Or if Benedict had just plain stolen them.

Abby? I agreed with Stella on that one. No chance.

Zoë? People knew her for her sculpture, but I remembered hearing her read once, and she had a gift for poetry too. But would she give her poems to Benedict? Not if she thought Abby Lake was still around. I remembered her reaction to *While Weeping for the Wicked*. The way she'd stroked the cover and fingered the pages. It had seemed obvious she hadn't known about the book. So, Zoë. Obsessed and crazy, yes. Angry and vengeful because he'd stolen her poems, no.

Even Kostas, old buddy and mentor, hadn't known that Benedict had published *While Weeping for the Wicked*. Maybe Zoë gave her poems to Benedict before she found out Abby was in the picture. Maybe she found out and flipped. Zoë with her chunks of marble and her strong hands and her blowtorch. From what I knew about her, if she'd found out Benedict was using her poetry to get rich and live happily ever after with Abby, Benedict might have been seriously singed.

Kostas was a bit put out at being dropped off at Evening's End.

"Dear lady," he said, "I'd be more than happy to share your home again tonight."

"That is very kind of you, but I will make certain she is safe," Marc-André said.

The fact was, I would rather face a crazed killer than keep bumping into people in my own house. Liberty and equality were in bad enough shape. Fraternity didn't even rate.

* * *

We didn't spot a single vehicle near my home. Yahoo. I felt the pressure of Marc-André's hand as we sprinted to the front door. Nothing like the absence of the media to pump up your libido.

Alone at last, and alone with the right person. Tolstoy kept a discreet distance. Marc-André and I careened through the front door cheek to cheek, followed by lip to lip, hip to hip and zip to zip. It worked for me. Twentysome years of marriage to you-know-who had dulled my senses, but I could still identify the melting tingle and the urge to rip someone's clothes off.

There were only two problems. They were seated in the beanbag chair and Woody's wheelchair, respectively. But not respectfully.

"Look who's here," Liz said.

"I get to say that," I said.

Woody snorted. They were always snorting, those two. Together, they sounded like a barn full of hogs. "The look on your face, kiddo."

Marc-André's forehead creased.

"I didn't see your car," I squeaked.

"You could thank us," Liz said.

"For what?" Sneaking into my house? Stamping out my brand new sex life?

"Funny. How about for getting rid of those hounds outside?"

"Ah," I said, "May I ask what you told them?"

"Never mind. You don't want to know. They're gone, aren't they? And by tomorrow you'll be old news again, and no one will give you the time of day."

Woody shook his silver braid and waved his arms. "Wasn't my idea. You ask me, you're missing a major opportunity here, kiddo. Good time to get that new book out with all this attention."

"And listen," Liz said, "I don't like hearing my best friend has been involved in another murder every time I turn on the television. I want to hear things like that directly from you. I've left you some messages which I expect you to listen to. Sergeant Whozit's on there too. He sounded hot under the collar."

Not only had she taken over my answering machine but, from the look of things, she was settled in for the evening.

Marc-André squeezed my hand. Liz spotted the movement. I could tell she rated him at least a nine. I rated him off the scale.

"Anyway, you don't need to worry about a thing. Woody and I are concerned about your safety, even if you're not. We are going to spend the night. That should keep dangerous people away."

"Thanks, but no thanks, Liz. Do you need a lift?" I said.

"She's parked around the bend in the road. Part of the surprise," Woody said.

Liz's eyes glittered. As far as I was concerned, she could glitter all she wanted. The magic had gone out of the moment.

"You've had a tough day," Marc-André said. "Why don't I call you in the morning?"

Just as well. Two more minutes in the room with Liz and Woody, talking dewlaps and satanic rituals, and my sex life would be finished before it started.

I turned to Marc-André and smiled. "Absolutely."

Twenty-Seven

"You are supposed to be in school. And after school, you are supposed to be at Stella's. And please don't tell me it's a PD day." The irritation in my voice resulted from spending the night with the understudies rather than the leading man.

Half the pajama party had just left with Cyril, but I was still stuck with Liz, and now the second shift was arriving in Kostas's ancient green car.

Josey and Kostas paid no attention to my grumbling. "I'm playing hooky," she said, holding a plastic bag close to her chest.

Behind her, Kostas beamed. Naturally. He probably invented hooky as a boy and would be glad to see it flourishing. "Good news. Those television fellas have all left, dear lady."

Josey, still clutching the bag, sprinted past me and headed for the bathroom "Wait a minute, I've got something to show you."

Liz snorted from the beanbag chair. She lounged with a cup of coffee, instead of her usual Courvoisier, which she would never find unless she decided to do my laundry. The life of a country doctor must be great.

I gave her a dirty look. It didn't seem to be making an impression. I was working on a more effective facial expression when Josey reappeared.

"What do you think?" she asked. It would have been easier

to answer truthfully if she hadn't been wearing her first major knitting project.

I could only hope Liz wouldn't choose that moment for one of her candid evaluations.

"I finished stitching it together. It's a sweater."

I clutched my coffee and opened my mouth. Nothing came out. Kostas gave me a glance which I interpreted to mean, I'm sorry I didn't know this would happen or I would have warned you. Personally, I would have expected more from the Father of Hooky.

I took a deep breath. "Heavens, what an ambitious project."

Liz appeared to be captivated with the view from the window. Planning to build an ark maybe.

Tolstoy headed for the kitchen.

Josey twirled to give us all possible angles.

The arms were definitely different lengths, and both somewhat longer than Josey's. The sweater had various undulations and bumps I felt certain were not part of the original design. The front seemed made-to-order for someone with three breasts. The patterns resembled the works of Jackson Pollock rather than traditional Irish knitwear.

Kostas said nothing, leaving me to dig myself out. Sure, I like to be alone, but not abandoned. I thought fast. Josey's frown deepened.

"The colours," I said, after a medium eternity, "are gorgeous."

"They are nice, aren't they? Kostas gave me the wool and he dyed it himself."

You'd think I would have been prepared for that sweater, its component parts and its construction, since we'd all been confined to small spaces while Josey was knitting it. I exhaled with relief. But I wasn't getting off that easily.

"But what do you think about the sweater itself?" Josey asked.

Time for Kostas to take the reins. "My dear girl," he said, "it's an excellent first effort."

As an artist-in-wool, naturally he was aware of the sensitivities of the novice knitter. An excellent first effort. I'd had no idea, but I did know Josey, and Josey was one of those people who is born with a knack for doing things easily and well. Josey would not like anything that could be described as "an excellent first effort".

"It's pitiful," Josey said.

"No," Kostas and I cooed in unison.

"Yes, it is. Do you think I can't see? No one in their right mind would ever be caught dead in it."

True enough, but neither Kostas nor I had the courage to agree.

"I can't believe you guys wouldn't tell me the truth."

"We didn't actually...lie."

"You didn't tell me the truth. You treated me like some kind of little kid or something and you...you...you patronized me."

I spoke, since Kostas's mouth was busy swallowing.

"I don't think so. We, and I speak for both Kostas and myself, felt this was a formidable task, and should be recognized as such. Whether or not anyone would actually wear it is a secondary consideration."

Josey snorted and pulled the sweater off.

"What's more," I said, "you learned to knit, something that some of us haven't been able to do in forty some years. And you finished it under most difficult conditions. You should respect and admire the sweater for what it is."

Josey's lip curled as she dropped the sweater to the floor.

"I couldn't have done as well," I said.

"I never thought you could," she said.

Liz barked with laughter.

"Sure, it's your practice piece," said Kostas.

Josey whipped around. "You never mentioned anything about a practice piece before."

"Did I not? But dear girl, I'm an aould man and apt to forget things now and then. Everyone begins with a practice piece."

"Remind me sometime," Liz said, "to tell you the results of my first surgery, before I really got the hang of it."

Tolstoy returned from the kitchen to put in his two milkbone's worth by sniffing the longest arm, then curling up on it.

"The key thing," Liz said, "is to avoid litigation. I think you're safe in this case."

"It doesn't matter," I said.

Tolstoy smiled. Kostas and I opened our mouths, but too late. The front door banged behind Josey.

*　　*　　*

It was a real pleasure to see the back of Liz and Kostas, and even Josey, although her exit left a whiff of guilt.

I could deal with that because at last I was gloriously alone. Once I took my mind off Marc-André and the night that might have been, I needed to think. Even though Abby was dead, I couldn't shake the sense of being pushed around. Manipulated. The biggest manipulation of all had been the placing of Benedict in my bed. Playfully. I still couldn't get over that playfulness.

I'd really liked my tidy explanation featuring Abby as

Benedict's killer. In my theory, she'd slipped the body into my bed as a way of thumbing her nose at Benedict after his death. And thumbing it at me in anticipation of mine. But I had no way of knowing what went on in Abby's tormented mind before she died.

If Abby had killed Benedict out of jealousy, why had she been killed? What possible role could Dougie Dolan be playing in this whole circus? What about Mary Morrison's comments about dangerous Dougie taking the blame for things other little lads had done? So Dougie Dolan, small-time thug, had spent a lifetime playing second fiddle to Benedict. And some thirty years later, Benedict had been flouncing around, squiring a pretty lady and announcing to anyone who'd listen he was into some big money. Could that have sent Dougie Dolan over the edge? If so, why the interest in me? Had Benedict spoken about me to Dougie? Blathering on over a jar with that "love of his life" drivel? Was Dolan snaking after me because he believed I knew something about Benedict's windfall? That made some sense, but it didn't explain anything about why Abby had been killed.

I sat at my desk and stared at my paper analysis for many long minutes, until it hit me. If Abby had been on her own wacky mission to wipe me out, it might explain why Dolan had killed her. What if Dougie Dolan thought he needed me alive to extract Benedict's secret?

What was happening with Dougie anyway? Had he been arrested? It had to be good news if Sarrazin wasn't hassling me any more. Just to be on the safe side, I called the Sûreté. Officer Winnie wasn't available. Neither was Sarrazin. I left a message for each of them. And one for Sarrazin care of Dr. Duhamel's answering service. Just in case.

I took a certain amount of pleasure in leaving a long,

complicated message, including a summary of Philip's latest settlement offer, with the young woman who answered the phone for Natalie, the reluctant lawyer.

I had one thing left to do that day: Find out where the Flambeau fit in. That geedee literary award had to be connected. Stella didn't think the poems had even been written by Benedict. Had the rigging of the contest been tied to the writing off of Benedict? I was long overdue to learn whether Mme Flambeau could shed any light on who had really written those poems.

* * *

"*Désolée*, but I have not had any success with Mme Flambeau. I have already checked with all my contacts. She is even more reclusive than usual. She has not been seen at the Foundation itself. There isn't much going on there. I do not think anyone even staffs the office properly." That was not the way Hélène would run a foundation, let me tell you.

"No kidding," I said. "I've left plenty of messages with those people, if indeed there are ever really people there. It's pretty frustrating. I think Mme Flambeau must be the key to this whole thing. So you can see how important it is."

"I do, Fiona."

"Can you give it another try? All I need is an address."

"Of course. But I have been very busy. You know we are planning a new fundraising tour of historic St. Aubaine. The brochure is ready and..."

"I'll help."

"But I need people to fold and stuff and stamp."

"I'll fold, stuff and stamp."

"...and people to go to the Bureau de Poste."

"I'll go to the Post Office. Someone must know where this Flambeau woman is."

"I have one more possibility. But you know those envelopes will need to be sealed too."

"Absolutely."

It took her fifteen minutes to get the address.

I called Cyril Hemphill and told him to get over on the double.

"I'll be off like a prom dress," he said.

*   *   *

Tolstoy is a country dog. He didn't take well to the mobile parking lot that is Boulevard Métropolitain or to the *Autoroute* Décarie and to the speed, traffic and honking horns on the other asphalt entrances to Montreal.

Neither of us was prepared for the heat: a steaming day that might have been expected in July but was inappropriate for mid-September. A trickle of sweat tap-danced down my back. And *I* wasn't wearing a white fur coat.

The only happy traveller was Cyril Hemphill. "Thinking about getting the AC on the old girl refitted." He'd be able to do that on what it was going to cost me to get to Montreal and back. Lucky my credit was still good with Cyril.

I gave Tolstoy a sympathetic pat on the head. "I'll be glad when all this is over," I said to Cyril.

"I imagine you will."

"It seems like it's been going on forever, and I feel like everyone in St. Aubaine still thinks I might have killed Benedict."

I met Cyril's eyes in the rear-view mirror. "Don't you worry about that, Miz Silk. I set them gossips straight. They might want to think you done it, but they know darn well the truth is at the time of that murder, you were tits up, pardon my French."

Why thank you, Cyril.

My hair reacted to the heat and humidity by kinking into corkscrews and standing away from my head, like Little Orphan Annie Meets the Sauna Creature. I allowed myself to be distracted by this image in the sideview mirror while Cyril somehow got lost in Notre Dame de Grâce, St. Henri, Côte de Neiges and Lasalle. I took some small comfort in thinking Dolan could never have followed Cyril's cab through all those detours.

Tolstoy and I were both pretty wilted by the time the cab wheezed its way through upper Westmount toward the stately home where we hoped to find Mme Flambeau. Like many of its neighbouring properties, it could probably be picked up for three or four million. Finally, Cyril squealed into the circular driveway and parked in front of some expensive shrubs. You could have stashed another dozen or so cars in that driveway, but Cyril's cab was the only one there. I hoped someone was at home, and the Flambeau vehicles were safely parked in the three-car garage.

Mme Flambeau. I prepared myself for an emaciated woman with metallic blonde hair, two-inch red nails, a fistful of diamonds, ninety-dollar black Swiss stockings and a heart full of murder.

As an alternate plan, I'd prepared myself for a cool aristocrat with a streak of silver in her brunette pageboy, pencil-thin in a plain dark wool dress the price of a sports car. Of course, she might also possess well-toned arms that could hoist dead old Benedict into my four-poster. I had not prepared myself for a woman who looked like a loaf of homemade bread dough that had been allowed to rise a third time.

When she answered the door, I assumed she was the housekeeper. Mme Flambeau answered her own door, but only because she was about to take three small yappy dogs for a walk.

Tolstoy flipped. Maybe it was the little bows in their topknots that set him off. It was the closest I've ever come to feeling irritated with Tolstoy.

"Forgive him," I said, grabbing his collar before he swallowed one of the yappers. "I urgently need to see Mme Flambeau. My dog is usually well behaved, but he's just driven from St. Aubaine in a totally non-air-conditioned car. And..."

"I'm Mme Flambeau. Did you say St. Aubaine?"

"Yes. I'm a..."

"St. Aubaine." A smile cut through the doughy face, revealing a first-rate upper plate.

"I had a friend in St. Aubaine," she said. "A dear, dear friend."

I managed not to shout a-ha. "Benedict Kelly?"

Her face glowed. "You were also a friend of Benedict's?"

I'd been expecting a French accent, but what I heard was pure Ottawa Valley Irish. This woman would have been right at home sitting on the passenger side of a pickup on any rural road outside St. Aubaine. Far more at home than perched here on top of Montreal.

Mme Flambeau stepped into the spacious foyer, yanked open an interior door with her free hand and shooed the three yappers through it. She called to someone unseen: "Please take the babies out. I have company."

Some of the company hurled himself at the door after her babies.

"I'm so sorry. He's usually a perfect gentleman," I said. "He's not himself after that hot car. I'm sure he wouldn't hurt them. It's that testosterone thing."

Madame Flambeau's watery blue eyes swam with worry.

"You're not an arts reporter or a critic, are you, pet?"

"Anything but."

"A poet?"

"Certainly not."

"Any other kind of reporter?"

"Just an old friend."

"A friend of that lovely boy. I normally don't receive visitors. But all right. You can come in," she said. "You look..."

Polite wording must have failed her, but she stopped herself from saying drenched, sweaty or half-dead.

"Do you think my dog could have a drink of water, please?"

"Of course, poor doggie, come along. Didn't you send Snickers and Diggums and Booboo up the walls, you naughty boy."

The naughty boy wagged his tail.

"What kind of dogs are they?" I asked, seeking to bond.

"No kind at all, pet. Just found them at the pound. Three survivors from an unwanted litter. I couldn't bear to leave them."

"Ah. Tolstoy is a pound dog, too," I said. I didn't mention that he was also a purebred Samoyed. "I was lucky to find him just at a point in my life when I really needed a friend."

From somewhere outside the stadium-sized house, we could hear hysterical yips. Someone swore sharply in French. I followed Mme Flambeau along a hallway that brought Versailles to mind and into a kitchen that made Hélène Lamontagne's showpiece seem like a closet. To begin with, she had at least two of everything: two large Aga ovens with spectacular range hoods, three sinks with high-arching brass faucets, two islands, each one better equipped than my entire kitchen, two cooktops, two dishwashers and two over-sized sub-zero fridges with covers that matched the cupboards. Two sitting areas: a bar-type with high, cushioned stools and a kitchen table set for six with upholstered chairs. Two hanging racks with burnished copper pots. Every surface was marble the colour of rich cream.

Only one fireplace. Only one copper cappuccino maker.

Mme Flambeau filled a large red ceramic bowl with water and set it in front of Tolstoy.

The temperature in the house was set to chill butter. I could feel the sweat on my back changing to ice crystals. Tolstoy, dog of the north, was beginning to revive. I shivered.

"Coffee?"

Coffee. Oh, excellent. "Thank you." Five minutes earlier, the idea would have made me pass out, but now I was grateful.

"Instant okay, pet?"

I sacrificed the truth for expediency. "Absolutely, that's all I ever drink." *Instant?* A kitchen that must have set the owner back two hundred thousand dollars and we're drinking instant?

"Let's have it here. This is the coziest room in the house."

I remembered the hallway and nodded.

Mme Flambeau took her instant with evaporated milk, as if she'd never left the farm. I took mine black with three sugars, to be on the safe side. We sat at the kitchen table. It was like being alone in a large restaurant.

"Huge house," I said. "But I suppose you get used to it."

"I never have, pet," she said. "Alphie picked it out. It doesn't seem fair to his memory to get rid of it. But I never really feel at home."

Who would with all that marble? "To tell the truth, I probably never would either."

It was time to reveal my purpose before the instant coffee chilled over.

"So I'm surprised you didn't recognize me. I've been in all

the papers and television."

"I never read them, really, pet. I find them upsetting."

"There's been a lot about Benedict in them lately."

"Tragic. But I couldn't bear to read about it. I wouldn't have known anything except that a reporter called to ask how I felt about his death. Imagine that. How would they think I would feel about it?"

A woman after my own heart. And she didn't read the papers. That meant I didn't have to go through the bed thing. I gave Mme Flambeau my brightest smile. "I am in charge of Benedict's memorial service and the scattering of his ashes."

"Oh, that lovely boy, poor lovely boy." Her eyes welled. "The scattering of his ashes. Just to think of it breaks my heart."

It was enough to make you sick. "I wanted to talk to you about the Flambeau Prize and why you chose Benedict, and what you liked about his work. That would really help me greatly."

This was the first thing I'd said or done to surprise her. "Help you to do what?"

"Oh, to devise the speeches, you know, the eulogy, things like that. Make sure nothing important gets forgotten."

She liked that, I could tell.

"So," I said, not letting my smile dip, "let's begin at the beginning. How did you first meet Benedict?"

Mme Flambeau's face took on such a faraway look, I thought she might have slipped from consciousness. After a long minute, I spoke again. "Was it at some literary event?"

"Oh, no, pet," she said, "I never go to them."

The smile fell right off my face. Didn't go to them? Wasn't this the godmother of the underfunded arts in Quebec?

I lifted my eyebrow encouragingly. And worked the smile up from first gear.

"Of course not. Then...?" Tolstoy helped out by placing his

chin on Mme Flambeau's feet. She smiled at him. Perhaps because he showed no signs of ever yapping.

I seized the moment. "So it was...?"

"Here in the neighbourhood."

Neighbourhood? Neighbourhood would not have been on the list of the first thousand words I would have chosen.

"I see." Here in the neighbourhood. Of course.

"He was lost. He took a wrong turn. I was walking my dogs, and we just ran into each other."

It took all my willpower not to roll on the floor shrieking with laughter. Lost. I loved that. What, had he taken a wrong turn while stumbling out of a Vieux Montréal bar, crawled a couple of miles and fallen up the geedee mountain?

"Oh, yes," I prompted.

"He'd been supposed to meet a friend who didn't show up, and he was stranded. Isn't it terrible what people will do to each other?" Her doughy cheeks took on an angry red blush, like strawberries on a shortcake.

"Oh, it is," I said. "It really is."

"So we got to talking, and he mentioned he was a poet."

"And you mentioned you were a supporter of the arts."

"My heavens no, pet," she said. "I didn't. I didn't want him to be influenced by it." The strawberry blush spread down her neck.

"Naturally, I can see where you wouldn't."

"I want to be accepted for myself. Not for Alphie's money."

"So he didn't know who you were and..." Amazing. I wondered briefly if I might improve my financial standing by selling her a bit of the swamp by the side of my cottage.

"No. no. He had no idea who I was. It was only later he found out, and by that time I already knew all about him. By the time his niece drove from West Quebec to get him, I'd learned a lot about the struggle of poets. Dreadful, isn't it?"

"Absolutely."

"Really, our society abandons its poets." She wiped at something in the corner of her eye.

"So true. Um. You mentioned his niece?"

"Yes, thank heavens Benedict had his family to stick by him."

"For sure. Um, did they?"

"They did. His nieces anyway. They both adored him."

"Of course. Which one picked him up?"

"I only met the one. Pretty girl. Abby."

I was very, very glad Mme Flambeau did not watch the news.

"And then, that marvellous, marvellous book came out, and he presented me with a copy."

"Ah." *While Weeping for the Wicked.*

"It affected me deeply. I read a lot of Victorian poetry, you know. It was almost as though it had been written with me in mind."

Probably had been. I wouldn't have put it past the late scoundrel. Why not? He'd set up everything else. Why not pinch a bunch of suitable poems and rig up a book to appeal directly to this gullible woman with the billion or so surplus dollars? What could go wrong?

"As though he could see into my very soul. To see my spiritual side. Recognize what is really important." Her eyes filled with tears.

He would have had to work at that. It would have taken a bit to get past the image of fresh baked bread and scrubbed floors.

"Remarkable," I said.

"More coffee?"

Before I could refuse, she was on her feet bustling over to

the nearest sink. Refilling the kettle. Plugging it in next to the cappuccino machine. Her shoulders were set, her face turned away. Benedict the naughty poet had meant a great deal to Mme Flambeau. And she had meant a payload of cash to him.

I was pondering the whole insidious setup when she returned with the two mugs of instant.

"And you decided to award him the Flambeau Prize."

"So yes. I did. The money was sitting there, getting topped up every year. I don't like a lot of this modern poetry, and I have to confess I got behind on my reading, so it hadn't been awarded for a while."

Or ever, actually. "Benedict certainly could have used the boost."

"I know. He had no money at all. He had holes in his shoes. Did you know that?"

I hadn't. What's more, I didn't believe it for one minute. Bridget would never have tolerated it. But Benedict wouldn't have found it convenient to mention his loyal supporter and meal-ticket to Mme Flambeau, keeper of the Flambeau bundle.

"Must have been rough," I said.

She nodded. The tears spilled over.

"There's no money in poetry. None at all. Especially if you're true to yourself. As Benedict was. Lovely and true."

Lovely and true, my fanny. I reached over to pat Tolstoy so my face didn't show my opinion. But Tolstoy jerked his head and growled. Piercing yaps could be heard from the deck area. I grabbed his collar before he disgraced me again.

"Oh, dear, here come the babies."

"Time for me to go, anyway." I knew darn well I'd end up paying for any time Cyril Hemphill spent lounging in his sauna-like cab.

Mme Flambeau reached out and squeezed my free hand.

"Thank you, pet. It was good to talk about poor dear Benedict, and I would be thrilled to help you with his scattering."

"Excellent. Think whether you'd like to read from his poems or give a little eulogy. I'll call you if you give me your number. It's unlisted, I believe."

I waited at the front door while Mme Flambeau wrote out her phone numbers: home, chalet in the Laurentians and cellphone. As she handed me the slip of paper, I shook my head in fake sorrow. "It's a such shame poor Benedict didn't get to claim that money before he died."

Mme Flambeau's neck snapped back. "Pardon me, pet?"

"The prize money. Too bad he never got it. Think of the happiness it would have bought."

"That's the one good thing, pet. He did get the money."

"What do you mean? He *did?*"

"Oh, yes. At least, he had a bit of joy and recognition."

"But the prize hadn't been awarded when he died."

"He was in such a bad way. I didn't have the heart to make him wait. He didn't even have decent clothes to wear to the ceremony, poor boy. Or even enough money to come to Montreal."

"Oh, right. So..."

"I gave him his cheque early. The ceremony would have been just a bit of show. He had his pride."

"Of course, that was very kind of you. Too bad he didn't get a chance to cash it."

Her smile was radiant. Transforming. "Oh, pet, but he did cash it. Immediately. At least the poor boy had that."

Twenty-Eight

I spent the trip home fanning myself peevishly and wondering if Mme Flambeau could have found out about Benedict and Abby. If yes, would she have been humiliated enough to kill him? By the time we hit St. Aubaine three hours later, I had to conclude that I couldn't imagine Mme Flambeau as the killer, no matter how much provocation she might have had.

Sarrazin was lying in wait when Cyril swung into my driveway. That took my mind off Mme Flambeau. Cyril duly noted the presence of the police on my doorstep. I could imagine the news would be all over St. Aubaine within the hour.

It didn't matter. I needed to speak to Sarrazin anyway, but after a six hour round trip in Cyril's steam-mobile, I preferred to do it following a shower, a shampoo and a chilled, boozy drink.

On the other hand, Tolstoy was thrilled to see Sarrazin.

"I have something to tell you, but you'll have to stand upwind," I said, approaching the house.

Cyril looked interested. Speaking in front of Cyril would be one way to make sure your every word was relayed to the immediate world. Probably enough to bring the media spilling back.

"Goodbye, Cyril," I said.

Cyril pulled away, disappointment smearing his face. He spun a bit of gravel as he left.

"Give me a minute," I said.

Without waiting for approval, I headed into the house, opened every window and put on the big fan in the living room. I filled Tolstoy's bowl with cold water and took the last two Blues from the fridge, hoping Sarrazin would refuse one because he was on duty.

"Nope. I'm not on duty," he said.

So if he wasn't on duty, what did that mean besides one less Blue for me? Did it mean I wasn't safe from his questions 24/7, twelve months a year, Christmas Day no exception? Unless I wanted to speak to *him*, in which case he would be stunningly unavailable.

Even with my accrued resentments against Sarrazin, it wasn't fair to park my smelly self next to him on the porch swing so I perched on the rail.

"I imagine you're here to tell me you've picked up Dougie Dolan before he kills someone else."

He shook his head. "Not this time."

"I can't believe..."

"Yeah, yeah. We'll get him."

"Did you get a chance to talk to Rachel Kilmartin then? I think she knows something about Dolan. She may even be able to tell you where he is. The whole thing has to do with the Flambeau money. Here's the big news. I've learned Benedict actually received that honking big cheque before his death. And what's more, he cashed it."

"That a fact?"

"Yes, it is. So the thing is, where's this money? That's what Dolan's after. Maybe he killed Abby so she couldn't get to it. Maybe the police are finally going to have to do something about it."

Through the open living room window I could hear the

phone ring four times. The answering machine picked up.

Sarrazin and I listened to Kostas's message.

"Sorry to have missed you, dear lady. But I wanted to let you know the good news. We'll be celebrating Josey's birthday tonight."

I wasn't in any shape for a party.

"Call our mutual friend for details."

Our mutual friend.

It took an effort to turn my attention back to Sarrazin. He was picking the dead heads off the deep red daylilies by the porch.

"You're good friends with Mr. O'Carolan, I see."

"Yes, I am." Even though I'd never even heard of the elderly elf two weeks earlier.

"That's why I came by." Pick. Pick. Pick. "To discuss him."

No, it isn't, you miserable picker, I thought. You came by because I had something to tell you, and I left a dozen messages, and now you realize that I'm an innocent victim not a perpetrator. "So what is it?"

"So," he said, "since you're close to him, I guess I don't need to tell you his real name, you'd already know it."

"Oh, absolutely."

*   *   *

I ran the water for my first long luxurious soak in weeks. Forget the shower. I tossed in Strawberry Secret bubble-bath, poured a healthy dose of Courvoisier into a snifter and added some ice.

I put "Bolero" on the stereo and boosted the sound up to stun.

As I stepped into the bath, secure in the knowledge Sarrazin was probably arresting Dolan at that very moment, I chuckled over the nonsense with Kostas's name. Sarrazin was just getting back at me for leaving that nasty message at Dr. Duhamel's.

All this crap will soon be over, I told myself. Time to practice sexy thoughts. Think about Marc-André. It would pay off in the writing, if nothing else.

But the current problem oozed its way back into my mind. So where was the money? In an account somewhere? I was pretty sure Sarrazin would check that out in the morning.

Where had the late scamp cashed that cheque? It couldn't have been in our village, where nothing is secret. I would have heard about that from one of the key news carriers, Woody or Cyril or even Gisèle at the Caisse Pop. So not in St. Aubaine.

Of course, *where* was not as interesting as *who*. Who could have had that cash? Most logically, his loving "niece", Abby. But Abby was dead. And now we had two hundred and fifty thousand reasons why that might be. Even the St. Aubaine police would have noticed all that cash on the crime scene, so forget the Jetta as the hiding place.

Had Dougie Dolan snatched the money from her car or her apartment before the police got there? That might account for why he seemed to be keeping a low profile since Abby's murder. He was probably tanning on the beach in Rio.

Unless someone had snatched the money from him. Or snatched it from her first.

Bridget wasn't the only person who should have had a share in Benedict's crooked good luck. What about Stella, raising those twins with Benedict's face?

What about the poet who really wrote *While Weeping for the Wicked*? What about Benedict's old buddy and mentor, Kostas O'Carolan, with his roof falling down and his car on blocks? Oops, what about the fact Josey's birthday party was that night, and I had only an hour before the stores closed?

For some reason, my lovely bubbly bath felt chilly.

*   *   *

The Chez was hopping, hot and crowded. It would have been a perfect spot for a birthday party if "Big Girls Don't Cry" had not been playing on the juke box. Every chair, vinyl bench and stool in the restaurant was occupied. I spotted a lot of baseball caps. I wasn't sure what kind of influence Kostas had exerted to get four booths set aside for us, but I hoped it was legal.

Laughter boomed along with the cheerful crash of crockery from the kitchen. I was wearing cologne, although it was drowned by competing scents of sweat, tax-free cigarettes and *plats chinois*. I smiled into Marc-André Paradis' eyes. The whole scene, and particularly the Marc-André part of it, took my mind off things.

The numbers were growing. Kostas had recruited Marc-André, Bridget, Stella minus her husband, and Hélène minus hers, Woody and Mary Morrison. Liz brought Natalie. Perhaps she was expecting things to get out of hand. "Don't worry," Natalie said. "*He'll* get the message this time."

I could only assume she meant Philip.

"While you're at it, how good are you with bail jumpers?" I said.

She shook her head. "Bad idea."

"Not me, someone else who might use your help."

Natalie made a face.

Rachel had eluded the invitation, even though I'd banged on her door again on our way to the Chez. Maybe she'd already had a visit from the police. I could always check with the bearlike presence in the furthest booth.

Josey was in her glory solemnly describing the night we'd spent in the cave. She made it sound colder, damper and more dangerous, the sort of thing movies are made of. You could almost hear the bullets whizzing past your ears. You could feel the furry spiders sidling up the inside of your pant legs. You could smell the decay and taste the blood from bitten lips.

At our table, good humour ran high. Everyone was glad to be together. Kostas talked on about the fine people of St. Aubaine. Although with the racket in the restaurant, I could hardly hear a word.

Mostly, I smiled moonily over my Blue at Marc-André.

I smiled at Josey, too. Whenever her morose, round, freckled face swam into view. Birthday or not, Josey hadn't smiled at anyone, not even Kostas, since she'd finished her sweater. I knew damn well a greasy spoon with a crowd of middle-aged drinkers wasn't the best place to celebrate a fifteenth birthday.

"Peggy Sue" chirped out of the juke box. Right after the chocolate sundaes and the lemon meringue pie, Kostas rose. "My dear, dear friends," he said. "I notice your glasses are all full. May I suggest yis use them to toast to the health of a grand young person here among us."

Josey swivelled her head to spot the grand young person.

"Someone we have grown fond of. A colleague of great courage and curiosity. A friend and an ally."

Not necessarily the words I would have chosen to describe anyone celebrating a birthday, but they did suit Josey.

Three blue-haired ladies at the next booth were hanging on every word Kostas said. Mary Morrison glanced at them and leaned toward me with a whisper.

"Some think he's still quite the lad."

Kostas preened. The phrase "everybody has a sex life except

you" took on enhanced meaning. His voice resonated as he extolled Josey's virtues: honesty, hard work and the ability to deceive the police. It sunk to a seductive murmur: loyalty and quick thinking under fire.

The ladies shot back three identical smiles.

Kostas raised his pint. "Let's hear yis. To Josey Thring," he thundered, "a damn fine friend. Happy Birthday."

It nearly brought the roof down. Everyone in the Chez, including a few who were well past the point of standing, shouted Happy Birthday. Even total strangers hollered out, "To Josey, helluva friend" or "*Bonne fête, Josée*".

Hélène broke into the French version of Happy Birthday. She was joined by a group at the bar.

Josey's eyes remained like portholes long after the rest of the crowd had lost interest in our celebration.

"Open this first," Mary said.

Josey ogled the small wrapped gift without comprehension.

"Open it," I whispered.

Inside, a small pewter rectangle with seagulls on it framed the photo of Josey and me taken on our first visit to Mary.

"Thank you," Josey said.

"And now, a legacy from the O'Carolan clan to our friend Josey." Kostas thrust a large, unwrapped packet of papers at Josey. "Here are my secrets of knitting, all of the traditional patterns, and many more I've designed and worked out meself. I'm passing them on to you because I know you have the talent to be an artist-in-wool and a passion for perfection, being a Virgo, and I can trust you to treat them with care and respect." He slipped into his seat with a thud.

Josey bit her lip. She reached out and touched the hand-written patterns, many on yellowed, crumbling paper.

I swear her eyes teared up a bit when she opened Marc-

André's package. A history of West Quebec, with some references to the Thring family, and a collection of topographical maps of the area with the best hiking trails highlighted in yellow.

She could build an appetite hiking and then use Woody's gift of a fistful of McDonald's gift certificates.

Even Liz had forked out for a complete set of tickets to the One Act Play Competition.

Hélène knew Josey well enough to select a small hand-tooled red leather wallet with six compartments and matching address book, promising many happy hours of organizing.

Josey fingered the four-leaf clover motif on the silver key chain from Bridget and flicked the 350 pages of *Create Spectacular Crafts from Useless Junk* and *Bathtime Made Fun* from Stella. Personally, I figured Stella's offer of a secure home was the best present of all.

My own gift, a pair of Bausch and Lomb binoculars in a leather case, seemed mundane in comparison to the others. Even if I'd had to add my emergency cash roll to the remains of my annuity cheque to pay for them. If Josey's birthday gift wasn't an emergency, I didn't know what was. I'd considered myself lucky to get my foot through the door of the Outfitters Shop as the proprietor flipped the sign to *FERMÉ*.

"Thank you, everyone," Josey said again. "I never thought I'd ever get beautiful gifts like this. I'll never forget tonight."

Everyone found this speech to be exactly the right sentiment and length. But I was worried about Josey. Her skinny shoulders were stiff. Her mouth was clamped tight. Her hair stood in spikes. As she headed for the door with Stella, I reached out and touched her arm.

"What's wrong?"

"Nothing."

"Please," I said.

"Really, everything's great. It's just that..." She goggled at me with those saucer eyes. "Jeez, I never had a birthday before. I've never even been invited to one. I'm not sure what you do when you get stuff like that. And everything."

I could understand. Probably the only birthdays Josey ever saw were on television. It made you think.

"You were fine," I said.

Her shoulders relaxed. "I didn't forget anything?"

I shook my head.

"Good." Back in the Chez, somebody put on "It's My Party".

Marc-André took my hand unobtrusively when I returned. I felt like nothing else could go wrong. But as they say, you don't buy beer, you only rent it. It was only matter of time until I had to go to the ladies' room.

The setting felt warm and friendly. Safe. When Kostas headed for the men's room, I toddled after him to the ladies'. Maybe I'd ask him if he'd ever had another name. For fun.

"Where are you going?" Marc-André said.

"Ladies' room."

"I don't know," he said. "It's kind of away from things. Downstairs past the storage."

"I'll be fine," I said. "The place is crawling with people, and Kostas is just ahead of me."

I passed by Sarrazin's table. "We had a word with Rachel Kilmartin. It's only a matter of time till they locate Dolan," Sarrazin said as I slipped by.

Only when I rounded the corner towards the Hommes and Dames and couldn't see Kostas anywhere, did it occur to me that maybe I should have dragged Marc-André along. With all those people around, how could the hallway be so empty now?

I hesitated. How stupid, really. An almost-forty-five-year-old woman could not go back and ask a man to accompany her for a pee break. I straightened my shoulders and lifted my head high. The back corridor smelled of mildew and cats. The air felt cold and damp enough to give me goose bumps. I tried to reassure myself the scuffling noises in the storage area were only rodents. With a strong sense of unease, I scurried into the Dames and flicked on the lights. My dog might have helped, but he was outside panhandling for French fries.

I don't mind admitting I checked all three cubicles. I locked the door of my chosen cubicle and braced my foot against it.

You're a dope, I told myself minutes later as I gripped the sink. Why didn't you wait and walk over with a group of women?

I peered through the door into the hallway, hoping I hadn't missed Kostas on his way back. If only someone in the crowd would answer the call of nature.

I felt a wild surge of relief when I saw Marc-André stride into the hallway towards the men's room. The relief ended with the flash of an arm behind his head.

"Shut up or I'll pull the trigger. You better believe it." I'd never heard his voice before, but I knew it had to be Dougie Dolan. And I believed what I heard. I drew in my breath when they passed the door. Dougie Dolan was strong-arming a struggling Marc-André. I caught a glimpse of the gun pressed to his temple. My heart ricocheted around my chest. I shrank back behind the door.

Through the crack in the door, I could see Dolan direct Marc-André into the storage room. Out of sight. My breath was ragged and loud. Dolan would most likely kill Marc-André if no one did anything. And no one else knew anything needed to be done. Screaming was out of the question. Nobody but Dolan would hear. And Dolan had a gun.

Across the hall, glass crashed on the floor. I had no weapon, and Marc-André was in serious trouble. I didn't even have my carryall, which might have packed a mean punch. I stumbled around searching for something to help Marc-André until I spotted the toilet tank lid. Why not?

I decided to make a run for the stairs to get help.

The scuffling stopped inside the storage area. I tiptoed past with the toilet tank lid raised above my head, just in case.

"I want that Flambeau money. Tell me where it is, you little bastard. Tell me where it is."

"What are you talking about? I'm telling you, I don't know anything about it."

More glass shattered. Fumes from cleaning fluid filled the air. He had guts, that Marc-André.

"I finished that pig Benedict, and I'll do you with a smile on my face if you don't tell me where it is."

I couldn't hear Marc-André's words.

A crash shook the wall. I edged towards the storage area, the toilet tank lid in attack position. The thing must have weighed ten pounds. I figured it could do serious damage. I poised ready to swing if I had to and also ready to make a run for the stairs.

I peeked into the storage area and took my chances with the back of the yellow head. I whacked it with the porcelain lid. Dougie Dolan pitched over neatly, landing on his weapon.

"Run for it," I shrieked, "before he gets up."

Marc-André lay quiet, blood trickling from his temple.

I raced up the stairs, howling and swinging the lid. Plates went flying as Sarrazin jumped to his feet.

"It's Marc-André. Dolan's trying to kill him."

Sarrazin tore down the stairs. I galloped after him. Behind us, you could hear chairs being knocked over and people screaming.

As we charged towards the storage area, the door sprang from its hinges. Dougie Dolan was hurled backwards onto the floor. Marc-André leaped towards Dolan, grabbed the gun and fired.

Dolan crumpled. The sound of the shot screamed in our ears.

Marc-André's mouth opened. The gun slipped from his fingers and clattered on the floor as he slid down the wall, leaving a streak of red. He crouched there, his head in his hands.

I'd never seen a man shot. Dougie Dolan jerked, a red stain spreading on his shirt.

Sarrazin and I stood still, stunned, just long enough to miss Dolan's lunge for the gun. Before Sarrazin could grab it, the gun barked again. Marc-André yelped and fell sideways.

Dolan gurgled. Red froth bubbled from his lips. The gun clattered to the floor.

I checked frantically for signs of life in Marc-André. Dougie Dolan, the man who had put us all in danger, lay dead.

And Marc-André's lifeblood was seeping from his wounds. Sarrazin said, "*Merde.*"

Twenty-Nine

Liz rode in the ambulance with Marc-André. Sarrazin rode ahead with a slap-on light transforming his ordinary Ford.

Kostas and I located Mark-André's keys and drove the BMW to the hospital. We needed to do something. Sitting in the *salle d'urgence* waiting for news seemed as good as anything else.

Sarrazin joined us in the waiting room before midnight, confirming Dolan's death. Heaving himself into the miserable molded plastic chairs. Giving the giant philodendron in the corner a look of pity. Getting my informal version of events outside the storage room.

"It was all about money," I said. "The two hundred and fifty thousand dollars Benedict got. Dolan wanted it. He thought Marc-André had it. Or knew where it was hidden."

"Did he?"

"I have no idea. He didn't say anything about it to me. He was fighting to save his life. But I would have thought not."

"Do you know where it is?"

"I wish."

"You'll have to come in to the Sûreté tomorrow to fill out a full report." He picked a pair of dead leaves from the philodendron on his way out.

As the automatic doors closed behind him, I faced Kostas, saying what I had to say.

"What about you? Do you know?"

"I don't, dear lady. I don't."

"But you did know what was going on." It wasn't a question.

Kostas squirmed. "Some of it, dear lady. Some of it only."

"Which one of you wrote the poems?"

"Marc-André."

"I see."

"No, dear lady, ye probably don't."

"Try me."

"I blame myself. I should never have told him."

"Told him what?"

"The poems were old ones, when Marc-André was learning to write. He outgrew them. Wasn't all that interested in light and romantic stuff. He began to write more in French than in English. I rescued that notebook from the fireplace just in time. If I hadn't, probably none of this would have happened. Or at least if I hadn't left it lying around."

Of course. "So, Benedict visited you and found it?"

He nodded. "I didn't think anything of it at the time. Talked a bit about Marc-André and how he'd moved on. Didn't even notice the notebook gone. I can't tell you the shock I had, dear lady, finding out that scamp had made out they were his own. I think he was trying to get the old girl to bankroll him. You know."

"No kidding. And how did Marc-André react?"

"He was mad as hell when he recognized a stanza of one of his own poems on the radio when they announced the Flambeau Prize. You can imagine."

I could. "What happened then?"

"He was going to confront Benedict, especially since everyone told him Benedict had been bragging about some big deal. But he never got a chance. That Dolan did it for him."

"And why did Dolan come after Marc-André?"

"I can't be sure, but I think somehow, someone might have let it slip he was the real poet and rightly steamed about it. Word must have leaked out."

I had a pretty good idea who "someone" might have been. "And where did I come in?"

"Ah, dear lady, I feel a bit ashamed, now. Our fondness for you isn't in the least bit simulated. Of course, we didn't know you at first, but we decided we'd have to find out about you. Play along with the scattering. In case you were not what you claimed to be. I mean, he was found... Do you know what I mean? We weren't sure, but we wanted to keep an eye on you."

"That's why the attention? That's why you got me the car?"

He nodded a miserable little nod.

I wasn't in a position to lecture. I'd used them as much as they'd used me.

"One more thing. What is your real name?"

You would have thought I'd slapped him. It took a very long time for him to answer. "Hector Baggs. My mother always called me Heckie. Not much of a name for a poet and an artist-in-wool. Not like Seamus Heaney or Benedict Kelly or Marc-André Paradis. It was nothing but a handicap. I'd no choice at all but to change it into something more interesting."

"So you're not from Ireland?"

"Not in the least, I'm afraid not. But then, no one's perfect, dear lady."

*   *   *

It was three in the morning before Liz was able to determine that Marc-André had a chance. Aside from the good news, I was glad to see her, since Hector (my mother always called me

Heckie) Baggs and I had not been the most congenial company for each other.

"We can go home," Liz said. "They won't let anybody see your precious poet yet. And certainly not you, Little Miss Kiss of Death."

I dropped Kostas off at Evening's End. What was an extra half hour drive on slippery back roads in the driving rain with Liz snoring in the back seat? I wasn't in any hurry. I wouldn't be able to sleep anyway. I declined Kostas's offer of protection.

"Dolan's dead now. I'll be okay."

I declined Liz's offer too. For all the good it did me. She insisted on coming home with me. I couldn't sleep and wasted the rest of my night at the computer.

*   *   *

"Darling," Brandon sputtered, struggling to keep from slipping on the slimy rocks. "Can you ever forgive me? I can't imagine living my life without you."

Cayla studied him silently, the sea wind whipping her hair like a rebellious halo. Tears stung her amazing azure eyes. He was so handsome and so faithless and, so...unable to take care of himself.

How long, she thought, would he even survive if he tried to live his life without her? He'd get trampled by the first runaway horse he encountered or he'd slip into an abandoned mine shaft under the main street or he'd stroll through a plate glass window or...

"Angel bug, please answer me. This is it. The big commitment. Heart and soul. For all time. Violins. Orange blossoms. Matching towels. Theirs and theirs. Can't you see it, Cayla? Say something. I can't..." His face crumpled with barely suppressed emotion. "I

can't face my bran flakes every morning without you."

Cayla reached her hand across the windswept rock to touch him. His presence electrified her. Her breathing became fast and shallow.

"Oh, Brandon," she cried, as they sought each other greedily, hands and mouths touching. "Brandon, darling, be careful of the sea weed. Eaaaaaaughhh!"

"Darling, it's really quite shallow here," Brandon said, emerging. Water dripped from his nostrils. "And quite romantic, don't you think?"

Sure, why not, Cayla thought, as she clung to him and wiped the sea water from her eyes, I can always buy another sweater if this one shrinks.

"Snuggle bun," Brandon coughed, as they sank together beneath the playful waves, their hearts beating as one, "wouldn't it be wonderful to be married here?"

"I think inland might be better," Cayla said, spitting out a bit of sand.

"Darling, whatever you want. I'm so happy we're..."

"Brandon," Cayla asked when they surfaced for air.

"Hmmm?" He nuzzled her damp ear.

She traced the lines of his nose, stopping short of the nostrils, which were draining.

"Yes, Cayla," he gasped.

"You do have insurance, don't you, darling?"

"You know," I said to Liz as the sun came over the horizon. "There's supposed to be good money in cook books. I'm thinking of making the switch."

Liz agreed. "Cookbooks? Good idea. Then I suppose it won't matter if you sleep alone."

With Dougie Dolan dead, I was safe at last, a good feeling. As a bonus, I was yesterday's news. No one had picked up on the toilet tank lid as a front page teaser. Instead, the media hounded Sarrazin and hung out in front of the hospital. I raced around St. Aubaine with impunity. I felt great—except for worrying about Marc-André.

I got home to find Josey sitting in the porch swing, wearing the binocular case and struggling with ten different colours of wool and a new pattern. "I heard from Kostas this morning that Marc-André is going to be all right."

"Let's hope. And you're supposed to be in school." I said without much enthusiasm.

"I made you a present."

"School. Now."

"It will only take a minute, and then I can concentrate on getting to school."

I considered that. "All right. What is it?"

"Go ring your doorbell."

"Please, Josey, I've had a rough night."

"Jeez, Miz Silk. Don't make such a big deal about everything. Just press it."

I walked to the door and pressed.

Josey's disembodied voice echoed. "Miz Fiona Silk cannot come to the door right now, but leave a message after the beep and she'll get back to you, if she feels it is sufficiently important." The machine beeped.

"You're amazing, Josey. This is the nicest thing anyone's ever done for me."

Her cowlicks stood on full alert. Triumphant.

"And to show my appreciation, I'm going to take you to

school in a decent car for once."

The cowlicks seemed to wilt. She focused her attention on the new binoculars. She ruffled Tolstoy's ears, but she didn't say a word to me, leaving me to ponder my ingratitude.

"Let's go," I said.

My brand-new take-charge tone would have had more effect if I'd been able to find the keys to Marc-André's Beemer. Luckily for me, they finally showed up underneath the driver's seat.

"Don't look at me," Josey said. "I didn't put them there."

Then it hit me. A car could be an excellent place to hide a large envelope or a small package, say a couple of hundred thousand dollars and change. If you didn't trust your local tellers to keep a secret. Or your friends. And most especially if you thought your house might be searched by a pro like Dolan. Of course, you'd have to hide the car too. I'd assumed all along that Benedict's killer had ditched his sports car in the river or something. But what if Benedict had twigged to the fact that Dolan was on the rampage and squirrelled away the MG with the moolah in it? Ready to scoot off into the sunset the minute the coast was clear. No more farfetched than anything else about this whole business. It was just the sort of thing Benedict would do. And it wasn't as if I had any better ideas.

"Tell me, Josey, if you were going to hide a car, where would you put it?"

"Easy. Where there's lots of other cars. Isn't that what they do in the movies? Put them in parking lots? Airports."

"The police have been looking for his car in the usual places. No sign anywhere."

"Maybe it's in the woods. Some place far away and inconvenient."

I shook my head. "Benedict didn't do inconvenient things. To himself, that is."

"Hey, Miz Silk, what about Paulie Pound's? There's hundreds of cars there. Paulie's always hanging around the Britannia, so Benedict would have known him."

"Right. But the police have already searched his premises."

Josey snorted. "Sure, and those St. Aubaine constables couldn't have missed anything."

Absolutely.

"I suppose if you're an extra hour late for school, it won't be the end of the world."

"I think this might be more educational," Josey said.

*　　*　　*

Long before St. Aubaine was reborn as a scenic tourist trap, Paulie Pound's scrapyard at the old quarry site by the northern edge of the village was a blight on the landscape. Jean-Claude Lamontagne had launched periodic battles to put Paulie out of business and increase the prettiness quotient of the surrounding acreage, which he owned, coincidentally.

Paulie Pound didn't give a flying fig for Jean-Claude. Nor did he give a flying fig for what we did in his scrapyard once the ten dollars was pressed into his already greasy palm. Paulie was on his way to the Britannia.

"You're the Thring girl, ain't ya."

Josey nodded.

"Remember, I know everything what's in this yard, girlie. It's all numbered. It's all on the computer."

Josey's eyes bulged.

I got the subject back on track. "So Benedict Kelly was here not too long ago?"

"Yup."

"Was he here alone?"

"Yup."

"Did he bring anything in?"

"I never paid him for nothing."

"Right. Mind if I we look around?"

He spit a steam of tobacco juice into the nearest puddle. We took it to mean we had his blessing.

Heaps of rusted metal, gutted trucks and cannibalized cars stood in rows and rusting piles. But neat rows and neat rusting piles. Every American and Japanese make you could remember for forty years. With the exception of the Edsel. Naturally, there was no jaunty red MG. Half an hour later, soaked to the skin and filthy, we had worked our way past every vehicle right to the bank of the old quarry that edged the scrapyard. No more rows, no more cars. No more good ideas. We were ready to call it quits.

But I'm a patsy for a subliminal message. The sign CAPITAINE PATATE on the side of an ancient cube van that had served out its days as a chip wagon for instance. The battered van hunkered on blocks, next to a pathetic pile of useless car parts.

Mmm, fries, I thought.

Josey picked up a broken steering wheel and a car ashtray from the pile. "There's nothing much here," she said.

"Right. Let's head back home, get cleaned up and then we can head back into town to get some fries at the Chez," I said. "Before you go to school."

"Or instead of," Josey said. "I love fries."

Tolstoy, who does not care for being wet but is a big fan of fries, barked in agreement.

I said. "Everyone loves fries. Come to think of it, Benedict used to practically live on them." Then it hit me, like a clonk on the head with a bar of rusty metal. I crawled over some debris to the back of the chip van and tugged at the handle to the double doors. I didn't expect them to open as easily as they did.

Inside the van, the driver's and the front passenger's seats had been removed, leaving a good-sized space, missing the cooking equipment but still smelling faintly of old grease. The window on the driver's side was broken and jagged. The van was empty, except for a large lump under a tarpaulin. We climbed in and lifted the near end of the canvas. Sure enough, the cheerful red of the little MG shone through, clean and gleaming.

I scratched my head. "How the devil would he have gotten the MG inside this chip wagon? It's up on blocks."

"Was the car working?" Josey said.

"I imagine it was. Benedict loved that car."

"Then I suppose he just set up a ramp and drove it in."

"A ramp? Where would Benedict get a ramp that would hold the weight of a car?"

"This is a junkyard, Miz Silk," Josey said.

"So?"

"Well, how do you think Paulie Pound gets half these cars here?"

"How?"

"He's got a towtruck, and he's got a flatbed truck and he's got a ramp. Getting stuff moved around is no problem."

"But Paulie Pound said that Benedict didn't leave anything here."

"No, he didn't. He said he didn't pay Benedict for anything. That just means that Benedict didn't sell him anything for scrap. He wouldn't sell this beautiful car for scrap anyways, would he?"

"No. And knowing Benedict, he didn't want to pay to store it either."

"He must have just wanted to hide it."

"Right."

"I wonder why he wanted to hide it, though?"

"I have a pretty good idea."

"What, Miz Silk?"

"He was socking away everything of value to him. His car and his newfound money. Who would think to look here?"

Josey nodded. "Paulie Pound might. But if Benedict was thinking he could get his mitts on a ramp when old Paulie was getting hammered down at the Britannia, easy enough to do. Drive the car right in, put the ramp back. The price is right, and the secret's safe." She smiled like someone who had a couple of secrets safe herself.

Right.

Perseverance paid off. It was a tight fit inside the van with the car and us, but we managed to crawl into the MG and start our hunt. Shoved down behind the distressed leather of the driver's seat, a neatly stapled Jiffy bag.

I broke a finger nail opening it.

"Is it...?" Josey said.

"Yes! Lots and lots of lovely moolah."

"Jeez."

The van doors slammed behind us.

We stood there stunned, then I gradually felt my way to the door and tried to open it. No luck. Someone had wedged it shut.

A minute later, I heard the screech of tearing metal. My head thumped a bar on the side. Josey bellowed.

"Someone's ramming us!"

It took a minute before I could see straight, but then I had barely enough light to make out Josey clutching her knee. Her face was pinched in pain.

"Josey, are you...?"

"It'll be okay, Miz Silk. Just dinged it on the car."

She bit her lower lip, and her face couldn't have been whiter if she'd dipped it in a flour bin. Ding, my fanny. She was going to need a doctor for that knee.

"But what about you, Miz Silk? Your head's bleeding."

Oh, good, that meant we were alive for the moment.

Rain battered the chip van. Overhead, seagulls screamed. The back door was jammed. How long before Paulie Pound would head down this way? Months? Years?

The van shook again with a crash. Tolstoy scrambled and barked.

"What if they shove it into the quarry?" Josey said.

"No chance. Whoever it is wants this money. And they will want it nice and dry." I sounded a lot more convinced than I felt, considering how close we were to the edge. I tucked the envelope under my shirt. "I think they're trying to knock us off the blocks."

What kind of a lunatic would ram their car into the chip wagon? That gave rise to other questions.

"Josey, do you think that some of these abandoned vehicles could be hotwired?"

"Are you kidding? Paulie would have stripped the engines out of them long ago. There's nothing worthwhile at this end of the yard."

I managed to get over to the side of the van with the broken window. Carefully, using the tarpaulin to protect my hands, I lifted out pieces of glass, as Josey sat clutching her damaged knee. "We have to crawl out," I said.

"I can't. I can't move my knee." Tears trickled down her cheeks. "Why is this happening?"

But at least whoever was ramming us had stopped. Hoping like hell whoever that was didn't know about Josey and Tolstoy, I squeezed through the window to run for help.

256

Thirty

She held the revolver steady as she got out from behind the wheel of Marc-André's beautiful Beemer, now with its front end seriously crumpled, and approached the side of the van. Her ankle must have hurt like hell, but somehow I thought she had other things on her mind.

"Bridget!" I shrank back against the side of the van.

She smiled, but I didn't like the cold light behind her smile. "Tell her to get out."

"She can't," I said. "She's hurt her knee. She needs a doctor."

Bridget laughed. "A doctor?"

"Leave her alone. She has nothing to do with any of this."

"Shut up," Bridget said. "It's time for Benedict's lost love of a lifetime to join him. But first, I'll have that money."

Hatred twisted her lips and eyebrows. Everything that had been beautiful about Bridget had vanished.

Rain slapped at our faces and drenched our hair. I didn't have to know anything about guns to know the one Bridget gripped with both hands meant serious business.

"I was never Benedict's lost love. But I am your friend."

Her clothes were soaked and her hair plastered to her head.

"Friend," she spat.

I reached out to her. The twitch of the gun made me jerk my hand back.

I met her eyes. "I can imagine what you went through."

"Can you? I loved that little shit for more than thirty years. Every time he got drunk, he'd cry about you or some other lost love. What did I get? Taken for granted, ignored, betrayed." The muscles on her jaw knotted. "Do you know what happened after all that time?"

I shook my head, and water sluiced down my neck. But I did know. I could read it on her white face, in her burning eyes. Bridget's love had mixed with twenty years of laundry and vomit and bailouts and lies. It had twisted into hate.

"Bridget," I said, "I understand."

"No. You do not understand," she shrieked. "Have you ever made your lover's bed and found some other woman's panties?"

She was right. I wouldn't have handled that well.

"That wasn't the worst of it. I got used to the women. He needed variety and excitement. Even so, I believed he and I were it forever, and the other women would come and go. But the bastard," she said, gasping for the words, "the bastard..."

I shook, soaking wet, silhouetted against the sheer grey rocks and dead cars, a target for her rage against a dead man.

"I didn't fit into his plans. I was good for laundry and cheques and making excuses to his friends. I was good enough to praise him and his idiot poetry. But not good enough to share the Flambeau money." The hand holding the revolver trembled.

"Oh, Bridget," I said.

"But you didn't know that, did you?"

I shook my head.

"Only Abby knew. He told her when they were in bed."

"But..."

"Oh yes, I heard him. In his squalid little hovel. He was supposed to have been in Kingston giving a lecture on poetry at Queen's University. 'Integrity and the Irish poet', he called his talk. Isn't that a laugh? I wanted him to have something to eat when he got back, so I went to his place."

Her eyes glazed. "The Queen's lecture was a lie like all the other times. I heard them talking and laughing. About the Flambeau money. About what they'd do with it."

Behind me, I heard Josey moving inside the van. Or maybe it was Tolstoy.

"I waited, you know, for him to tell me. How I wouldn't have to spend eighty hours a week on my business any more, always scared this would be the week I couldn't cover costs. He never mentioned sharing the money with me. Never mentioned me at all. That's when I knew I hated him." Her words echoed over the quarry.

"And you had Dougie kill him?"

"That was a mistake. Dougie was an idiot and overheated as always. Like a walking time bomb. I wanted him to shake the story out of Benedict. Tell us where the money was. Not to kill him, at least not then."

"Right," I said.

"Such a shame about poor Benedict," Bridget laughed. Bridget laughing was creepier than Bridget sneering or crying.

"But Dougie always despised Benedict, didn't he?" I said, playing for time.

"Oh, he did. Very much. Just hurt him, I said, enough to find out where he's stashed it, but don't let the beating show on his face."

"And he couldn't stop."

She shrugged. "Benedict taunted him. Dougie blew a fuse. I can't say I felt sorry that Benedict died. I enjoyed watching Dougie work him over. I hated to leave for my bridge game, but lucky I did. Couldn't have had a better alibi when I needed one."

Bridget swayed in the rain, laughing loudly at the memory. My stomach knotted.

"It was a damned nuisance, because we still didn't know where the money was hidden. That's where you came in."

"You put Benedict's body in my bed."

"Dougie did the labour. I was the artistic director. I stage-managed the whole thing from the pay phone in the Emergency Ward. Did a lovely job too. Wasn't it a wonderful image? That champagne and the rose? The little smile on his face? I'm so sorry I didn't get to see the finished product."

"How did you know I was out?" Stall, stall.

"Don't be stupid, Fiona. This is St. Aubaine."

"How did Dougie get in?" Keep stalling.

"There isn't a lock made that Dougie couldn't get through. If he could have been counted on not to make some stupid mistake once he was in, he could have made a bundle."

"But it had to be you who left the note in Benedict's cabin."

"Of course."

"But why me?"

"They always figure it's the nearest and dearest in the death of a loved one. I had to provide a distraction. I thought of little old 'lost love' you. Lucky me, I found the thank-you note you wrote me for ordering those Irish coffee glasses. I stuck in a couple of extra x's and o's, Dougie popped it over to Benedict's place, and there you go, evidence."

It made as much sense as anything else. Behind me, I heard Josey softly rustling inside the van. Was there anything she could do to save herself and Tolstoy?

"So, no insurance?"

"Of course not. I can't believe you were that stupid."

"And those bequests from Benedict?"

Her smile came straight from the heart of a glacier.

"To bring out the people I didn't know about. I knew Benedict hadn't carried this off by himself. And I figured Abby didn't know where the money was. She was too stupid to keep something like that from slipping. Dougie was to follow you. The answer had to be with someone connected with Benedict somehow. I figured the ones you brought gifts to would tell you about others and sooner or later the ones who knew about the money would reveal themselves. And Dougie could chat with them. And it worked. See?"

"That's why there was nothing for Marc-André. You didn't even know he existed," I whispered.

"I knew some bloody poet somewhere cooked up that book. It was just a matter of time until he crawled out to get the cash."

"And Rachel," I said, "what part did she play in it?"

A snort. "Silly cow. She's always done everything I asked her to. Gullible as they come. I told her to keep quiet about Dougie."

I exhaled slowly. I could figure out what was coming next.

"So that's it," she said. "And now you've done what I hoped you might. So, I guess I don't need you any more."

Josey. Would she feel a bullet after I did? Did you even live long enough to feel them? Somehow I managed to keep the fear out of my voice.

"But, of course," I said, "I think you'll be at some risk when they find my body. After all, you arranged for me to hold the scattering, you knew all the victims, Benedict, Abby. And me. Rachel's talking to the police now."

"Do you have any idea how deep this quarry is? They'll never find your body. Most likely they'll think you found the money and ran."

I was running out of stall tactics. Behind me, Josey tapped at the van wall.

"So, Fiona, I'll be simply devastated when I hear the news of your duplicity. After I stood by you through everything." She raised the gun.

I tried not to wet my pants.

The mocking smile set off fireworks in my head. Did Dougie have to be the only time bomb? Why did I never get to be a time bomb? Bridget had her back to the quarry. If I were going to die, could I at least take her with me?

My hands clenched and unclenched behind my back. My mind raced. A straightforward body tackle might do the trick. It wouldn't take much to tip Bridget into the pit behind her.

Keep talking. "I suppose Abby was part of your plan."

Bridget sneered. "She was part of her own plan. To find the money. To get rid of you in the process, I imagine. Our little Abby became a wee bit unhinged, don't you think?"

"Oh, yes."

"Dougie and I worked out she was tracking you because she suspected you had the money, but she was so overcome by jealousy, she had to harm you. She couldn't control herself."

"But why was she so jealous of me?"

Bridget chuckled. "That was the funny thing about it. You see, the only three people in the world who really knew Benedict wasn't in your bed when he died were Dougie, me and you. The idea of Benedict spending his last night with you really tortured her, so that had its satisfactions. But she became a liability."

"And so you had her killed?"

Bridget shrugged. "Dougie killed her. After that craziness at the Findlay Falls, we couldn't take a chance she might actually do you in while you might still be useful to us."

I couldn't believe Bridget would plan to spend the rest of her life with old ticking time bomb Dougie.

"Were you planning to get rid of Dougie in the end?"

"Of course." The icy smile emerged again. "Once he'd served his purpose. Dougie was dangerous and greedy, and I didn't want to split the money with him. I've had enough of men taking more than their share. Lucky for me, someone else finished him off."

I worked to control my shivering. "You couldn't trust Dougie, but you can trust me. I don't have anything to do with the money."

She laughed again. "Very good. But, of course, I can't trust you in the least. Even if you weren't carrying that Jiffy bag, you know too much. I'm always cleaning up after other people, it seems. And now..."

A shout distracted Bridget. Rachel's voice rang out. "Bridget! Dear God, no. Don't shoot her!"

Bridget jerked towards the sound. At first my heart soared. Bridget couldn't shoot Josey and me in front of Rachel. But it didn't take long to conclude that there was a point beyond which Bridget had nothing to lose.

Bridget raised the revolver and pointed it in Rachel's direction. Rachel stopped moving.

"No," she screamed.

I lunged for the pile of scrap metal searching for something to use as a weapon. I grabbed the first thing I spotted in the scrap pile. A crumpled hub cap. Except for the weight, it felt like a Frisbee, the one thing I could throw with some accuracy. I aimed towards Bridget and hurled the hub cap as hard as I could. It struck her chest with enough force to knock her backwards. She whipped around and teetered on her bad ankle. It didn't stop her from firing off a wild shot at me. Her second bullet ricocheted off a pile of rusted metal in Rachel's direction.

"Get away, Rachel," I yelled.

Bridget lurched behind a truck carcass. She raised her arm again toward Rachel.

"Stupid interfering bitch. Will I never get rid of you?" The next bullet pinged off the truck door.

I searched for something else to use against Bridget. A rearview mirror!

"Bridget. Oh, God, no, Bridget, how can you say such things?" Rachel stumbled toward Bridget, wailing. "You know how I feel about you."

I prayed Rachel would stop worrying about Bridget's affections and get herself out of the line of fire.

Bridget whirled and fired in my direction. The shot connected with a rusted-out station wagon ten feet away. She twisted back to Rachel and raised the revolver, holding it straight with both hands.

As I flung the rearview mirror at Bridget, the revolver fired. I heard a jagged scream from Rachel as she lurched behind a pile of tires.

Bridget lowered her gun. I snatched up a stickshift and lobbed it. Bridget's presence filled my eyes and my mind. Another shot rang out, this time inches from my head. Bridget crouched and staggered closer. My knees shook. The blood pounding in my skull drowned out all other sound.

I grabbed a broken steering wheel and aimed. And missed. Bridget's eyes met mine. Without blinking, she raised the revolver, before I could stoop to find another projectile.

Something that looked like a pair of binoculars flew from the van and smashed into Bridget's knee. She squawked and crumpled. The gun flew out of her hand and landed in a heap of twisted metal parts.

I lunged toward the gun. So did Bridget. I jerked into a crouch and jumped. A jagged bit of scrap metal gouged my thigh as I landed. The knifelike pain in my leg brought me to a stop, gasping. Tears stung my eyes, and I fought to catch my breath.

Bridget inched toward the bumpers, her faced contorted.

My head swam. I dragged myself toward her, reaching out. Bridget edged forward.

I grabbed a piece of metal bumper and hurled it. I heard a grunt from Bridget. I didn't turn my head. I kept inching forward, focusing on the gun. Sharp metal bits cut my hands, but I reached the gun before Bridget. I collapsed on my belly with my arms extended, both hands clutching the weapon. Blood dripped from my shredded palms. Pain surged through my leg. I felt waves of nausea, and I tried not to retch.

I levelled the gun at Bridget's face. Blood and water dripped from my sleeves. My hands shook.

I kept my mind on Rachel, probably dead or dying among the car bodies, and on Josey and Tolstoy trapped in the chip van.

Bridget's bruised and bloody face, full of hate and pain, swam in and out of focus. Her arm hung at a bizarre angle. She lurched two feet in my direction.

Someone will come, someone will come. Don't press the trigger, I told myself, no matter how much you want to. I was startled by how much I wanted to.

The gun felt like it weighed a hundred pounds. I barely held on until I heard the sound of a siren. Josey's faraway voice drifted from the van. "Don't let go, Miz Silk."

Bridget watched with the eyes of a fox, waiting for the chickens to do something stupid.

Flashing lights reflected now in the windows of the dead cars. Someone must have called the police. Possibly Paulie Pound, worried about losing some of his valuable scrap. In St. Aubaine, gunshots lead to phone calls.

"You hang on, too," I managed to shout.

No one answered. Car doors slammed. Voices called.

Bridget's eyes met mine. I knew what she was thinking as she limped to the the edge of the quarry.

"Bridget, don't."

Nothing prepared me for the feeling as she stepped calmly off the edge.

I lowered the gun and wept.

Thirty-One

Outside my little house, chill rain pelted the windows. With luck, soaking the latest tribe of media. Of course, they had nothing to complain about. Kostas had given them an excellent interview, covering mostly sweaters—with samples shown. He'd made a fine warm-up act for Woody. Liz had lounged in the background, looking remarkably well-preserved.

I basked in being warm, dry, bandaged, and newly revaccinated against tetanus. Not to mention alive, vindicated and untelevised.

Kostas puffed. "I've been saving those sweaters for yis."

Josey's sweater featured a girl with round, blue eyes, her hair spiky and uneven, something the uninformed might have attributed to the geometry of knitting. I saw Josey there, right down to the bandage embroidered on her knee, captured by Kostas O'Carolan, artist-in-wool.

My own sweater reflected the red, yellow and orange of fall foliage.

Josey kept staring at her sweater. One of her more inscrutable expressions occupied her face.

"It's nothing, of course," Kostas said, with becoming modesty, "compared to what you'll be doing yourself, my dear girl, if you keep on progressing at the rate you are."

Josey nodded with the solemnity I would normally have associated with someone embracing Holy Orders.

"And you'll be in touch, my girl, at me new address?"

"You have a new address?" Josey asked. "Where?"

Kostas twinkled a bit more than usual. "At the home of Miss Mary Morrison, where I will be ensuring her security and preventing her last years being spent in loneliness and misery."

And preventing Kostas's last few years being spent in a tumble-down cottage with a leaky roof and no hot water.

"I will miss Evening's End and me view of the river, but there are compensations. And me dogs are welcome at Mary's."

Josey approved. "That worked out well," she said.

No kidding.

"Indeed, and I do believe it calls for a little celebration."

I fished my bottle of Courvoisier out of the washing machine and kissed it good-bye. I whispered in Kostas's small pink ear, "Don't worry, Heckie, your secret's safe with me. In fact, I've already forgotten it."

"Dear lady, I am grateful. And shall we toast to absent friends?"

*   *   *

Rachel lay back on her hospital bed, her eyes closed, the streaks of tears harsh against the bone colour of her skin. Her arm was in a sling, and I knew more bandages strapped her ribs.

She opened her eyes and struggled to a sitting position.

I had mixed feelings about Rachel at that moment. Rachel, who'd known that Dougie Dolan was a walking time bomb.

"Ah, please don't hate me, Josey dear." Josey's expression remained guarded. "I know it's hard to understand, but I loved Bridget," Rachel said. "She told me Fiona really was responsible for Benedict's death, and Dougie was going to follow and get proof. But once I got to know you and Fiona a bit, I figured out Bridget and Dougie might have been mixed up in something terrible. I had to face it. That last morning she sounded really out of control."

I thought I heard Sarrazin mutter, "*Merde.*"

Josey patted Rachel's good arm. "If you hadn't followed Bridget and distracted her, Miz Silk and I might both be dead now. Tolstoy too."

Sarrazin cleared his throat. Maybe he felt as I did. If Rachel had spoken earlier, Abby Lake would have been alive and Marc-André breathing without life support. And Dougie Dolan, a guest of the government instead of the graveyard. On the other hand, I wouldn't have wanted to try to explain Bridget's death to Sarrazin without Rachel as a witness.

Thirty-Two

The Gatineau river shone fast and silvery.

"I guess this guy's had enough funerals now," Josey said.

She gazed through her binoculars and over the inlet as Benedict's ashes drifted on the breeze and settled on the lapping water. A clump of ash caught in a small eddy and whirled around for slow seconds before sinking.

The air was full of fiddling and sniffling. A cluster of O'Mafia read their poems before the dozen fiddlers tuned up to pay their last respects to a wild Irish poet and legendary lover.

Zoë stood off from the crowd, red head high and shoulders squared. Dignity personified. Unlike Mme Flambeau, puffy-eyed and shuddering and unable to utter her formal good-byes. Lucky for her, Josey took pity, providing her with a steady supply of fresh tissues and a shoulder to lean on.

Even Stella showed up, holding her twins by the hand.

Kostas, hoarse from booming his epic forty-two verse memorial poem to Benedict, stood with his pudgy mitt on Miss Mary Morrison's shoulder. I was pleased to note the absence of Sarrazin, probably tied up with the coroner. But then Sarrazin's absence spelled good news, since Uncle Mike had made a rare public appearance. Josey had dusted him off and propped him up next to Natalie. If all went well, they could keep each other busy and out of trouble.

Around the fiddlers, women blew their noses and cried. Even I felt a ache in my throat for Benedict, whose wicked ways had cost his own life and three others, Abby, Dougie and in the end, Bridget.

The sun dipped behind scudding clouds and the river reflected the hillside. I held my breath as Benedict's ashes drifted and merged with the waves. The last tangible remnants of Benedict Kelly, poet, philosopher and lounge lizard, swirled and sank into waters as green as any graveyard.

Mary Jane Maffini is a lapsed librarian, former co-owner of the Prime Crime Mystery Bookstore in Ottawa and author of the Camilla MacPhee series (*Speak Ill of the Dead, The Icing on the Corpse, Little Boy Blues, The Devil's in the Details* and *The Dead Don't Get Out Much*) and the Charlotte Adams series.

Her short story "Cotton Armour" in *The Ladies Killing Circle* won the Crime Writers of Canada Arthur Ellis Award for best short short story in 1995, and she was a 1999 finalist for best first novel for *Speak Ill of the Dead*. She was a 2001 double nominee for the Arthur Ellis Awards for best short story, and her story from *Fit to Die* won the Best Short Story Arthur in 2002.

Lament for a Lounge Lizard was shortlisted for the Arthur for best novel in 2003 and was followed by another Fiona Silk mystery, *Too Hot to Handle,* in 2007.

Maffini lives in Ottawa, Ontario.